The Ugly Princess

A Karlathia Chronicle

Elizabeth K. Burton

ZUMAYA OTHERWORLDS

AUSTIN TX

2011

THE UGLY PRINCESS
© 2003, 2011 by Elizabeth K. Burton
ISBN 978-1-934135-20-4
Cover art and Design © Tamian Wood

"Zumaya Otherworlds" and the griffon colophon are trademarks of Zumaya Publications LLC, Austin TX.
Look for us online at
http://www.zumayapublications.com

Library of Congress Cataloging-in-Publication Data

Burton, Elizabeth K., 1948-
   The ugly princess / by Elizabeth K. Burton. — 2nd print ed.
      p. cm.
   "A Karlathia chronicle."
   ISBN 978-1-61271-048-8 (trade pbk. : alk. paper) —
ISBN 978-1-936144-47-1 (electronic/multiple format) —
ISBN 978-1-61271-046-4 (electronic/epub)
   I. Title.
   PS3602.U76974U45 2011
   813'.6—dc23
                          2011035250

Acknowledgments

Phil, as always, and with all my love, for making it possible for me to finally achieve my dream.

Catherine Asaro, who suggested my short story really read more like the synopsis of a novel.

All the people who don't read fantasy—except for this one.

And special thanks to Calimacil Inc. of Sherbrooke, Quebec, for permission to include their gorgeous Sword of the Templar Godefroi as part of our cover design.

Chapter 1

THE TRUTH MIGHT NEVER HAVE COME TO LIGHT HAD THE king not gotten drunk at his wedding banquet and choked to death on a pheasant bone.

The events leading up to and instrumental in the unfortunate moment began three months earlier, just after the summer solstice. The day commenced much like every other, with King Edrick roaring into the private dining hall already well into his first bottle of brandy. He engulfed his usual enormous breakfast, then strode off to his private council chamber to see if there were any pressing matters of state he needed to attend to.

I was in my small office near the kitchens attending to the monthly accounts when one of the downstairs maids dashed in to inform me a courier waited in the main reception hall. As such messengers were only employed for matters of the utmost urgency, I immediately went to greet him.

"I have a message for His Grace," the man announced before I had barely stepped into the room.

"I will take it," I said, quickly assessing the layer of dust on his uniform, thick enough to nearly obscure the patch on his shoulder and the shadows of fatigue under his eyes. He had ridden long and hard, and I saw no reason not to relieve him of his task and send him off for a meal.

"My orders are to give the message to His Grace."

"Corporal, do you know who I am?" I dislike resorting to a military tone, but I dislike even more standing about arguing with people who should know not to.

"Yes, milord."

"Then you are aware I am privy to all the king's business. Now, your message, if you please."

He wrestled with it for a brief moment but, in the end, he truly did have no choice. Thus, I was the first to learn that the Queen of Abernal was dead.

I expect self-introduction is in order before we go any further. My name is Bartrim Ruford, and I am the Seneschal of House Rediman, the twelfth member of my lineage to occupy the post. It, like all those of any importance in the king's household, is hereditary, guaranteeing the monarch dependable help and a fair number of people steady employment for generations. At least, that is the official explanation for the system. When said monarch is like Edrick, it tends to work somewhat less smoothly than its originators had intended.

His Gracious Majesty Edrick Rediman, the fourth of his name to reign in Abernal, was, shall I say, difficult to appreciate but fairly easy to please, provided one had considerable skill at diplomacy and an even greater willingness to compromise one's ethics. Fortunately, I had been blessed with a more than ample portion of the former and so was able to avoid many instances of the latter.

I had assumed my position some five years prior to the events we will be discussing and had, so far, kept His Majesty's good will.

For two decades, an outpost stood at the foot of the Stone Mountains. It had one purpose—to apprise the king by the swiftest means available that his detested wife was dead. I now led the dusty courier to the council chamber, where we interrupted a discussion among His Grace and his three

Ministers of Council of the comparative charms of two new ladies just arrived at court. I then hastened to find my wife.

Danella and I knew the king would want to celebrate the news he had just received and hastened to prepare a small feast for His Grace and a few select friends. He had waited twenty years to hear that his estranged wife had finally been killed in some skirmish or other so he could replace her and get a male heir. Well, a legitimate male heir, anyway. He had produced plenty of the other kind, not being any more inclined to celibacy than he was to restraint in dining.

The news that the longed-for day of liberty had, at last, arrived provoked instantaneous results. Envoys departed before the following noon to all the neighboring monarchs with nubile daughters, and a week later Edrick was betrothed to the lovely Yolanthe of Nadwich. Despite our surprise at the alacrity with which the queen-to-be was selected, Danella and I immediately began preparations for the nuptials; and I dispatched invitations to all the relevant lords, ladies and royals. As the weeks prior to the arrival of the lady and her parents passed, the palace actually had a rather more light-hearted, festive air than I could recall having enjoyed for many years.

I, of course, made all the necessary arrangements to welcome the future lady of the house, just as my late father had done for her predecessor. Not surprisingly, the said preparations included gently persuading my sovereign to temper some of his more abrupt mannerisms.

"Are you calling me a boor, Ruford?" he snarled when I suggested having the princess taken immediately to his chambers on arrival so he could "try her out" was somewhat less than romantic.

"Heaven forbid, Your Grace. You are, as everyone knows, the consummate gentleman. However, the lady Yolanthe is fresh from the convent and likely shy for that reason."

"Then best she get over her girlish megrims now. The sooner she's in whelp, the better."

"Well, of course, there is the matter of her father, who is rumored to be an overly pious man much enamored of the concept of premarital chastity."

The mention of his prospective father-in-law, who in addition to piety had a treasury reputed to be twice the size of Edrick's he might, if provoked, decide not to share with his new son-in-law, gave my royal master pause.

"So, have her brought after he's in bed," Edrick suggested, though his voice had lost some of its earlier assurance.

"A possible alternative, Your Grace, but Queen Barba has asked to share her daughter's chambers to assist with last-minute preparations. And I suspect even were that worthy lady to be a sufficiently sound sleeper to allow your wishes to be fulfilled, King Benifaz will have more than one...observer...in his daughter's retinue, ready to report in detail if the princess's virtue were in any way compromised prior to the exchange of vows."

He sat slumped, one hand gripping his favorite goblet, the other clenched on the arm of the chair. The course of his thoughts as he struggled to reach a plan with a greater chance of success made his face twitch. Finally, to his obvious disgruntlement and my sincere relief, he accepted the inevitable.

"'Tis but four days," he conceded. "Do what you think best."

So it was that the king met his betrothed with all appropriate courtesy in the Great Hall, the only remaining remnant of the original castle, as per custom. She was a lovely vision, small and slight with deep violet eyes and red-gold hair flowing freely to below her waist. She was exquisite and had a palpable air of sweetness.

She took one look at her betrothed and went white to the lips.

Her royal parents chose not to officially take notice of her reaction, although Queen Barba shot her husband's back a glance that should have drawn blood. I subsequently noted, however, that she kept her eyes downcast and her face carefully schooled when there was the least chance her spouse might observe her demeanor. My interpretation of this behavior did not speak well of His Grace of Nadwich, a summation which...but more on that at the appropriate time.

Edrick was five years past his fifth decade, while the lady was two years shy of her second. He was squat and broad and not much inclined to regular bathing; and despite his respect for Benifaz his small, black eyes stripped off Yolanthe's traveling ensemble like razors. Recognizing the need for intervention, I made haste to suggest she might be overtired from her journey and hustled her off to her temporary suite of rooms to recover. Edrick licked his lips as he watched her go, and I'm saddened to admit I was glad the nuptials would take place in only four days. Otherwise, I suspect, he would have reverted to his original plan in spite of Benifaz's money.

"Poor lass," muttered Danella as we retreated to the kitchen to begin preparation for that night's betrothal banquet.

I quite agreed with her, but the deed was done. One could only hope the lady would manage to produce the required heir as soon as possible, after which time she would likely be spared most of her spouse's intimate attentions. Edrick preferred women with fewer inhibitions than a princess trained in a religious community was likely to have.

Still, to give the man credit, he did behave himself reasonably well for the remaining days before the wedding. The ceremony went off without a hitch, and the bridal feast began as the sun retired for the evening. I made certain Yolanthe's wineglass was topped off, but I doubted even that was going to be enough. As course after course arrived and Edrick grew more and more drunk, I caught her staring at him with a look usually reserved for confrontations with savage beasts.

When the final toast to the bride had been made, Queen Barba and a cluster of Abernali ladies escorted her from the festivities upstairs to the king's bedchamber, where she would wait in nervous nakedness in the royal bed to do her duty. Custom demanded Edrick allow at least an hour before joining her, so a variety of entertainers had been hired to help him while away the time. As a troupe of bawdy clowns sent the assembly into roars of laughter, a course of lemon-ginger partridge was served, a dish that was one of His Grace's favorites. Snatching a drumstick, he bit it in half, chewing bone and all as he hoisted his cup and gulped wine.

I had left the hall to see that the buffet table in the ballroom, where the wedding guests would retire once Edrick had gone, was adequately supplied, so I was not present for the terminal event. However, the man who had served the partridge informed me later that His Grace, in the midst of a bellow of laughter, suddenly fell back into his chair. He sat staring into infinity with his mouth agape as the already high color in his face grew darker still. He seemed to be trying to speak, but the group's attention was on the clowns so all failed to notice his peculiar behavior. He clapped his hand to his throat, a signal he had instituted to alert the wine steward he desired a refill on those occasions when the noise level was too high for conversation. This was promptly provided, but Edrick continued to gesture madly. The rest of the staff, unable to interpret what it was he seemed so desperate to obtain, mingled about in confusion until the king gurgled, turned a singularly unregal shade of purple and fell facedown into his mashed potatoes.

It was at that moment I returned to the banquet hall. One of the clowns had observed the king's curious behavior and stopped to stare. His fellows, their practiced routine thrown awry, stopped as well and turned to see what had interrupted them. Slowly, the room fell utterly silent as I hurried to see what was happening.

Benifaz leaped up and gawked at his son-in-law as if he suspected Edrick were simply evincing yet another disgusting aspect of his character. He confirmed this a moment later in the tone of a man just discovering manure on his best boots.

"Good God! The man's passed out!"

As such an event had occurred numerous times in the past, it was not an unwarranted conclusion. The king's ministers exchanged looks of mingled exasperation and chagrin from their seats. Until the marriage was consummated their plans to continue in their positions of power were uncertain. Edrick's apparent incapacity to perform that duty—not to mention his having mortally offended the new queen's proud and easily offended sire—was not encouraging.

I, however, had a dreadful feeling that was not inspired by politics or thoughts of my future, and so, apparently did my lifelong friend the Royal Champion. Sir Christopher Evergild had failed to observe Edrick's distress, as he was stationed according to Edrick's orders well behind the throne-like chair the king used when dining formally. Despite his height, his view was thus blocked by the ornate back of the royal seat. At Benifaz's exclamation, however, he leaped forward—too late.

Chris pushed through the gawking servants to lift Edrick from dinner and lean him against the back of the chair. The king's eyes were wide and blank amid the potatoes and gravy and his head lolled in a way no living man's would. I laid my fingers on the place on his throat where his pulse should be. As I had suspected, there was none.

"Gentlemen," I said to King Benifaz and the Ministers of Council as quietly as I could and still be heard, "the king is dead."

Benifaz slumped into his chair, never taking his eyes off the corpse. The gaggle of ministers put their heads together and muttered as I gently cleaned my late sovereign's face with a napkin while Sir Christopher held him steady. They gazed in horror at the corpse of their monarch and former source of steady revenue and then stared with even greater dismay at each other.

The silence that had to this point held sway was shattered as three hundred voices all erupted at once. Many of the gentlemen and not a few of the ladies leaped to their feet in an effort to see. Some who were less mindful of their dignity went so far as to climb onto their chairs.

Finished with my cleaning chore, I motioned for four of the footmen to remove His Grace, surreptitiously slipping the royal signet from his hand. I then stepped down from the dais to the center the room under the high dome that crowned the hall. From here, I knew, my voice would carry to all.

"Ladies and gentlemen!"

The uproar ebbed as all eyes moved from the exiting cortege to me.

"His Grace King Edrick has suffered an accident—may God grant him eternal peace."

For a long moment no one moved; and then, one by one, the guests stood and left, some to their chambers, others to their carriages. In a matter of minutes, the only guests remaining in the Great Hall were Benifaz, who was staring into his cup of wine; the ministers, who were staring at each other; and Sir Christopher.

No one had really expected Edrick to survive long enough for any son he might sire to reach majority. The ministers had intended to ensure at least one—and preferably all—of them were named as regents when the hoped-for male heir inherited the throne.

Now, they were appalled. The king was dead, his marriage unconsummated, thus precluding the possibility of there being a posthumous heir. The line of succession, by default, fell to his late majesty's only living child.

"There must be someone else," muttered First Minister Marlan Overlack to Third Minister Zephus Settleson.

"You know better," growled Second Minister Ludlow Entreput, tossing back a double measure of brandy. "It was you who advised him to kill all the ones from the wrong side of the blanket off, remember?"

"But, ye gods," interjected Settleson, slumping back and covering his face with his hand. "*Her!*"

Already the servants were clearing the tables, so of course I must stand on the dais where I could adequately supervise. That my position also offered me the capability of overhearing their discussion was hardly accidental, not that they would have paid me much attention in any case. Many if not most courtiers overlooked the presence of "the help," and quite often they included me in that designation.

That cloak of servitor invisibility apparently covered Sir Christopher as well. He had returned to his place behind the king's chair, from which I knew he could hear every word.

"We know where she is," Overlack said, his voice cold and ugly. "And there are cousins. Accidents happen."

Settleson slid his hand down below his eyes, which were suddenly bright with speculation. Entreput smiled, a most unpleasant expression.

"Indeed," he agreed, pouring another two fingers of brandy but this time sipping it meditatively.

He poured for his fellows, also, and they raised their glasses in a toast. I did not care to consider what they pledged, but I suspected it had nothing to do with anyone's health—especially *hers*.

Chapter 2

*AS HIS MAJESTY HAS NO NEED OF MY SERVICES AT THE MO-*ment and the Ministers of Council are occupied in mutual commiseration, this would seem an opportune moment for me to provide some information regarding the history of Abernal and the royal family.

Abernal is a fairly small country situated on the southwest coast of the continent of Karlathia. It is bounded on the east by Nadwich and on the northwest by the Empire of the Decirons. Tucked between them are the various mountain valleys and plateaus claimed by the Moldori, a society of savage horseman about which more later.

Ours is a reasonably wealthy country. There are two fine ports to the south and some productive coal, iron and silver mines to the north. In between lies some of the finest farming country on the continent.

House Rediman assumed the throne of Abernal some five centuries ago. The founder of the house was elected by popular acclaim following his resounding defeat of a score of barbarian tribes, which he then united into a single political entity.

The people of Abernal, not approving of allowing too much power in too few hands, also established a system that required their new king obtain permission from several representative bodies before making any sweeping decisions. One was the Guild Consortium, with a membership that represented nearly all the common folk. The other was the Council of Ministers, six representatives of the titled and academic communities.

Some generations later a descendent of the first Rediman attempted to establish himself as absolute ruler and was promptly shot through the left eye by an arrow while hunting. His son, being of a somewhat wiser order, made official in the form of an irrevocable charter the two bodies that yet represented—supposedly—the will of the people.

It will have been noted that the late Edrick's council contained not six but three ministers. Following his ascension soon after his first marriage, Edrick replaced the first three ministers to retire with Overlack, Entreput and Settleson; and when the remaining three also became vacant he simply left them that way. By careful nurturing of his relationship with the Consortium, he had thus managed to achieve what amounted to absolute rule without anyone's lodging a protest.

Edrick had reigned for nearly three decades; and to give him his due, Abernal enjoyed relative peace and prosperity most of that time, as we had for much of the fifteen generations that preceded him. The reason for this was quite simple.

Their bellicose ancestor notwithstanding, the kings of House Rediman preferred alternatives to bloodshed for settling state disputes. This was in large part because law and the custom established by their First Ancestor demanded the monarch lead the armies in the event of any extensive hostilities.

In addition, the Redimans all seemed to understand extended peace meant full coffers. This distaste for placing themselves and their treasury in jeopardy had led to the establishment some two centuries earlier of the position of Royal Champion, currently held by Sir Christopher. Disputes that could not be settled in the council chamber were referred to combat between the Champion and a representative of the other party.

Fortunately, our neighbor monarchs had been, for the most part, no more inclined toward blood and battle than our own. Oh, they maintained their armies—they were lazy, not stupid—but as long as the diplomacy-by-single-combat system worked they accepted the results with relatively little complaint.

This gentleman's agreement, however, went by the board with the Moldori. They were a serious nuisance, constantly invading this country and that, stealing livestock, abducting women (or men, depending on the majority gender of the particular raiding party), burning villages and whatnot. They swooped down out of their mountains on their speedy horses, took what they wanted, ruined what they didn't and were gone back to safety before the kingdoms they attacked could rally disciplinary action.

Edrick's father, the third Edrick, was determined to obtain relief from these pests. So it was that in his youth the now-deceased fourth Edrick was contracted in marriage with Marvaya, the eldest daughter of the High Chief of the Moldori. The alliance was arranged by the young prince's esteemed sire on the advice of his ministers, two of whom owned lucrative mines very close to the border.

To their later chagrin, however, the Council of Ministers failed to view the lady prior to completing the contract. When she arrived the day before the scheduled nuptials, they and the prospective bridegroom discovered she had a number of ritual scars on her face. She also had a tendency to snarl and draw knives at any perceived insult—and she was easily insulted. She was small and dark and had the wiry strength and agility of an alley cat, which complemented her temperament beautifully.

"Send the bitch back!" the prince roared in the privacy of the royal apartments. "She looks like a field plowed for planting."

Had the royal treasury been up to the reparations that action would have required, he might have gotten his wish. Observing the groom's less than enthusiastic reception of his betrothed, the agents of the High Chief were quick to suggest an arrangement might be made to dissolve the match—for a price. The amount required would have fed the entire kingdom for at least a year.

So, Crown Prince Edrick exchanged vows with the dark-eyed lady, who glared at him with something less than ardent appreciation. (No proof has been found to support the rumors of the time that she had, in fact, referred to him as "that fat pig" and threatened to turn him into a soprano if he failed to satisfy her in the marriage bed.) At the wedding banquet, she was seen to match him cup for cup; yet when the ladies came to snatch her away she strode off with nary a stagger.

Always willing to make the best of a bad situation, particularly where women were concerned, the prince retired to the nuptial chamber later that night, having consumed sufficient wine and spirits to make the sight of his bride less burdensome. He emerged the following morning bruised, battered and bloody, swearing never to set foot near the princess again without benefit of full body armor.

Not long after that the old king died, and ten months after the wedding the new queen was delivered of a daughter. Her royal husband took one look at the infant and ordered it and the queen out of his sight.

"You might know a bitch pup would be as ugly as the dam," he snarled and then ordered his new ministers to find a safe way to get rid of them both.

Before any concrete plans could be developed, however, the queen, having done her duty as she saw it and being apparently lacking in maternal sensitivities, gutted the two guards assigned to keep her in her quarters and vanished from the palace one night. Several proposals were put forward in regard to dispatching the infant; but more cautious heads pointed out that she was, after all, the only completely Abernali heir to the throne until another arrived to replace her.

The Moldori witch must be divorced to allow Edrick to take a new wife on whom he could beget an heir. Once her replacement was in hand, it could then be arranged for the Ugly Princess to toddle off a high balcony or slip in the bath.

Considering her repulsiveness, they pointed out, it would be an act of mercy.

To the ministers' dismay, however, there were several impediments to their achieving Edrick's goals. For one thing, there were no women of marriageable age in any of the local royal families; and His Grace was quite specific about the need for regal blood in his son's veins. Furthermore, he stressed in a tone to chill the blood, she had better be a beauty.

Those, as it turned out, were the easy parts. What brought the entire program to a halt was the clause in the marriage agreement requiring a substantial payment before a divorce could be acquired. The amount, not surprisingly, was approximately twice that suggested by the High Chief's agents prior to the marriage. It was clear the man knew his daughter—or Edrick—well.

The sum in question being totally out of reach, and the threat of increased raiding by the Moldori an obvious consequence of any alternative choices, Edrick was forced to accept his fate. Until either he or his absent queen died, he would not be acquiring a new bride.

This did not, of course, improve his attitude toward his tiny heiress. He refused to give her a name and threatened dire bodily harm to anyone who so much as mentioned her in his presence. It was my mother who smuggled a priest into the far corner of the palace where the infant lay to have her christened.

As months passed, rumors grew. It was said the princess was a monster, her limbs twisted and her face deformed. She was allegedly given to fits of screaming rage, to have bitten the nipple from the breast of her wet nurse, to have claws and horns and scales. When such gossip was repeated in my mother's hearing her face would redden with anger, but she never contradicted the stories or defended the infant.

"I know who it is spreads such tales," I heard her tell my father one night. "And who will be blamed but me if anyone says otherwise? I can only tend the wee mite as it is by his sufferance. I'll not risk being shut away from her for having a loose tongue."

Her efforts and her restraint were in vain, however. When the princess was six months old the king decided there was no need to keep her in the palace.

"Stout walls and well-paid servants can be had anywhere," he shouted.

So, the Ugly Princess was sent to live in a dark, damp keep high in the foothills in the farthest corner of the kingdom, attended by a contingent of Trolls. They are a gentle people, but one that most humans find it difficult to look at for any length of time. That, said Edrick, made them the appropriate folk to look after a deformed child.

She remained there for twenty years, more a folk tale than a reality to most of the country, unseen by any but her faithful servants. Given there was at least the possibility of her assuming the throne, she was educated as befit a princess, although all of her tutors were ancients who always seemed to die just as their term of employment was nearing its end.

Now, at the instigation of a dead bird, the Ugly Princess had become an ugly queen.

"There's only one thing to do," decided First Minister Overlack. "We will simply marry her off to Benifaz's nephew. He doesn't care what a woman looks like as long as she's breathing, and she will no doubt be so grateful to have a man she won't be any trouble at all to convince we know best. And he's part Rediman through his grandmother."

"And what assurance do we have His Nibs of Nadwich won't decide to do without our services?" snarled Third Minister Settleson.

"If you have an alternative suggestion, I'm certain we would all be pleased to entertain it," replied Overlack in the same tone.

As nothing apparently suggested itself, they were forced to find the plan acceptable and drank a toast to the future.

Sir Christopher Evergild leaned against the high back of Edrick's chair and listened as the men he had come to call the Three Spiders plotted the future of a woman none of them had ever seen. The servants were still clearing away the wedding feast, and he could see Bartrim standing just within earshot of the conspirators, appearing to be interested in nothing but assuring the clearing away was done properly.

Chris envied Bart that ability to dissemble. He, on the other hand, had a face that gave away everything, which is why he was grateful King Edrick had been so fond of thrones he wanted to eat sitting on one. The huge ornate chair had a back seven feet tall and half that wide, and the dais behind it was wide enough to provide a spot where he could retreat when necessary, which was pretty much any time Edrick ate. Otherwise, House Evergild would have lost their two-century-old position when Chris parted company with his head for sneering at the king's manners.

"So," Marlan Overlack said, now the decision to take control of the exiled princess was made, "we will send a delegation at first light to escort the...queen...back to the palace. You, Settleson, will draw up the marriage lines and we will have her sign them as soon as she arrives. The wedding can proceed as soon as Demtri can be fetched."

"Good God, Overlack," Zephus Settleson whined over the gurgle of yet more of the royal brandy pouring into his cup. "I'm in no condition to attend to legal matters tonight."

"Besides," chimed in Entreput, "the woman's been locked up for twenty years. One more day isn't going to make a difference."

Chris didn't have to see the Second Minister's face to know it was twisted into a sneer of contempt. That tended to be his normal expression, and it colored his voice even when he was straight-faced.

"How reassuring to know our heads of state have the situation so firmly in hand."

Chris started, his hand flying to the dagger that was the only weapon Edrick would allow him to wear at the table. An instant later, he glared at the lanky man standing beside him.

"One of these days, Bart, you'll sneak up on me like that, and I'll carve you a new smile under your chin," he muttered.

"Promises, promises. What would your father say if he knew you could be snuck up on? Anyway, they've swooped off to circle the corpse, so you can come out now."

Chris followed him out of the Great Hall and down the passage to the kitchen, where all the food that remained was being packed into hampers. It would be taken to the local abbey to be distributed among the poor, something that wouldn't have happened were Edrick still breathing. As far as the late king had been concerned, there were no poor in Abernal, just people too lazy to work; and he had seen no reason to encourage them in their sloth.

"Sit down, Christopher, and eat," Danella Ruford said, setting a plate and a mug of ale on the staff's dining table as if she had known beforehand he would be arriving. Perhaps she did—he had more than once suspected his best friend's wife had a touch of the Sight. He'd always persuaded himself otherwise, because he liked her too much to let suspicions come between them.

He wasn't going to turn down the meal. He hadn't eaten since midday, and if the germ of a plan forming in his head decided to sprout it could well be longer than that before he ate well again.

"So, now what?" Bart slid into the chair beside him, re-filling Chris's cup and then pouring one for himself.

"I have to get to her before they do." He said it almost without thinking, only that moment realizing the seed had not only sprouted but grown to maturity as he ate.

"It's said she's mad as well as ugly, Chris. What if it's true?"

"Madwoman or monster, she's still the queen, and I'm her champion. Once I've sworn fealty, the Spiders can't touch her without risking my stepping on them." He drained his mug and got up, calling one of the pages over with a quirk of the finger. "Go to the stables and have them saddle me a good horse for a fast ride."

The lad dashed off, and Chris used the back stairway to climb to his rooms. Stripping off his ceremonial armor, he dressed in leather breeches and a light hauberk then tossed a fur-lined oiled-leather cloak over his shoulders against the chill rain that had started falling just after nightfall. He would have preferred to leave the chain mail behind, but the tradition of his office demanded he wear it when in the monarch's presence.

His dagger he thrust into the sheath in his boot then buckled on his sword. Finally, he looped the gold chain bearing the badge of the King's Champion around his neck.

He had been five years old when the princess was born, but he remembered very little of those first months of her life. His father had just started him on his sword training and that had been more important than some baby—and a girl baby, at that.

Nor had he thought much about her after he was old enough to understand her story. Oh, he had heard all the stories about her deformity and her insanity; but that had nothing to do with his purpose in life, which was to guard the king after his father retired.

Suddenly, she was his purpose in life, and the tales of horror that surrounded her kept nibbling at his brain. What would he do if he arrived at that antiquated stone-heap and found a raving lunatic?

"Don't make trouble where there's already enough," he mumbled as he pulled on his gloves.

There was a knock, and Bart stepped inside carrying a saddlebag.

"Danella says there's enough there to get you to Norburgh. We'll have the Lady's Nest in the Queen's Tower cleaned and ready by tomorrow sunset at the latest. And you'll want this." He held out the royal signet.

"I see at least a day and a half there and likely twice that back, plus whatever time she needs to prepare for the trip," Chris said, tucking the ring into the pouch on his belt. "And that's if we ride straight through. I'll send messengers to give you some warning."

The two men returned downstairs together then shook hands at the door to the kitchen garden.

"Keep an eye on the Spiders," Chris said.

"Godspeed, my friend."

The rain came down steadily, pounding against his head and shoulders as he followed the stone-paved path through the garden and beyond its wall to the courtyard and the stables. The stablemaster was waiting with a restless gray stallion, and he, too, wished Chris "Godspeed."

He trotted his horse down the long, straight drive toward the main gate, which the night guards began to swing open as soon as they heard his approach. The wind drove the rain into his face, forcing him to pull his hood down so far it was all he could do to see the road. His mount protested, much preferring a warm, dry stall; but Chris patted the stallion's arched neck and then set him to a hard gallop with a kick of his heels.

Chapter 3

THE DEEP-LAWNED MANSIONS OF THE NOBILITY THAT SUR-
rounded the palace gave way to the three and four-story
buildings of the Registon business district. The chill rain had
driven all but the vermin—two- and four-legged—and the
constabulary indoors; so the wide, brick-paved avenue that
led from Abernal House to the bridge over the Woodrath
River was empty enough for his horse's hoofbeats to echo off
the buildings. It was still early enough that lights glowed
from the windows where people lived above the mercantile
establishments.

Riding being something he could manage dead asleep,
Chris let his mind wander, once again reviewing Edrick's
death, probing to see if there was anything he could have
done, should have done, to prevent it. But Bart was right—
he had been shackled by Edrick's commands. So, although
the sense of duty some people swore was a component of the
blood of the Royal Champions gave him a momentary pang
of guilt, his logical mind overruled the charge he had failed
his responsibility.

That wouldn't apply, though, if he allowed the Spiders to
carry out their plans.

He often wished his father hadn't retired well before the usual age when Royal Champions surrendered their sword of office to their successors. Or that he had chosen Mikel for the job, even though Chris's elder brother had no real interest in it. Chris had no qualms about his skill with arms. If he had to fight to defend the new queen the outcome wasn't in question. What he wasn't good at, as he had been reminded again tonight, was dealing with the likes of Overlack and company.

He knew he should be aware of all the undercurrents running through the palace—through the entire country, actually—but he always seemed to be one step behind. It hadn't really mattered before, because he could rely on Bart. Now, though, his gut instinct told him he would need to be able to anticipate and respond all on his own, and he wasn't sure he was ready.

According to tradition, he should have had years of working with his father, honing his skills both military and diplomatic, before taking office. The customary age for a Champion to pass his sword to his successor was sixty; and some, like his grandfather, kept the job even longer.

Instead, at fifty-five, Davvyd Evergild had suddenly announced that the title of Champion and commander of the king's army was now in the hands of his twenty-year-old younger son and left Registon for Tidecastle, his domain on the southern shore. His only response when Chris or anyone else questioned his abrupt departure was that he felt his son was more than ready to replace him and saw no reason not to enjoy a few additional years of freedom from the demands of the title.

Chris rode through the sodden night until he felt the horse begin to tire. The highway was empty, the houses beside it dark and silent. The villages he passed through might have been deserted, only the occasional tavern shattering the night with raucous voices when the door opened as he thundered by.

In Riverway, the first city north of the capital, he exchanged the exhausted animal for another at the army garrison, informing the commander of the king's death and his own errand. Then he was off again, riding toward the darker shadows to the north and east that were the mountains where the princess dwelled. The rain slacked off from time to time, but it was never far away; and his cloak eventually became soaked through.

Dawn was coming, although the shrouded sun did little to ease the dreariness, when the second horse began to falter. He was in the broad belt of farms that looped across the center of the country and there was no garrison nearby. Fortunately, since nearly every farmer engaged in horse breeding to one extent or another, he found a stable in the next town. Cantering into the yard, he shouted for the hostler as he slid from the saddle and walked his mount to let it cool down.

"Help you?" the man said from the door of the stable.

"I need a sturdy remount with as much speed as can be had."

Even through the dim light of early morning Chris could see the man's eyes light up with greed. He would have already recognized that his customer was in a great rush and so not likely to want to waste time bargaining.

"I've a likely mare that might suit for twelve gold." He turned and called into the barn, and moments later a boy came out to take over the cool-down chore. Chris strode inside and was shown the animal. To give the man credit, he hadn't lied about her quality.

"She'll do," he said. "Get her geared. I'll leave her at the garrison in Norburgh and you can send someone to return my mount and fetch her back anytime after tomorrow."

And then he tossed back his sodden cloak to reveal his chain mail, which left the hostler standing with his mouth gaping, his protest silenced. Only one man in Abernal dressed like a relic, and when he did his word was law. Fifteen minutes later Chris was back on the highway.

All that day and through the night he rode, pausing only to tend to the necessities of nature and change mounts. He ate as he rode and drank when he stopped, falling into a mindless semi-dream of fatigue. At Norburgh, he again informed the commander of the change in ruler and requested he keep the news to himself until Chris could return with the new queen. He didn't miss the way the colonel's face stiffened in consternation.

The rain continued, with the brief moments of respite usually lasting just long enough for his cloak to begin to dry before he was drenched again. It was midmorning when he at last reached the foot of the high hill where the princess's prison stood. Compared to the many-windowed, elegant structures that had long ago replaced most of its ilk, it crouched like some ancient monument to war with its crenellated parapets and slit-windowed watchtowers. What would it be like, he wondered, to spend your whole life locked within those forbidding walls surrounded by nightmarish creatures whose sole function was to keep you there?

A narrow but well-tended road curved gently to the top of the hill. The rain, which had appeared to be over when he started the easy climb, returned with renewed vigor halfway up. By the time he reached the heavy, iron-banded gate he was exhausted, chilled, wet, hungry and not in the best of moods.

"Hallo, Captain of the Guard!" he shouted as he sat in the downpour, his tired horse blowing from the exertion. "I have important news for Her Highness."

"Then tell it and be off, man," snarled a gravelly voice from a guardhouse set over the portal. A broad-shouldered Troll in studded leather armor as antiquated as his mail leaned out just far enough for the roof overhang to keep him out of the wet.

Chris pushed back his cloak so his badge of office gleamed even in the dim, rain-soaked daylight.

"I am Sir Christopher Evergild, hereditary champion of the Royal House of Abernal, Troll, and what I have to say is for Her Highness's ears alone. Now, open the bloody gate!"

The last vestige of his patience was abandoning him, and it made no difference that he knew Trolls were better known for their stubbornness than their spirit of cooperation. It was why Edrick had contracted with them to guard his daughter in the first place, knowing no amount of pleading or bribery would gain anyone access to her.

But he had no way of knowing what was happening in Registon. By now, the Spiders could be on their way here, ready to use the power Edrick had granted them to co-opt their new monarch before she had the opportunity to understand what was happening. The last thing he needed was this idiot of a guard standing in his way.

"Matters not if you're the king himself. Orders is the gate stays closed, so closed she stays."

As if collaborating with the Trolls to ensure his frustration and discomfort, a brisk breeze began, aggravating the clammy chill that was rapidly seeping to his bones and blowing the rain into his face like needles.

"If you blockheads don't open this gate, I'll have your hides for doormats," he roared in the voice that had given many an opponent on the field of honor second thoughts. "By whose order do you deny entrance to the royal champion?"

"Your pardon, Sir Knight," replied a decidedly non-Troll voice from within the guardhouse, and in the shadows behind the guard Chris caught a slight movement. "Unaccustomed as we are to visitors, we may have become a trifle...overly suspicious. Pray, enter and be welcome to Raven's Cry."

If velvet had a sound, it would brush the ears with just that softness and warmth. It wrapped around him and sent a liquid quiver through his chest that slid down through his belly and lodged in his loins in a most embarrassing manner. Astonished, Chris searched to penetrate the darkness; but between the rain in his eyes and the angle, he was blind. Still, the great iron-barred gates were swinging open with a loud squeal to reinforce the welcoming words. He spurred his horse within and dismounted, handing the reins to the Troll child who ran out to meet him.

He wasn't certain what he had expected to find. This rough castle was nothing but a prison, and his experience with prisons was that they were rarely pleasant. However, the courtyard was as clean and neat as possible, given it was only partly paved with cobblestones; and although he could hear the sounds of livestock coming from what were likely barns to his left, there was no sign of waste anywhere nor was the stench of manure overwhelming. It was a clean place, nearly homey, a place where those who lived in it cared for appearances.

The keep appeared at some point long before to have been truncated, so that only two stories topped by a modern slate roof remained. Three steps led from the ground to a stone porch, half of which was covered by a wide overhang so that those inside might stand in the doorway without regard to the weather. There were casement windows above and below, though no light came from any of them. Someone had gone to great pains to make this as comfortable a dwelling as possible, and Chris didn't believe for a moment it had been Edrick.

Yet who else? Except for the tutors Bart had told him about, the only ones permitted within the walls were the Trolls. If they were responsible, he needed to make some considerable alterations to his ideas about them.

Just then, one of them, wearing armor of leather and plate, a thick scimitar on his belt and an iron mace in his hand, leaped down from the battlements, taking the thirty-foot drop as if he were hopping off a stair. His bowlegs made him seem menacing as he drew closer and Chris let his hand fall to his sword hilt. Then, as the creature came near enough for his face to be clearly visible, the sense of impending threat vanished. In fact, Chris could have sworn the creature looked ashamed.

"I'm to apologize, milord," the Troll guard mumbled, dropping to one knee without regard for the inch-deep mud. "'Twas wrong to keep ye out when ye come on king's business."

"Better too much devotion to duty than too little," Chris heard himself say, wondering a moment later if he always sounded that pompous. Then wondering why he was wondering. "The lady who just spoke..."

"Sir Christopher?"

It was another Troll, a female this time, come from the keep and standing in the shelter of the portico. Behind her, the door stood open, but there was no light to be seen from within despite the overcast of the day. Chris strode to meet her, careful to look her in the face to avoid insult. It was not a pretty sight. She nodded once, as if approving his courtesy.

Other than having the same number of eyes, nose and mouth, Trolls looked like nothing human. The bones of their faces were irregular, as if they had been broken at birth and had not healed properly. Their noses were flat and broad, the nostrils little more than slits; and their great round orange eyes had slit pupils too much like a snake's for comfort. Prominent brows cast the eyes into shadow, and inch-long fangs overlapped their undershot jaws and thick gray lips. Coarse shaggy black hair covered their heads. Like the guard, the woman—unquestionably the housekeeper, now that he was close enough to see her—was shoeless, her long, clawed feet seeming almost rooted in the stone floor.

"My lady has ordered a bath and a room and a meal for you, milord," the Troll-woman said, her voice surprisingly soft for a creature whose face looked like nothing so much as weathered granite. "If you'll—"

"I must see her at once. I must tell her—"

"This is the lady's house, milord," she said firmly. "She will decide when you must see her. Until then, we beg that you let us make you comfortable."

26

Chris started to protest. He needed to deliver the signet and warn the princess—the queen—there were others whose intentions were less than honorable on their way to collect her. But there was something in the steady way the Troll-woman looked at him that confirmed doing so would only be a waste of breath. That he was shivering from the cold and had to struggle to keep his teeth from chattering was added incentive. What he had to do would take only a few moments, and a hot bath and a warm fire sounded like paradise at the moment. Settleson's entourage couldn't possible arrive before tomorrow, even if they rode straight through as he had.

So, allowing himself to be persuaded, he sighed and followed the housekeeper inside.

Chapter 4

THE HEAVY OAK DOOR CLOSED WITH A SUBDUED THUD, AND he was suddenly standing in pitch dark. He had heard Trolls were able to see with little or no light, but he had never had enough contact with them to verify it. Until now.

He might have been in the center of the earth. His every soldier's instinct started screaming, his hand moved to the hilt of his sword as the rest of his body automatically adjusted for defense. He heard the rustle of her skirts, felt the stir in the air as she moved past him...and lit a candle.

Taking a deep breath to settle his nerves, Chris followed her down a short passageway, where a coarse runner removed much of the mud from his boots, and into the keep's Great Hall through another thick door. Here, a banked fire gave enough light for him to make it to the stairs without stumbling over either of the huge wolfhounds lounging about. He felt their eyes on him, judging him and, apparently, deciding he would be allowed residence on at least a provisional basis.

What little else he could see of the room reinforced his first impression that Raven's Cry was accoutered for comfort rather than grandeur. A dining table built for sturdiness rather than elegance and a dozen matching chairs stood to his left, and the area in front of the hearth was set up as if it were a small room. A thick wool carpet in an intricate pattern of dark blue, cream and rose covered the stone floor just beyond the danger of sparks from the fire, and a pair of handsomely painted silk screens were set up on either side to foil the drafts. A sofa, several well-upholstered chairs and side tables with lamps created an intimate space, while tapestry frames and baskets of sewing and yarns spoke of the most common activity that occurred there.

The room the Troll woman escorted him to was equally pleasant, and it had already been set with a roaring fire. He knew they would have seen him coming as he climbed the hill—that was the whole point of the keep's location, after all—but the warmth of the room suggested the challenge at the gate and the guard's subsequent apology had been for show. Did that mean they were expecting him? Or that he wasn't the first to have ridden past that supposedly sealed gate?

The two tall glazed windows had floor-length drapes of dark-blue satin pulled back to allow light inside. After the darkness, even the dim gray of the rainy morning was a relief. He crossed to look out, just in time to see a figure shrouded in a voluminous black cloak cross the courtyard for the door.

He tossed his saddlebags onto a carved wooden chest at the foot of the bed and took off his dank cloak, draping it over a ladderback chair to dry.

"I am Droj," his escort said. "I am the chief housekeeper. If you have need of anything, ring the bell." She nodded toward the bed, where an exquisite needlepoint bell pull hung within easy reach of the pillows.

Another servant, this one a male, entered then, followed by an entourage bearing a large metal bathtub and the first of many buckets of hot and cold water to fill it. Droj nodded to him once and left him in the care of the newcomer, who introduced himself as Tugor. As Chris stripped off his clothes, Tugor unpacked the saddlebags.

"This needs pressing," he said as he held up Chris's field uniform, its navy blue wool crushed into a network of creases and wrinkles from the damp. "I will see to it and arrange for your luncheon."

Chris, now pleasantly submerged in lavender-scented hot water, smiled as the Troll bowed and departed. *He might look like a piece of rough-carved granite*, he thought, *but he sounds just like Bart.*

The first indication I had that trouble greater than just the machinations of the Spiders was afoot arrived early the morning after Christopher's departure. It appeared in the person of a sobbing youngster, one of the lads who clean the ashes from the fireplaces. He dashed into my office, the tears streaming from his eyes making tracks in his grubby face.

"The king wants you, sir," the lad blubbered. "He said he would be in the little room."

There being only one king present in the palace in a position to make demands, I immediately grasped that Benifaz was, all uninvited, assuming the position of interim ruler of Abernal. However, that did not explain the boy's distress, although the way he rubbed his backside suggested a possibility.

"Is something amiss, Will?"

"He asked where you were, sir, and then when I told him he called me an ins'lent brat and—and—he made Arty beat me."

When one attends royalty, one learns to hide one's inner thoughts quite early in life from both employer and employees. One of the first lessons my late father taught me was that no matter how difficult it was, the royal seneschal must not allow his (or her) opinions of the behavior of those served to be communicated to those doing the serving. Nevertheless, there are times when such control is difficult to maintain, and instances such as this of utterly unnecessary cruelty are the worst.

At Danella's insistence, we do not beat our young folk here. It is her belief—and to date the results support her belief—that rewarding good work is a much better incentive than punishing poor. For Benifaz to have ordered such a thing done over the lad's simple misunderstanding of his meaning—that he was to fetch me, not provide information as to my whereabouts—appalled me. I can only imagine how Arty, a kindly old footman who loved the youngsters dearly, must have hated being forced to perform the brutality.

"And he said I'd get more of the same if you didn't come quick."

Pausing in the kitchen only long enough to arrange for Will's upset to be somewhat assuaged by a liberal application of cookies and milk, I hastened to the "little room," a private dining chamber situated off the formal one. Benifaz sat stiffly in the king's seat at the head of the rectangular table, slowly breaking his fast. Not surprisingly, he did not acknowledge my presence until it suited him, an action intended to make clear to me who was in charge. As I have no problem with my own company, it is a maneuver that fails to affect me.

The lengthy silence did provide the opportunity for me to study the man. Fate, always on the lookout for an opportunity for irony, must have rejoiced at being able to replace Edrick with Benifaz. He was a small man, lean to the point of emaciation, though certainly not from lack of eating if the quantity of his present repast was any indication. He wore his iron-gray hair trimmed close to his head, making his jutting blade of a nose even more prominent and in no way enhancing his total absence of chin. His mouth was small and pursed, as though he had been born sucking lemons.

He cut his food into tiny bites, chewing each one thoroughly before swallowing. He did not mix the fare on his plate, finishing one item entirely before proceeding to the next. When he drained his cup, he neither called for more nor signaled for it—he simply sat immobile until one of the servitors present moved to attend to the lack. He ate meticulously and with total concentration, and he kept me standing until the last crumb had been consumed.

"I see a serious lack of discipline among the servants, Ruford," he said at last, pushing his empty plate aside to rest his clasped hands on the top of the table. A servitor slipped silently over and removed the dish to a tray set by the door for that purpose then lifted the tray and disappeared with equal silence. "In my household, when a boy is asked the whereabouts of someone, he does not simply reply with those whereabouts. He hastens to fetch the individual required with alacrity."

As there was no reply I could make to the statement without revealing my thoughts on a man who would hurt a child for such a stupid reason, I made none. However, Benifaz was the sort who is always ready to take umbrage, even when there is no cause.

"Have you nothing to say? I see from where the boy's attitude arises. Well, be assured there will be changes now that Edrick is no longer here to cater to your slovenly handling of his affairs. I am aware the law prevents me from discharging you, but there are other means available to ensure proper attitude and adequate attention to duty."

"As Your Grace has already attended to the matter of the boy, I did not think any response necessary. If I erred, I apologize."

It was clear that answer did not please him any more than my silence had, but he was unable to find specific fault with it and chose to get at last to the purpose of his commanding my presence.

"As there is no one else here of sufficient rank to do so, I will take charge of seeing everything is kept in order until an heir can be found. The first order of business is to have Edrick's remains seen to."

"The brothers of St. Thanaton were called within the hour of His Majesty's passing. He was set to lie in state in the cathedral an hour past dawn."

Benifaz's cheekbones had acquired a bit of a flush, and his black eyes were hard as onyx. I concluded it would behoove me not to underestimate him—he could do a great deal of harm between now and the time our new queen arrived to send him on his way.

"I have sent for Edrick's Ministers of Council, who should be arriving momentarily to discuss the disposition of the throne," Benifaz continued. "You will see that we are not disturbed."

It was on the tip of my tongue to tell him there was nothing to discuss, that the rightful heiress would be arriving within the week; but a sudden remembrance of Settleson's words the night before kept me silent. Christopher's absence would be noted all too soon.

So, I simply bowed and withdrew, passing the three bleary-eyed councilors as they responded to Benifaz's summons. The night staff had already advised me the trio had been up until nearly dawn making inroads in the royal cellars before retiring to their beds. As eager as they were to snatch power while it dangled in front of them, I doubted they appreciated such an early awakening.

My first stop was the kitchen, where I collected a somewhat mollified and definitely cleaner Will. I did not intend that Benifaz should have any opportunity to inflict any more damage on the boy, so I took him with me to the Queen's Tower, where I wished to confer with my wife. She had gone to the west wing of the palace immediately after breakfast to open and clean the Lady's Nest.

The central section of Abernal Palace was originally part of the sort of armored fortress that was the principal style of architecture in more bellicose times. After the institution of the King's Champion proved a success, however, Edrick's several-times-great grandfather had decided to display his confidence by building a house that was clearly a place for living rather than defense.

So, the walls and towers and battlements were torn down and what remained used as the core of a sprawling palace of two hundred rooms on three stories. A fourth story housed servant's quarters and storage rooms. At the end of each wing, hexagonal towers were constructed, one as the official residence of the queen, the other for the heir when he or she reached majority. Both had been closed since the Ugly Princess was dispatched to her mountain prison.

Now, a battalion of the staff, armed with buckets and mops and brooms and rags, were engaging the layers of dust and cobwebs that had settled in top floors of the Queen's Tower. Danella had set up headquarters in the Lady's Nest, the royal bedchamber at the very top of the six-story tower, where I found her alone carefully dusting a collection of fine porcelain figurines.

She is a beauty, my Danella, tall and slim yet with a figure that draws the eye with the compelling magnetism of a fine work of art. Her hair, sedately braided and coiled now but falling to her waist in a thick cascade when free, is the rich color of clover honey, her eyes green with flecks of gold that seem to swirl and glitter when she is pleased and flame when she is angry.

I knew the moment I set eyes on her the year before that she was the only woman I could marry, and it mattered not at all that she was the daughter of a merchant and not a scion of the nobility. My mother's reservations weakened after she realized Danella was well-versed in the tasks involved in running a large house. Her unimpeachable moral character, however, was what removed Mama's final objections. Though she made allowances for the weaknesses of human nature, Danella believed firmly in justice and assuming responsibility for one's actions. She asked nothing of our people she was not willing to do herself, and yet even when she brandished a scrub brush or broom she never lost her innate grace and dignity, the sort one can only be born with.

As there was not a single eligible young woman among our peers who showed anything like Danella's talents and character, our marriage received my mother's unqualified blessing.

I sent Will off to find something useful to do then closed the chamber door and joined her on the small settee. She set aside her dustcloth, alert to my mood as always.

"Something's wrong."

"Several things, I'm afraid, my dear. First, that poor lad who just left was treated to a dose of Benifaz's temper and will require extra cushions for sitting to his meals for a bit."

"I knew that nasty old man was going to be trouble. He has that look."

I have never understood precisely what "that look" is, although my beloved has been referring to it for as long as I have known her. I have also never known her to be mistaken about the unpleasantness of the characters of those who bear it, so whatever it is she is a mistress at interpreting it.

"That may be the least of it. He is meeting with the council as we speak, discussing the succession."

"Did you tell him...?"

"Of course not. However, I feel Christopher should be warned. The connivances of the Spiders are one thing, but the addition of Benifaz could prove dangerous. He insisted on bringing a full company of his personal guard with him for 'protection.' Should he get a message to his army commander at the border garrison, it would be simple enough to send a force to intercept Christopher and Her Grace on their way home."

"And it could be nearly a fortnight before they can return, for I can't see Chris forcing Her Grace to gallop the distance like a courier no matter what he told you."

"I think we must send a pigeon to the garrison at Norburgh. Perhaps he will be able to find some faster or less public route to bring her home."

The decision made, I kissed her and left the tower. The Registon battalion of the Royal Abernal Army, which included an office of the Royal Courier Service, was headquartered to the west of the city about a league beyond the city limits. After ensuring that everything was running with its customary efficiency, I obtained a mount from the stables and within the hour had scribbled a brief warning to Christopher.

"Benifaz meeting with Spiders re: succession. Suggest caution."

The captain on duty fastened the message to the leg of a bird and set it a-flight. I watched it wend its way north until it was no longer visible, and then I returned to the palace well before time for the noon feeding of the nobility.

Chapter 5

TRUE TO HIS WORD, TUGOR RETURNED THE IRONED UNI-
form along with a hearty meal, all arriving just as Chris had
slipped on his clean smallclothes. He postponed dressing and
filled his stomach with food as good as—and in some cases,
better than—any he had eaten at Edrick's table.

The hot bath and the food, however, only made him
more aware of his too-long hours in the saddle. He stretched
out on the wide bed, thinking to sleep for an hour or so.

He dreamed he was in a cave, wandering in a deep stony
labyrinth, searching for something...someone. He had no
fear, despite knowing he was lost, because finding that...yes, it
was someone...was more important that finding the way out.
He had a candle, but it was burned down to a stub; and he
could tell by the way the flame twitched it would go out
soon.

Then, ahead, he saw a pale glow coming from a side tunnel, and he hurried toward it. His heart pounded—the treas-
ure he sought was there, waiting. He reached the place where
the tunnels met and started to turn...

"Sir Christopher!"

Chris jolted awake and sat up. Droj stood over him with a lamp—and just as well. The sun had obviously been gone for quite some time, and except for the light from the fire he was once again buried in shadows.

"Milady asks will you join her in the Hall after you have eaten?"

He was tempted to say he would join her immediately, but he decided it was better to accept that the princess ran her house as she saw fit. Despite the urgency of his mission, offending his new monarch by trampling over her authority was not likely to start their relationship off on quite the right note.

"Please tell Her Grace I will be honored to do so."

Droj stared at him in silence, and he had no trouble interpreting the look in her eyes. She had noted the title he used—the one by which only the reigning monarch could be addressed. She said nothing, however, only moving about the room with a taper to light the candle lamps. Another excellent meal sat on the table before the fireplace.

Half an hour later she returned to conduct Chris back to the Hall. He had spent the time bracing himself mentally, determined he would face the Ugly Princess without a twitch, but he was spared the need. The woman sitting on the wingback chair by the hearth was draped from head to toe in smoky gray veils. In the golden backlighting of the flames, all he could see of her was a vague shadow that gave no hint of what lay under the tiers of silk.

She sat with incredible stillness, not moving even her head until he stood before her. One of the dogs sat beside her chair, her hand resting on its neck. Her gown was of plain gray wool—that much he could see—of good quality but hardly what royalty would wear.

Poor girl, he thought as he knelt before the ghostly figure. *She must be worse off than I've heard if she has to hide herself from Trolls.*

"Your Grace," he announced without preamble, "the King your father is dead. I have come to escort you to assume your crown."

He hardly expected her to display any grief, and she did not disappoint him.

"I suspected as much when the Royal Champion appeared on my doorstep. I'll confess, though, I had thought you were...older."

He recognized her voice as the one that had bade him welcome at the gate. Now, as then, it did interesting things to his spine. So did the light scents of vanilla and cinnamon and musk that surrounded her.

"My father retired five years ago," he explained.

"Ah," she said. "Please, Sir Christopher, be seated."

"I would swear fealty first, Your Grace. There may be... difficulties." He was thinking of the Spiders—and Settleson's strange reference to Benifaz of Nadwich—but she misunderstood.

"I would be surprised if the people were eager to have me." She kept her tone neutral, but even that was enough to make him feel guilty of having offended her.

"No, ma'am," he protested, "there is a plot to replace you the people know nothing about. Please, let me—"

"Yes, of course, Sir Christopher." She held out her hands, one palm up, the other palm down, so he could place his between them in the ancient ritual. He recited the words that bound him, body and heart, to the life of this woman; and when she responded with the words of acceptance he actually seemed to feel something connect between them.

That done, he took the signet ring from his belt pouch and slid it onto her thumb. Her skin was warm, soft against his palm; and when he bent to kiss the ring he was somehow kissing the back of her hand instead.

Chris was shocked to realize he was blushing, something he hadn't done since his father had caught him in the hayloft with...well, for a long time. He was suddenly grateful there was only firelight as he went to sit in the chair opposite her.

"Would you like some wine, Sir Christopher?"

"No, ma'am, thank you. What I had with dinner was excellent." *And why*, he wondered, *are we sitting here making small talk when there could be an army marching on this place? And where did she learn to comport herself so royally?* Not from the Trolls and not from the aging academics who had taught her to read and write.

"I will be ready to leave at first light," she said quietly. Even so, he started. If he didn't know better he'd almost have believed she'd read his mind. He dismissed that idea immediately—there had never been any signs of magical talents in any of the Redimans. No doubt she was just as able to read his thoughts on his face as Bart and Danella.

"If you require more time to prepare..."

"I have little here I cannot leave behind without regret, except for kind friends," she said with a touch of ironic amusement.

And why am I arguing with her when she just said exactly what I wanted to hear? Chris asked himself.

"I know you have rested, but I suspect not long enough," his queen continued. "Please, return to your room and I'll see you again tomorrow."

Feeling off-balance without quite knowing why, Chris stood and bowed, then did as he was told. Back in his room, he sank into a chair and stared into the fire, wondering.

He hadn't considered what the new queen might be like, but the last thing he would have expected was the calm, poised woman he had just left. In truth, knowing she had been literally raised by Trolls, there had been the possibility she would be an even worse savage than her mother.

That's when he realized he had neglected to ask an important question.

Idiot! You don't even know her name!

A discreet tap on the door interrupted his self-recriminations, and he called for whomever it was to come in. A young Troll brought in an armload of wood and set it carefully on the fire.

"Boy," Chris said, "I have a question."

"Aye, milord."

"What do you call your lady?"

"Milady, milord."

"No, lad, her name. What is her name?"

"The Lady Jahmelle, milord."

When Chris sat silent for a long moment, the boy took that as permission to leave. There was no sound in the room save the gentle crackle of the flames.

Jahmelle. What could have possessed Bart's mother to give the poor, benighted infant a name that could only have added to her pain should she learn its meaning? That was a cruelty he would never have believed Maryim Ruford capable of. Or had Edrick, in a fit of perverse humor, christened her that? That seemed more likely—it was the sort of twisted joke he would have found amusing.

Chris felt a sharp ache of sorrow and empathy for the woman who was now the reason for his existence. What must it be like to be forced to hide your countenance behind veils and darkness, knowing others would gaze at what lay beneath with horror or pity, and yet have to be addressed day after day, year after year, with a name that meant "beautiful?"

It took him a moment the next morning to remember where he was. His night had been filled with dreams that seemed dreadfully important as they progressed but which he now couldn't recall at all. The fire in his hearth had long since burned down to ash, and he debated whether to ring for someone to set it burning again before he forced himself out of the warm comforters. The stone floor was icy on his feet when he stepped off the rugs beside the bed, and as soon as he coaxed the last few embers back to life he dived shivering back into shelter.

How do people live like this? he wondered. *How could even Edrick condemn a child to live like this?*

He had never liked the old king, and not just because it had fallen to him and Bart to cover up the worst of the man's excesses. Edrick never missed an opportunity to make some cutting remark about him or his father on even the smallest pretext. Chris began to suspect he would have done away with the office of Royal Champion altogether had he been able to do so without the approval of the Consortium.

Nor would Chris have minded, although what he would have done afterwards he had no idea. The problem with his position was that training for it was all-consuming, lasted for most of one's life—and had little practical application to anything else. He did enjoy commanding the army and seemed to have a talent for it, but even there he knew he was a long way from being as good as his father was. There just wasn't any substitute for experience.

As soon as the fire drove off the worst of the chill he emerged again and dressed then crossed to the heavily draped window and looked outside. A brisk breeze was driving the clouds north, and the first crimson rim of the sun spilled its stain on the far eastern rim of the mountains. He wanted to reach Norburgh by tomorrow, and they would make better time in fair weather.

Had he been at Abernal House he would have headed to the kitchen for his breakfast, but he doubted the Troll servants would be as welcoming as their counterparts, especially to a human stranger. He yanked the bell pull, and a surprisingly short time later a maid arrived with a loaded tray. There was a steaming pot of rich coffee that was better than any he had ever drunk in Edrick's household accompanying the omelet, stewed plums and fresh bread. Whatever Her New Grace might lack in luxuries, she definitely ate well.

"What time will Her Grace be ready to travel?" he asked, resigned to having to wait at least another hour or two before she would manage to finish packing her odds and ends.

"Milady said to tell you to enjoy your meal, milord, and she will await you in the Great Hall."

Chris realized he was staring at the Troll when the woman raised her eyebrows in silent inquiry. Rather than look any more foolish than he no doubt already did, he shook his head and ate as quickly as he could. He decided he needed to stop anticipating how Queen Jahmelle would behave. Clearly, that way lay disaster.

Remembering at the last minute to light a candle, he strode below, only to find the windows undraped throughout the castle. Jahmelle was waiting, just as she promised, in her chair by the great hearth, her dogs lying one on either side of her. She rose as he approached and made his bow—she was taller than he had expected. Her veiled head came to his shoulder. She didn't get that from Edrick, which for some irrational reason pleased him.

"Did you rest well, Sir Christopher?"

"Very well, Your Grace, thank you." He looked around for her baggage, but there was only a single medium-sized shoulder pouch lying beside her chair. "I see your things have already been loaded. Just let me have our horses readied and we'll be on our way."

"All I will take with me is what you see," she said, gesturing toward the pouch. "My people will arrange for the rest of what I require to be sent along in time. As for having horses readied, I'm afraid that is going to pose a problem."

"Your Grace?"

"Your horse is the only one here. We haven't much use for them, you see."

She said it kindly, with no hint of criticism or resentment; but he still felt like an utter fool. Of course, there wouldn't be any horses. She hadn't been allowed past the walls. So, he had two choices: leave her here and ride back to the garrison for a second mount or leave now and ride double. Before he could even weigh the options, Jahmelle made the choice for him.

"Perhaps the sensible thing would be for us to share your mount until we can find another. If you feel he will be able to manage."

"Oh, certainly, Your Grace—he's a sturdy beast. Well, then, I'll—"

"There is one other thing you might need to consider."

"Your Grace?"

"I'm afraid I don't know how to ride."

"Don't worry, Your Grace, I'll make sure you don't fall off."

The minute he said it he felt his face go hot. It wasn't what he'd said but the way he'd said it—half-laughing and slightly arrogant.

She laughed. Not a giggle or a chuckle but a chiming peal of glee that banished his embarrassment in an instant and brought a smile to his own lips. There was nothing restrained about it, and he wondered how someone caged inside these grim walls her entire life could have the spirit and the sense of joy to own such a laugh.

"I will hold you to that, Sir Christopher," she said as she slipped her hand into the crook of his arm. She snatched up her bag before he could even reach for it and they started for the door to the outer bailey. "It would not do, I think, for the Queen of Abernal's first appearance before her people to be on foot because her backside is bruised from falling off her horse."

His mount was already waiting when they emerged from the central hallway. It would be better, he decided, to let her ride while he led, at least until they reached more level ground. That way he could also give her some riding basics.

This, however, presented him with another quandary. It would be hard for her to keep her seat riding sidesaddle, but he couldn't imagine her riding astride with her skirts hiked over her knees.

Once again she anticipated what he hadn't. She first made the gelding's acquaintance by feeding him a bit of carrot and rubbing his neck. Leading him nearer the stairs, she used the bottom step to help her reach the stirrup and swung aboard. She wore a divided skirt, cut so full the split was invisible when she was standing.

By now the household was assembled in the bailey and stood in a rough semicircle around them. To his surprise, many of them were weeping. So much for the tales of Trolls' hard hearts.

"My good friends," Jahmelle said. Her veils swirled in the slight breeze. "I know we never thought this day would come. I expected to spend my days here with you, sharing your joys and sorrows and your kindness and your wisdom. It seems, however, that the gods have other plans. I wish that I might take you with me, but I will have to be satisfied to take my memories instead. I love you all, and I will miss you."

Droj stepped forward and took Jahmelle's hand. She kissed it and squeezed it with undisguised affection.

"You are our own child," the Troll woman rasped. "Our hearts are heavy that we part, but they are also filled with joy that you have been set free. Know, sweet lady, that we are your people, and we will come at a single word if you have need of us."

She stepped back, and Jahmelle took one last lingering look before she turned to Chris and nodded once. He strode out through the wide-open gates, and as they started down the rough path he pretended he didn't hear her muffled sobs.

Chapter 6

I RETURNED TO THE PALACE, AND IT WAS CLEAR AT ONCE that ominous activities were afoot. The first indication was the pair of guards in Nadwickian uniform stationed on either side of the entrance to the formal reception hall. My curiosity aroused, I entered through the smaller reception area and peered surreptitiously through the doors connecting it to the larger room.

Normally, that cavernous remnant of an earlier time was used only to greet extremely important visitors. Now, however, Benifaz sat gazing down his nose from the high seat, surrounded by another half-dozen of his "personal guard." The staff scurried about trying their best to appear occupied by vital tasks. Those of the guests who had remained at the palace to attend the funeral milled about muttering to each other when they weren't cautiously eyeing the man ensconced in the place of power.

I started toward the kitchens, having decided additional information regarding what had occurred during my absence would be advisable. I passed several members of the staff, and their behavior served only to heighten my sense that matters were degenerating rapidly. Whereas they were accustomed to greet me with smiles and pleasant greetings, they now hastened about their business with frowns or grimaces of fear. That the atmosphere of the palace should have altered so drastically in just the hour of my absence disturbed me.

To further enhance my disquiet, Danella was waiting for me in my office, pacing in a way most unlike her usual calm demeanor. Her arms were crossed at her waist; and though I had but a profile view, I felt relieved the expression on her face was surely meant for someone other than myself. The moment she heard my step she halted and turned to face me.

"The message—"

"Has gone out and should be delivered to Christopher the moment he enters the garrison. I see His Grace of Nadwich has wasted no time taking full advantage of the situation."

"He has ordered that we cease 'fooling about' in the Queen's Tower and tend to our regular duties. He demands that all further meals be served in the formal banquet hall and that no one is to dine in their room. The meals are to be served at six of the morning, noon and seven of the evening for precisely one hour, and those who cannot manage to be present will do without. All the daily household chores are to be completed prior to the breakfast hour, which means we are now required to arise at three past midnight. Any said chore not done to His Grace's satisfaction will not only be done over but will earn the one whose task it was a flogging in full view of the entire household."

"The man does have a serious fixation with flogging people."

My beloved favored me with a quirked eyebrow and a grim glare, a sure sign my lame attempt at humor was not appreciated.

"He also stated that those responsible for overseeing the staff will share in any punishments inflicted."

I consider myself to be a man of even temper, not prone to succumbing to the baser emotions. However, Benifaz had managed to inspire me to outrage twice in the space of four hours.

I began to see, as well, that the alacrity with which he had accepted Edrick's proposal to wed his daughter had harbored a devious scheme, as Settleson's remark the previous night about "His Nibs of Nadwich" should have warned me. I now understood, perhaps too late, that the Spiders had been playing a double game, with the goal being giving Benifaz a foothold in Abernal he could then use to his advantage.

"He means to rule both countries," I muttered.

"How can he without starting a revolt?" Danella argued.

Before I could respond a footman appeared with a summons from our new lord and master. Accepting a quick kiss from Danella, I hastened to the entrance to the hall as swiftly as dignity would permit before assuming the appropriate demeanor for one of my status.

The Seneschals of House Rediman bear the hereditary title of baron and are counted slightly less than a king and a bit more than an earl, which meant I technically outranked most of those gathered to witness whatever drama was about to unfold. I felt the stares of the assembly on me as I strode purposefully to the high seat and made my bow.

I suppose I should have been alerted by this unusual scrutiny—as I've noted before, the nobility is as inclined to notice those of the servant class as they are to paying heed to the floor tiles on which they tread. By virtue of association, we Rufords had come to be included in that indifference, which had proven useful on more than one occasion in our family's history.

However, I had no past experience to set off internal alarms, so I attributed the attention I was now receiving from my peers as simply a reaction to the king's death and the events now unfolding. It is the price one pays for long years of relative peace, that falling into an inflated sense of security.

Leaning in seeming indolence with one elbow on the arm of the high seat, Benifaz gifted me with a choleric frown.

"Where have you been, Ruford?" he demanded loudly, ensuring he had the attention of all present.

"An errand in the city, Your Grace."

"There are servants for such things. Your place is here during this time of mourning."

"If Your Grace prefers."

"I do. What was the nature of this 'errand?'"

Think fast, Ruford!

"Cook discovered a shortage of raisins, and knowing Your Grace's fondness for rice pudding I hastened to replenish our supply."

The corners of Benifaz's mouth curved up in what on any other face might have been considered a smile. My personal reaction was that it rather appeared someone had tried to cut his throat and missed.

"How thoughtful of you to interrupt your busy morning to tend to this menial task personally."

"As it happened, the only greengrocer to have a fresh supply is not one with whom we are accustomed to doing business. I wished to confirm his goods met our standards, and that is something I prefer to do myself."

"We were not aware that raisins were to be found in the offices of the Royal Courier Service."

The course of this conversation was not leading in the most favorable direction. I suppose I should have expected that a man attempting to usurp a throne would have placed his prospective enemies under scrutiny. Clearly, I had been followed, and attempting to prevaricate further would only make matters worse. A careful lie of omission seemed the better part of wisdom.

"A simple message to Sir Christoper Evergild regarding the upcoming funeral services, Your Grace."

The Spiders were standing in a cluster to my right, their heads together and their eyes bouncing sideways at me between mutters. My response to the king's question must have been somewhat anticipated, for Overlack stepped forward and looked at Benifaz, who nodded to give him permission for whatever his role in this little charade might be.

For, of course, I had by now determined that this was some premeditated performance designed to present to the spectators what the conspirators had decided upon during their earlier meeting, while at the same time establishing precisely where the power in the kingdom now lay. Nor was it difficult to predict the content of the First Minister's address to me.

"Where is Sir Christopher Evergild? What could possibly have called him from his post at this crucial time?"

For a brief moment, I debated whether I should pretend ignorance of the purpose of Christopher's quest, but the gloating looks from the Spiders made it clear they already knew—or at least suspected—the answer.

"Sir Christopher has traveled to the dwelling of Her Highness, King Edrick's daughter and heir, to advise her of her father's passing."

There was a murmur from the assembled nobles as they discussed the ramifications of this. The legend of the Ugly Princess was a popular one amongst those with too much time on their hands, and I had no doubt those speculations had been enhanced in the hours since Edrick's death.

"And what is this alleged daughter and heir's name?" Zephus Settleson demanded on cue.

"As the Milord Minister is aware, Her Highness has not been at court since she was a child, and King Edrick, may his soul rest in peace, did not see fit to confide that information. Nevertheless, funds have been provided for her lodging and upkeep for these twenty years, under my father's supervision and my own."

Overlack sneered.

"This woman wouldn't be the first royal bastard to be supported by a doting father."

"The provision for Her Highness was made with the understanding that she is, in fact, Edrick's trueborn child. It is so specified in the contracts drawn up between the Crown and the High Chief of the Trolls."

Now it was Entreput's turn. One had to admit, given the brief time they had had to prepare their lines they were performing quite credibly.

"By what right does Evergild decide to name her heir apparent?"

"It is not Sir Christopher's place to name anyone anything, milord. However, it has always been accepted that the lady was King Edrick's legitimate heir. As such, it is Sir Christopher's duty to be at her side as her Champion."

His toadies having laid the groundwork, it was now time for the lead actor's next entrance into the scene.

"We have found no will bearing Edrick's signature naming this woman or anyone as his successor," Benifaz trumpeted, his eyes sweeping over his audience. "In the absence of such designation or any existing document attesting to the legitimacy of this unknown woman, we must, as the only suitable judge present, state that the succession is, therefore, not formally established. For that reason, we have sent for all those of near blood to our late and much-lamented brother, Edrick, and have ordered the royal genealogists to search the records to determine which of them has the closest level of consanguinity. When that has been determined, that individual will be named King of Abernal."

He dropped his gaze to me again, and the look he gave did not bode well for any of us. Of course, he knew that I knew, in my position as head of the Department of Genealogy, that his own nephew held that particular place, having had a princess of House Rediman for a grandmother. But the King of Nadwich was far from finished with his pronouncements.

"We have also issued a warrant for the arrest of Sir Christopher Evergild and the unnamed woman he presumes to pass off as the daughter-heir of the House of Abernal for the crime of high treason. Two companies of the Royal Nadwickian Army have been summoned from the border garrison to assist in their apprehension. As you have seen fit to abet him in his crime, we now order that you be stripped of your title as hereditary Seneschal of House Rediman and be confined to prison until your trial on the same charge. Guards!"

I realized I was staring at Benifaz, my jaw gaping like that of a yokel at his first fair, as two of his hulking troopers seized me by the arms. We had anticipated some opposition to the princess, based on what we had overheard. I understood that Benifaz was using the whims of fate to gain control of Abernal. I cannot even say I was, at this point, surprised he would blatantly deny what everyone in the kingdom knew, that the princess in the far-off castle was Edrick's true daughter.

But that he could accuse the Royal Champion, the very symbol of honor, of treason and intrigue and do so clearly expecting his accusations to be accepted without question or protest stunned me. I realized in that moment of enlightenment I had grown overconfident in the system that had kept us safe all these years. Were we, and the people of Abernal, about to pay a ruinous price for our trust in a system that others, it seemed, had been all along exploiting to their own ends?

My warning to Christopher suddenly seemed no better than a whisper in a windstorm. Indeed, if the garrison to which my message was dispatched accepted this unabashed usurpation without protest, Chris and the lady would likely be bound in chains the moment they rode through the gates.

Chapter 7

THE SUN, AS IF FEELING GUILTY FOR ITS MANY DAYS' AB-
sence, chose to atone with summery radiance. By midmorning Chris abandoned his cloak, as did the princess, stopping
for a moment to bundle them on the back of his saddle. He
debated asking if she wanted to shed her veils then told himself she wasn't a child. If she were too warm, she'd do something about it without his prompting.

However, though the day grew even warmer, she didn't
seem bothered by the heat. Nor was she inclined to chatter.
They descended the road down the slope without another
word once his riding instructions were done.

"Sir Christopher, I believe the trail widens just ahead. I
would like to stop there for a bit of a rest, if we may."

A quick glance told him it was noon, and guilt washed
over him.

"Whatever you wish, Your Grace. And I apologize—I
should have stopped before this."

"I sensed you felt we needed to hurry," she said, "and I've
been enjoying the view."

It was a perfectly innocuous thing to say, and yet those
few words hit him like a punch in the belly. He hadn't been

enjoying the view. He'd been thinking about the heat, and the hours ahead until they reached the bottom of the mountain, and how he was going to get her to the palace in a reasonable time when she couldn't ride, and how far the Spiders' delegation might have traveled. He had seen nothing since their departure save the trail and the inside of his own head.

He looked up and tried to imagine how what he saw must look to her, whose world had been bounded by the thick stone walls of her keep. Below them, a broad swath of alternating harvested fields and pastureland separated by fences of split rail or stacked stone spread away on all sides, turned golden by the lengthening nights and early frosts of autumn. There were swatches of forest as well, copses the landowners carefully preserved to provide a place for game to thrive. Horses and cattle both dairy and beef grazed here and there, and off on the right where the ground was too hilly for cultivation a black-and-white shepherd dog dashed after a straying ewe and sent her trotting back to the flock.

The road—little more than a trail from here to where it met the Eastern Highway—wound gently beside a narrow, rushing stream. The sky was a rich, bright blue with nary a cloud, and a very gentle breeze carried the scents of warm grass and freshly watered earth. Above them, a pair of hawks circled, searching for prey as they drifted on the warm thermals the sun pulled from the stone.

Abernal was a beautiful country, but he had grown habituated to its beauties because he saw them every day. What must it be like to look on it as she was, with eyes that had never seen anything like it?

They reached the place she had seen, a broadening of the road with a stone fire pit that indicated it was a common resting place for travelers; he dropped the horse's reins and went to help her down. Before he reached her, she tried to dismount on her own and nearly fell when her stiff legs wouldn't hold her. Chris reflexively caught her by the waist to steady her, discovering she not only had one but that he could nearly span it with his hands. Whatever her other physical flaws, the Ugly Princess wasn't overweight.

"I begin to see that staying on a horse has perils as well as does falling off," she commented, a touch of the humor that fueled her wonderful laugh bubbling in her voice.

"Just keep moving, Your Grace. It will ease up—but I suspect you'll be a little uncomfortable until you're used to it."

"Sir Christopher," she chuckled as he helped her walk off the stiffness, "I suspect you are a master of understatement."

The Trolls hadn't stinted on their food supplies, and even without a fire they ate much better than Chris was used to doing on trips like this. There were small rolls of fresh bread wrapped around thick slices of clove-spiced ham, tiny raw carrots cleaned and lightly salted, and a small stone jug of fresh cider still cool from the cellar. He tried not to stare at her as she deftly tucked the meal in under her veils. The ones she wore today were shorter, draping only to just below her collarbone, but they were just as opaque as the ones she had worn before. How did she see?

"Quite well, actually," she said, and he felt a chill go down his spine that wasn't at all like the pleasant one he'd experienced the first time her heard her voice. Was she a witch to know what he was thinking?

"No, I don't read minds, Sir Christopher. Although I've had few visitors during my...stay...at Raven's Cry, they invariably wonder how I manage with my veils. Judging by the way you've been watching me from the corner of your eye, it was apparent you were doing so as well."

It was a logical explanation, but Chris wasn't sure he believed it. Jahmelle of Abernal was an unknown quantity—and there were plenty of tales that ascribed more-than-human powers to Moldori women. Still, he couldn't very well call his monarch a liar.

"The veils are a special weave created for the use of the Moldori Dream Dancers," she continued. "Are you familiar with them?"

"I'm afraid no one knows too much about the Moldori, Your Grace." Well, other than that they were a pack of uncivilized bandits who stole what they wanted when they wanted it and fought like rabid wolves when they were cornered. But it wouldn't do to tell his monarch that, either, given her genealogy.

"The Dream Dancers are the spiritual leaders of the Moldori—the entire race, not just the clans," Jahmelle explained. "The cloth reveals nothing to the outside observer, but the wearer can see through it as if it were clear glass. It's really quite remarkable."

Christopher finished his cider and began repacking the food. She pitched in without hesitation, and in minutes they were again on their way. This time, however, she chose to walk alongside him. He had hoped she might talk more about the Moldori—he was, after all, the commander of the royal army and any information about potential enemies was useful. He refused to hear the teasing little voice that said what he really wanted was to listen to her rich voice with its soft, husky undertone.

However, she preferred asking questions to providing information, and he couldn't fault her for it. He was surprised at her range of knowledge, not just about Abernal but about other things. It seemed she hadn't wasted all those years of captivity but had instead spent them studying anything and everything. The limit of her knowledge, though, was that none of it was current.

"Had my father been ill long?" she asked him after a lengthy discussion of the events of the previous five years.

"No, ma'am, he wasn't ill at all. He had an accident while dining and choked to death." He wondered briefly why he chose not to mention Edrick had been dining at his wedding banquet then decided it wasn't relevant to their present situation. The marriage hadn't been consummated nor Yolanthe crowned, so she couldn't be a factor in any plot against Jahmelle.

"You mentioned something about a conspiracy...?"

"The three Ministers of Council—"

"So, King Edrick never replaced the other three?"

"No, ma'am, and the Spi—the ministers were overheard last night plotting to replace Your Grace with your cousin."

"Have they allies in this?"

How to answer that one? Did the Spiders have an ally in Benifaz, or had they simply assumed any attempt to place his nephew on the throne would necessarily require his participation? The King of Nadwich was notoriously afraid of assassination, so he hadn't really thought it strange the bridal party had arrived surrounded by a hundred soldiers. Perhaps he should have.

"I don't know for sure, Your Grace."

Dusk was creeping out of the east as they finally reached level ground, bringing the chill back. After retrieving their cloaks, Chris looped his sword belt over the saddle horn and mounted, the queen climbed on behind him and he kicked the horse into a canter. He knew of a decent inn midway between here and Norburgh, and he intended to get there before they stopped for the night.

They rode in silence for two hours as the night descended and the first moon, in its last-quarter phase, rose toward the zenith. Suddenly, Chris drew rein and listened. He hadn't been mistaken—the sound of hoofbeats, enough for at least a small cavalry patrol, came from the road ahead. A moment later he could see them—a scout, a color-bearer, one officer and a dozen riders.

He surveyed the land around them, looking for somewhere they could hide until he determined whether it was friend or foe approaching. *Just my luck*, he thought, *to be in the one section of the road with fields on both sides.* There wasn't even a drainage ditch where he could have the queen hide.

"It will be better for now if you're on the ground, Your Grace," he said, helping her dismount. "Go back about ten paces."

She obeyed without question as he drew his sword. Not that it would do him much good against men armed with pistols and muskets.

"Ho, there!" a man shouted. "Who goes?" The patrol stopped just within musket range, but as near as he could tell only the scout had his weapon ready to fire. And he had it resting across his arm rather than aimed.

"Sir Christopher Evergild on the queen's business."

"Thought so," the other man shouted, and only then did Chris recognize the voice.

"You're out a bit late in the evening, aren't you, Ted?" he said as he sheathed his weapon. He rode back and helped Jahmelle remount.

Edgard Truville, captain of the mounted infantry company at the Norburgh garrison, led his men forward until he and Chris could clasp hands. The older man grimaced with distaste.

"Yes, well, I thought it best to come find you after a company of Nadwickians arrived with a 'royal order' from the palace."

"Royal order? There's no one there to issue any royal orders."

"That was my take on it. I serve House Rediman, and as far as I know there's no 'Benifaz King' in that bloodline."

Suddenly, the captain noticed his friend was not alone on the horse, and in a matter of a moment he was on the ground on one knee, his hat in his hand. His men, all save the color-bearer, who snapped a brisk salute with his free hand, were so close behind in following suit there was barely a pause.

"God save Your Grace," he said.

"Thank you, Captain...?"

"Edgard Truville, at your service, Your Grace."

"Do I understand that Benifaz of Nadwich is in control of Abernal?"

"He's in control of the palace, Your Grace," Truville amended. "And he's issued an order for your immediate arrest for treason, Chris. Her Grace, as well. He's spreading it about you're trying to pass off some impostor as Edrick's daughter."

"How do you know he isn't, Captain? And, please, do stand up."

"Because Chris just wouldn't do that, Your Grace. I've known him all his life, and he's allergic to politics."

Chris felt her soft laughter more than heard it, and once again he wrestled with sensations that were utterly improper for a man to feel toward his monarch.

"Of course," Truville went on, "it happened we also got a message from Bart warning you to watch out for Benifaz, so there was that. I realized we hadn't done any night maneuvers for a while and decided this was an excellent time to correct that oversight."

"Bart?" Jahmelle asked.

"Bartrim Ruford, Baron Greenwater—Your Grace's Seneschal," Chris explained, realizing that in all their conversation he had somehow neglected to mention his friend.

So, his suspicion Benifaz had come to Abernal with ulterior motives was confirmed, although there was no comfort in the confirmation. Nadwich had been indecently eager to hand his only daughter over to Edrick, although he certainly knew about the late king's proclivities. Likely he had already contacted the Spiders before the betrothal agreement was even signed, enlisting their cooperation with promises of the power and wealth that was their only reason for existence. Giving them his promise of support in having them made joint regents should Edrick die while his offspring was too young to rule would have been more than enough to make them Benifaz's allies.

That, however, was a far cry from having Benifaz himself seize control, which now seemed to be the case. The question was: how to deal with the situation.

"And why," Jahmelle asked, "is King Benifaz in Abernal?"

Chris was glad it was too dark for her to see him blush. So much for saving the news of her mother's death and her father's remarriage for later. He should have known this could happen and just given her the information as gently as possible. For all he knew, she was already aware Queen Marvaya was dead—clearly she had some degree of contact with the Moldori. The problem was, she needed to have complete trust in him; and his failure to be completely forthcoming about what was happening—and why—might make that impossible.

Before he could speak, however, his dilemma became moot. The sound of a single rider nearing them on the road to the south had every man back in the saddle priming his weapon until a shouted codeword put them at ease. A moment later a second scout appeared, drawing rein abruptly at Ted Truville's side.

"You were right, Captain, they went back to the garrison and must have found out what we're doing," he said. "There's a full Nadwickian company coming—they're about five minutes behind me."

"Mount up!" Truville commanded, jumping into his saddle. "Follow us, Chris. We've a bivouac not far from here, and if we're lucky we can reach it before this bunch reaches us."

He swung his mount to the left and headed off with his men cross-country at a full gallop.

"Hang on, Your Grace!" Chris said, and followed an instant later.

Chapter 8

GRIPPED ON EITHER SIDE BY A GRIM-FACED NADWICKIAN soldier, I was half-dragged through the silent cluster of Abernali nobility. One of the staff must had gone to fetch Danella when it became clear disaster loomed, and I had time to send what I hoped was a reassuring look into her shocked eyes just before the doors closed behind me.

Confirming my suspicions Benifaz and his Abernali bootlickers had planned the entire episode well in advance, one of the city's prisoner transports waited in the drive. That the driver wore a Nadwickian uniform rather than the tan of the city constabulary was unnecessary reinforcement. Had I not provided the means for them to act by contacting Chris they would have devised some other excuse for removing me from the palace—the nefarious are notoriously creative when it comes to achieving their goals.

I feared my captors would bind my hands before tossing me into the confines of the square black wagon, but apparently I wasn't considered a sufficient escape threat for that. The interior of the van stank of sweat, vomit, sour beer and other things I preferred not to analyze. There were no seats, but I braced in a crouch rather than sit on the sticky floor.

The only light came from narrow slits near the roof, set there to allow ventilation, but I found the dark better suited my present mood.

I wasted no time cursing myself for a dimwitted fool, since that was a given. I had taken some pride in my skills as a politician, my position of necessity requiring I have a passing knowledge of who hated whom and which was planning an alliance with what. Never in my maddest nightmares, however, would it have occurred to me that Benifaz would blatantly insert himself into the succession process. It beggared my imagination, and I suspected I was not the only individual who would be stunned by his arrogance.

I was, however, the only one in a prison coach en route to a likely hanging for treason.

My next thoughts were for Danella, and I feared the worst. I knew from the Nadwickian's behavior toward his spouse and daughter he had little respect for women. Danella would unquestionably seek to alert Christopher to what was going on, and I feared what the self-appointed regent might do should he catch her.

I suppose those unfamiliar with the sort of society in which we Abernali had lived for so long will consider our reliance on our political neighbors' adhering to single combat as a diplomatic tool singularly naive. I will not argue.

The balance of power, however, is always precarious; and until this moment both the Deciron emperors and the kings of Nadwich had been acutely conscious that an unsuccessful invasion of any of their neighbors would likely have deleterious effects on their own life spans. The natural barrier of the arc of mountains that divided us from them, though not as precipitous as those found on the eastern half of the continent, had always been an effective deterrent when combined with the unquestioned superiority of the Abernali army.

So, we had become complacent, overconfident. Even I, who knew firsthand how enthusiastically Edrick and his three cronies had chosen to remain unaware of what was happening over the mountains, had gone on with my daily routines snug in a cocoon of ignorance. However, wallowing in regret would not resolve my present problem, not that I had any idea what might, short of Christopher's arrival with the queen.

The coach stopped, the door flew open and I was hauled out with no ceremony and even less consideration. We were in front of a jail near the river where the worst of the city's criminals were incarcerated, one to which an Abernali noble should never have been sent. The message was clear. Knowing he had insufficient evidence to truly prove a charge of high treason and knowing as well that he dared not flout the Abernali legal system—however much he might want to—without dire consequences, Benifaz intended I should not survive my arrest.

That my arrival was unexpected was also clear, to judge by the gaping jaw of the beady-eyed jailer who responded after the van driver pounded on the door. I suppose I should have found the care with which the other two soldiers prevented my escape, by compressing my upper arms just short of shattering bone, flattering.

"What's this, then?" the jailer said, his eyes skimming over me. "In the wrong place for the likes of him, ain'tcha?"

"Stand aside. This prisoner is ordered here by Benifaz of Nadwich."

"Who?"

"The Regent of Abernal, you idiot. He's to be held in the condemned cell."

For a moment, it looked like the man might argue, but something in the faces of my escort apparently discouraged debate. Taking a ring of keys from his belt, he led us into the depths of the building, stopping in front of an ironclad door with a six-inch-by-twelve slot in the bottom. Gesturing to a pair of armed guards in a small room opposite, he waited until they stood beside us then pounded on the door with his truncheon.

"Get back or get dead!"

He waited for as long as it would have taken someone with the ability to count ten before unlocking the door. He pulled it open, then moved quickly to the side to make way for one of the guards, who kept two loaded pistols trained on the shadow-draped figures inside until I was thrust within to join them. The door slammed shut and the rattle of the key sealed me in.

Once my eyes became accustomed to the dim light from narrow barred slits set well above the reach of anyone of normal height, I saw that the narrow cell held a half-dozen men of varying sizes, shapes and smells. None of the last was pleasant, nor was that effluvium abated at all by the added scents of the slops bucket, moldy straw and other elements of prison decor I preferred not to identify. The walls of shaped stone were damp and streaked with substances of no doubt unpleasant origins.

My cellmates clustered at the end opposite the door. Two leaned against the wall; one hunkered on his heels beside them, his arms on his knees and his head cradled on his arms, and the other three stood like rats disturbed at a meal by a new rodent they suspected wished to share their feast. They took in my attire, which contrasted vividly with the filthy rags they wore, and I saw a gleeful predatory gleam spark into all their eyes. I decided a show of initiative was in order.

"Gentlemen."

The one squatting snickered, and the two leaners pushed upright.

"Yer a right one, now, aintcha?" said the largest, a huge, barrel-chested creature whose wild black hair and beard seemed woven all of one piece and whose broken nose and blackened teeth, revealed by a wicked smirk, brought images of werewolves to mind. His cronies began spreading out in a wide semicircle to surround me. "Alwuz wondered what it'd be like to noggle with a nob."

I was unfamiliar with the cant word noggle and suspected I would much prefer to remain so. Without being obvious about it, I set myself for self-defense, as best I could unarmed against five opponents, and thought quickly.

"How much is Benifaz paying you?"

They paused in their sauntering advance and exchanged a look. The squatter, who had not moved from his place, slowly raised his head and met my eyes. In contrast to the others, this man had a look of sharp, if utterly cold, intelligence; and his attire, while no cleaner than theirs, was clearly of better material and cut.

"What does Ratface of Nadwick have to do with this lot?" he sneered as he stood with one easy motion and approached me.

"He sent me here to get rid of me, and I expect the guards and the jailer are being amply recompensed to see and hear nothing. Should you proceed with your intention to do me ill, however, you will be doing Benifaz's dirty work for free."

Of average height but with the well-honed muscle of an athlete, the man had eyes of steel-gray, set below sharply etched ebony brows on either side of a narrow blade of a nose. He was a handsome devil, but he reeked of danger. He also looked familiar. I wracked my brain, trying to recall if there were any disreputable scions of noble or wealthy houses that might have found their way to such a place as this. There was about him an unmistakable air of breeding, and something continued to twitch for attention in the back of my memory.

"Come along, Dagger," one of the others, a frog-faced, greasy little man I'd have laid wager was a pickpocket, whined. "Whitey's due to meet the hoodman at noon. A taste of such a fancy piece would send him off proper."

I knew then whom it was I faced, although I had not seen him since we were both boys. Dagger Jack Tarragent was a highwayman and alleged assassin whose family had once stood a step away from the throne—until Edrick and his council decided he didn't need rivals and arranged to ruin them.

Jon Tevor Tarragent's mother had been Edrick's second cousin. She and her husband died in a coach accident when he was but ten, and thereafter Jack was reared by his maternal grandparents far from court. The Spiders, at Edrick's behest, arranged for witnesses to swear Jack's grandfather, whose holdings included a rich silver mine and several prosperous cattle farms, was in league with the Deciron emperor and plotting to put Jack on the throne. The old man was beheaded on his seventy-fifth birthday, his aged wife left homeless and penniless. Jack would have joined his grandfather on the scaffold had he not managed to somehow elude his guards and escape.

Nothing was heard of him for nearly two years. Then a shipment of coin en route to Registon and the royal coffers in exchange for that month's output of the former Tarragent silver mine was stolen by a daring robber who sent the empty wagon to Edrick with a thank-you note. It was signed "Dagger Jack," and that robbery was the first of many.

Although Edrick was his favored target, Jack hadn't neglected the other three authors of his new career. Miraculously, he had escaped capture for the last ten years, and I admit I was astonished to discover he had finally been caught. The last I had heard, he was evading all those seeking him—and the substantial price on his head—with skill and daring, if not outright glee.

However, that tale was one for another time.

"You don't know, do you?" I continued, ignoring all but this man who obviously commanded here. I wasn't surprised. It was Dagger Jack's inborn talent for command that had earned him and all his kin Edrick's disapprobation. Well, that and all the silver.

"Know what?"

"Edrick's dead, Jack. Last night, at his wedding."

He fought to keep his face still, but his eyes betrayed him. They burned with savage glee.

"Tell me you poisoned him, Ruford."

"Actually, he choked on lemon-garlic pheasant."

He laughed. No, he *roared*, until tears streamed down his cheeks, and his pack of wild dogs were staring at him as if they thought he'd gone mad. Gradually, however, he gained control of his mirth.

"So, why are you here?" he demanded, sending the others grudgingly back to their original positions with a gesture.

"The Champion has gone to fetch Edrick's daughter. However, it seems His Grace of Nadwich has other plans. He's called the lady an impostor and accused Sir Christopher of high treason. And myself so as well, for aiding and abetting."

I was utterly unprepared for his reaction when I finished my tale with the information Benifaz had ordered the new queen's arrest. He began to curse, viciously and with considerable creativity. When he had vented his rage sufficiently, he paced the length of the cell then stopped an arm's length from me.

"She saved my grandmother's life, you know," he said, his voice rough and tight. "The Ugly Princess. I don't know how she found out, but one night a pair of Trolls came to the hovel Grandmother was hiding in and took her to a safe place in their mountains. On the way they stopped at Raven's Cry, and Her Highness promised she would be safe. Grandmama lived three more years and never wanted for anything save the only thing she ever really needed—my grandfather."

I felt my astonishment plastered all over my face. I had always envisioned the princess as a damsel sealed in an unassailable tower, surrounded by monsters and totally isolated. Obviously, that concept was in error. That Her Highness would have been no more than a girl of ten made the tale even more impressive.

"We have to get out of here," Jack stated, loudly enough to draw our companions' undivided attention.

"Agreed. Unfortunately, that seems to be the least likely potentiality at the moment."

"Not necessarily. They'll be coming to take Whitey to the gallows in a few minutes. Hear the bell?"

I listened and did, indeed, hear a tolling bell.

"They clang that thing to remind the condemned to meditate on his sins and atone before it's too late," Jack sneered. "There will be three of them—one to put on the irons and two to keep us in our place. They'll have muskets, with swords as backup. Was it City Guard brought you?"

"Benifaz's men. Then the jailer and two guards from across the way."

"And it's likely those three have been paid off?"

"A reasonable assumption."

"Let's hope you're right, because that will mean they'll be as far from here as they can so as to be adequately surprised by the discovery of the body." He stared into mental distance for a long moment. "So, are you still as good at hand-to-hand as you used to be?"

"Yes."

"And not given to false modesty, either. Here's the plan. Since you're supposed to end up a corpse, I think we can assume no one else will find out you're here right away. When that door opens, the two with guns will come in first. You stay against the wall next to the door, and when the third one is about to put the manacles on Whitey, put at least one of the other two out of commission and grab his weapons. We'll see to the rest. Once we're out, you follow me—and don't ask questions."

The rest of our cellmates were still clustered against the far wall, but now they looked like men with a future. That seemed like rather a false hope to me.

"Some of them could die," I murmured so only Jack could hear.

"We're all dead men, anyway," he replied, his eyes going flat and cold again. "You're in the Deadman's Palace, the condemned cell. At least this way some of us might make it."

I looked across at the others, and I saw he was right. Given the choice between death in a bid for freedom and death at the end of a rope, they had no choice.

"Well, then," I said so they could all hear me, "God save the Queen!"

There was a long silence as they stared at me then exchanged looks I couldn't interpret. Jack met my eyes with his steel-hard gaze.

"God save the Queen!" he repeated, and behind him the dregs of Abernal drew themselves up with what might almost have been pride.

"God save the Queen!"

"And God have mercy on us," Jack muttered as he walked back to squat once more on his heels and rest his head on his folded arms.

Chapter 9

THEY POUNDED ACROSS THE OPEN FIELD TOWARD ONE OF
the strips of forest, where the rest of Truville's platoon was
bivouacked. Chris knew halfway there he and his precious
charge were in trouble. His big-hearted mount, already tired
from the trek down the mountain and carrying double,
couldn't manage the pace of the others. Slowly, they fell behind, and when the panting gelding stumbled and nearly fell
Chris pulled to a stop.

"Ted!"

He heard a shouted order, and the platoon came to a stop
as their commander circled back to see what the problem
was. One look at the sweat-drenched horse was all he needed.

"Platoon," he shouted, "dismount! Mounts to the rear and
arm up!" Leaping from his own restive horse he led it over
and helped The Ugly Princess alight. "Teblen, Harton, front
and center."

The colorbearer, who by custom remained in the saddle
so the company's banner might be kept from enemy hands,
moved up as ordered while one of the troopers led his horse
forward and handed the reins to his captain. Truville aided

his queen onto his horse and quickly shortened the stirrups for her as Chris switched mounts.

"Private Teblen will take you to the camp," he explained as he worked. "We'll stay here to see if we're followed, but do me a favor and send the rest of the troop off as soon as you can."

"One platoon to hold off a full company?"

"Two, actually, but it's dark—they may not have noticed you. If that's the case, it won't come to a fight."

Behind them, the clatter of hooves on the road surface stopped. Turning in his saddle, Chris saw the glint of moonlight on the Nadwickians' weapons.

Jahmelle clicked her tongue and urged her horse to move, walking it slowly in a small circle and then up to the colorbearer's side. Of course, she had already shown she had an excellent natural seat, a gift of her Moldori heritage, perhaps. It was said Moldori infants could ride before they could toddle, the skill as innate as their black hair.

Exchanging a quick handclasp, Ted Truville went to command his troops and Chris kicked his horse into a full gallop. The queen's mount followed without hesitation, trained to go where the colors led; and they once more thundered across the moonlit pasture toward the distant shadow of trees.

About a hundred yards from where fires twinkled behind the screen of the forest the colorbearer stopped and shouted a password. From off to the left there came a response, and they started forward again. Moments later they coursed along an open pathway between the fires, the colorbearer shouting the call to arms. Instantly, men scrambled to their feet and began strapping on weapons.

They didn't stop until they reached the end of the open lane, where the commander's tent had been pitched. A sturdy lieutenant, commander of the second platoon, emerged from a smaller tent on the left as they reined up, stiffening to attention and tossing a sharp salute when he recognized Chris.

"Milord?"

"Get your men together, Lieutenant. Your captain is facing a full company from Nadwich in defense of your queen."

As if only just then noticing the third member of the group, the man started to make his obeisance.

"Not now, Lieutenant," Jahmelle ordered, and there was a tone in her voice that brought the man back to attention. Chris was impressed. Again. "It is more important that you go to your captain's aid."

Without another word the man dove into his tent to emerge moments later ready to ride and ran for the picket line to saddle his horse. Within minutes the balance of the troop was mounted.

Chris swung down and handed over his reins to a grizzled veteran, wearing the buff tunic and stripes of a sergeant-major, who stepped from Truville's tent. He lifted Jahmelle down. He knew she had to be exhausted and aching from the unaccustomed riding, but she still turned and ran her hand gently over her mount's sweaty neck.

"Thank you," he heard her say softly; and then she turned back, slid her arm through his and let him lead her into the tent. A moment later they heard the company speed off.

"I'm afraid this is a bit rougher quarters than I had in mind for the night," Chris said as Jahmelle limped across to sink onto the cot.

"To be honest, Sir Christopher, I think I could take comfort in anything up to and including bedrock at this moment."

A small table to one side of the tent held a pewter carafe and cups. Knowing his old friend as well as he did, Chris wasn't surprised to discover an excellent wine in the humble container, and he poured her a generous helping. She took it and lifted the edge of her veil just enough to drink.

"I'll see if I can't find you something hot to eat, at least."

"I'd like that, thank you. Won't you join me?"

"Best I keep my wits about me, Your Grace." He didn't add in case the Nadwickians break through, but he knew she heard the unspoken words.

A throat was cleared outside the opening, and Chris found Ted's man standing there with two bowls of fragrant stew and a small loaf of brown bread. Motioning for the man to enter, he looked outside at the deserted camp. The soldiers had carefully banked their fires with practiced efficiency so they could have warmth and hot food to return to without setting the woods ablaze.

Dropping the flap, he turned to find the queen seated at the table. She had drawn the sides of her shoulder-length veil up and somehow fastened them to the circlet that held them so they hung just below her chin. Half of him admired the way she managed to go on with normal daily activities encumbered by those draperies. The other half wanted to rip the bloody things off her, no matter what horror lay beneath.

"Please, Sir Christopher. You need to eat more than I do, and I'm sure the two soldiers on duty outside will warn you in plenty of time if you're needed. Thank you, Sergeant-major. What is your name?"

"Yours to command, Your Grace," the grizzled veteran replied. "Mikkel Carpent, at your service." With a snappy salute to both, he left them to their meal.

Chris debated the wisdom of accepting the queen's invitation then sat down to eliminate the empty place in his stomach. Who knew how long it would be before they ate again if Ted couldn't keep the enemy from the door?

Jahmelle removed her gloves, and after the first edge had been taken off his hunger Chris caught himself watching her hands. Whatever might be wrong with the rest of her, those hands weren't affected. They were long-fingered and elegant, yet strong and capable-looking, the skin the color of gold-tinged bronze. She used them with grace and deftness, plying the rough wooden spoon as if it were the finest silver.

She was not at all what he had expected. Granted, he hadn't really known what, exactly, to expect; but this poised, obviously well-educated woman certainly would have been his least likely choice. Even allowing that her isolation had made it impossible for anyone to know anything about her except what rumor and legend concocted, he would have thought being dragged from the only home she had ever known to assume a position she would never have dreamed might be hers would cause her some anxiety. Still, courage ran in her blood—whatever names one might have called Edrick, "coward" wasn't one of them.

"I noticed that none of the soldiers wear mail, as you do," she commented when they had both dulled the edge of appetite.

He started then became angry with himself. Half the Nadwickian army could have invaded the camp while he sat here mooning over her hands.

"Nobody in the world wears mail as I do," he sighed. "It's tradition. What I'm wearing now isn't too bad, but on formal occasions I'm required to wear the full regalia. I don't mind the clumsiness, but it's beastly hot."

He was suddenly aware he had just voiced to his sovereign a complaint he had kept closely guarded even from Bart. From the day he was old enough to know he would inherit the job of Champion, Chris had heard what an honor it was to wear the "uniform" that went with the position. It was, his father had said on innumerable occasions, a symbol of that honor, going back across the generations to the first of their line. Bearing its considerable discomforts in noble silence had become second nature...until now, apparently.

"I'm sorry, Your Grace, that was totally improper of me."

"Please, Sir Christopher, don't keep apologizing. I prefer honest answers."

Well, that's one trait she didn't get from her father.

Still, he seemed to be falling all over his tongue every time he opened his mouth around her. And there was still the matter of her unanswered question about Benifaz's presence in Abernal. He nodded politely and continued to eat, straining to listen for sounds that would tell him battle had been engaged.

"Something troubles you, Sir Christopher."

"I was just thinking this must be very...frightening for you, Your Grace."

"It has been a little more excitement than I'm used to."

He couldn't help but grin at her wry tone.

"I see Your Grace may challenge my title of Master of Understatement."

"I rather suspect what truly bothers you is that you feel obliged to remain here with me rather than go to your friend's aid."

"It's only one company of Nadwickians, Your Grace." Although he said it mainly to keep her spirits up, he realized as he said it that he actually meant it. He had received the same training as the men who were now fighting to protect their queen, training designed and implemented by his own grandfather as commander-in-chief of the Royal Abernal Army after he had retired as King's Champion. He was certain they were a match for any other force of equal size anywhere—and even for some larger.

As if his thought had conjured them, the sound of jingling harness outside signaled the return of their protectors. A moment later Ted ducked in through the doorway.

"Beg pardon for not knocking, Your Grace," he said, doffing his peaked cap.

"No apology is necessary, Sir Edgard."

The title hung in the air for a long, silent moment as Ted opened his mouth as though to correct her then realized it was not proper etiquette to correct one's monarch. The next moment it occurred to him she hadn't made a mistake, and he dropped to one knee.

Jahmelle stood and held out her right hand. Ted laid both of his on it, and she covered them with her left as he recited the oath of fealty all Abernali knights offered their monarch. That done, she stepped back to give him room to regain his feet.

"Congratulations, Sir Ted," Chris said, grinning at him and pretending not to notice the glisten in his friend's eyes. He knew Ted had always dreamed of being knighted—and had always known it was impossible, given his humble birth. He wondered if Queen Jahmelle had any idea she had just won Ted's undying devotion as well as his loyalty. "Our friends from Nadwich, I take it, opted not to interfere with your maneuvers?"

"I thought for a few minutes they might insist on sharing our camp, but their commander is apparently under strict orders to find the 'traitors' as soon as possible," Ted explained, standing at parade rest with his hands clasped behind him. "He opted to continue the hunt for another hour or so. Of course, I happened to let slip that I'd seen a coach turning off onto a back road toward Weston just before they arrived."

"And they didn't think it odd I'd choose to go west instead of east?" Chris asked.

"Actually, he asked that very question. I suggested you might have been taking the lady to Greenwater. That should keep them busy most of the night getting there and by the time they get back tomorrow we should be in Norburgh."

"Good plan."

"I thought so."

"I appreciate that you were able to avoid bloodshed," Jahmelle said.

"On either side, Your Grace," Ted agreed. "By the way, he mentioned in passing that Benifaz has apparently invited every lordling with an ounce of royal blood to come to the palace and be considered as Edrick's replacement. This bunch was originally traveling to spread the word and stopped at the garrison for a rest. One of them overheard one of our hostlers saying we'd gone out to find you, so they decided they'd come to 'help.'"

"The plan I heard was to give the throne to the Lump," Chris said.

"Apparently, that's changed. To give some sense of legality, they've declared the Lump is the legitimate heir, but I doubt he'd survive his coronation by more than a month. Once he's gone, Benifaz has a clear path to take over."

"The...lump?" the queen repeated.

"Duke Demtri of Nadwich, your grace's second cousin," Chris explained then realized he had once again committed an error of protocol. "Now that I think about it, though, pretending to be seriously considering other contenders might add a whiff of credibility to this whole mess."

"Well, with a bit of luck, we'll be at the palace gates before Benifaz can do too much damage. If we travel at full speed, we can be at Abernal House in three days." Ted bowed deeply to the queen. "I told the sergeant-major to fetch you some hot water for bathing, Your Grace, and I bid you goodnight."

"One moment, Sir Edgard." She turned to Chris, and he felt his belly sink.

"You were going to tell me why King Benifaz is in Abernal."

There was no help for it, and he squelched a sigh.

"I had hoped to spare you the news until this crisis was over," he said. "Benifaz was at the palace for the wedding. Your father married Princess Yolanthe after...after we received the news that your grace's mother was...dead."

He clenched his teeth and waited. The silence that followed his announcement seemed to drag on for eternity plus ninety-nine years.

"And when did this...news of my mother's death arrive?" the queen asked, her voice amazingly calm. Had his first impression of a warm and caring nature been wrong?

"Three months past, Your Grace."

"Ah, I see."

At that moment, Sergeant Carpent arrived with a bucket of steaming water, interrupting the increasingly uncomfortable conversation.

"Well," Ted said, his eyes darting back and forth between them. "We'll leave Your Grace to make yourself comfortable. Chris—a word?"

Wondering what Truville could have to say that was important enough to keep him from dinner, Chris bowed to the lady and followed his friend out into the night. He took with him the worm of doubt. He understood that royalty didn't display their emotions in public, but the queen's reaction was so devoid of anything he now wondered if at least some of the rumors didn't have a grain of truth in them. Perhaps, despite her earlier behavior, Jahmelle of Abernal was, indeed, a monster without any human feelings.

Chapter 10

NOW THAT HIS ANTICIPATED DANGLING DEMISE WAS TO BE indefinitely postponed, the hulking villain Whitey exhibited an amazing level of ebullience—for about half a minute. At that point, Dagger Jack sauntered up to the man, who stood a head taller and half again as wide, and slapped him resoundingly on the side of the head.

"Why don't you just go to the door and shout our plan to the nabbers, shit-for-brains?"

I was certain my new co-conspirator was about to end his underworld career as a stain on Whitey's enormous fists, but I had underestimated the power Jack wielded in his underworld fiefdom. The motley band all acquired a sheepish look and slunk off to the left side of the cell. Whitey slid to the floor, his long legs spraddled in front of him. The others leaned against the wall or each other. It was only after they had settled that I realized these positions had not been chosen at random.

Jack indicated with a lift of his chin toward the door that I should assume my own place then sauntered to the single bed in the room and dropped onto it. I squatted just a hair from touching the wall to the right of the door, having no desire to contact the greasy stones, and we stared at one another.

"True be you're Ruford Seneschal?" Frogface suddenly asked around the hangnail he was gnawing on.

"I have that honor."

"Cods, don't he talk ripe!" snickered a burly, scar-faced man in the corner to my left.

"Shut. Up."

Jack's voice was like a blade, cold, sharp and deadly. The snickering ceased, and Frogface developed an intense interest in his feet. It seemed barely a breath later I heard the tramp of boots on the stone floor of the corridor. I rose to my feet. So did Whitey, who stood with his back against the wall and made a valiant effort to appear terrified. He might have fooled a six-month-old infant, but I doubt it.

The only other person to move was Dagger Jack, who went to stand beside Whitey with his right arm draped over the big man's shoulder. There was the rattle of the key in the lock, and the portal flew open with a force that made the two-inch oak crack when it struck the outer wall. Two guards, pistols in both hands, strode in and stood on either side of the opening. They were followed by a jailer only slightly smaller than his prospective prisoner carrying a set of heavy manacles. As we had hoped, all three were strangers.

"Time to go, Whitey," the jailer snickered. "Your audience is waiting."

He started forward. None of the prisoners moved, and yet I was aware they were all crouched like predators.

"Should have stuck to snatch and grab, Whitey," the jailer continued. "There's a slew of rich folks out there just waiting to watch you swing, though I 'spect they'd like their valuables back first."

"As if they actually miss them," sneered Jack.

The jailer paused, and though I could not see his face his voice was sufficient for me to know he nursed a deep hatred.

"Your turn comes tomorrow, Dagger Jack, and be sure I'll see it takes a long, long time."

During this exchange, as the guards kept sharp eyes and steady gun barrels pointed at the assembly of felons, I crept silently up and snatched the daggers from their belts. An instant later, I applied the knobbed pommel of one to the base of the right-hand man's skull and he dropped without a whimper. His shocked companion hesitated just long enough for me to apply the same treatment to him. As their weapons clattered to the floor, the jailer started to turn, a movement cut short as Whitey's sledgehammer fist connected with his jaw. Jack extended his hand toward me in unspoken command. I held one of the daggers by the blade and tossed it to him, impressed at how easily he plucked it from the air.

My appreciation for his skill turned to horror when an instant later he leaned over and slit the throat of the wounded man. I must have gasped, for he turned back around, his face a stone.

"Problem, Seneschal?"

"Do you mean to murder them all?" My voice barely squeaked through my throat. While I had no particular affection for them, neither did I harbor them a grudge.

"That one needed killing, but we've no time for explanations at the moment."

By now the guards had been relieved of their weapons. At Jack's command they were chained together with the manacles, then Frogface tore up the rags that were his shirt and gagged them.

"Where to now, Dagger Jack?" he asked.

"Wherever you want," Jack said, tossing the man the ring of keys and thrusting the dagger into the sheath he had taken from its prior owner. "I got you out. Don't expect me to nursemaid you."

As if that were a signal, the gang of thieves and murderers slipped one-by-one out the door until only Jack and I were left. Motioning for me to follow, he led me down the hall, not toward the entrance but in the direction of the inner courtyard where the gallows stood. The door stood open waiting for Whitey, the bright noon sunlight streaming into the dim corridor; and as we drew nearer I heard the murmur of voices. Although executions are no longer held in public in Abernal, interested parties such as judges, victims and law enforcement officers are permitted to observe them. Whitey had, indeed, acquired a considerable coterie wishing to bid him farewell, judging by the volume of sound.

At first I feared Jack intended to go straight into the crowd; instead, he turned left into a side corridor that ended in a flight of stairs. My every instinct bade me run, but Jack moved at a steady, purposeful walk; and I had no choice but to ape him. The wisdom of his pace became clear when we passed an open door just before reaching the staircase. Inside a mess room a pair of guards—in fact, the two who had been bribed to allow my murder—were eating their lunch. Had we run past, we would certainly have attracted their attention.

The moment we reached the staircase, however, Jack pounded up two at a time—and for the first time I began to appreciate just how useful a finely honed sense of survival could be. One of the guards, however, must have glanced up as we passed and realized we didn't belong. We were about a half-dozen steps from the top of the flight when they exploded from the mess room and ran toward us, demanding we stop. Somehow, Jack had sensed our luck had ended.

By then, he had opened the door on the next landing, and I followed him onto the roof.

"Run!" he said, and shot off toward the edge.

I consider myself a well-conditioned person, but as Dagger Jack Tarragent led me across the city from rooftop to rooftop I realized there were levels of conditioning the average individual simply never needed to attain. *No wonder*, I thought as I struggled to keep up, *he's escaped capture for so long. He travels above the streets as easily as the rest of us travel below.*

I also learned his choice of route had clearly not been arbitrary. Although in the diverse sections of the city buildings tend to be all of a size, they are not all constructed in the same way. Newer structures tend to have flat roofs, sometimes with low parapets around them. Older ones, however, have gables or gambrel roofs.

Nor were the buildings evenly spaced. Time after time I feared we had reached a dead end, only to have my guide turn a new direction that allowed us to continue our flight unimpeded. Then we came to the first rope bridge connecting two buildings too widely separated for even the most athletic man to leap. There were several more; and where such spans were impossible, we simply clambered to the ground and carefully made our way to the next leg of our journey.

Finally, Jack descended to the floor of a narrow alley via a convenient downspout and made no effort to continue. At that point I had neither breath nor energy left to inquire where, exactly, we were. The buildings on either side of us were of stained ancient brick, which suggested one of the older quarters of the city, and the unpleasant smells arising around us reinforced that conclusion. The sounds from the street at the far end of our refuge were slightly muffled; but after a time, when I could hear something besides the pumping of my lungs, I recognized the distant bellowing of cattle, squealing of hogs and bleating of sheep and goats. We were in the Butcher's Circle near the river.

"Nice bit of dipping you did with those daggers," Jack commented. "I didn't know picking pockets was included among the knightly skills."

"Learned it...from a groom...with a nefarious past...who thought it would be amusing to enlist the son of the royal seneschal and the Champion as apprentice thieves," I explained as my lungs finally settled down.

"Christopher the White Knight? I find that a bit of a stretch."

The look I gave him expressed my surprise. I hadn't been aware Jack had even known Chris, much less well enough to evoke such a sneering tone.

"It never got that far. He reported the man to my father and we spent the next six months mucking out stalls until Dad saw fit to replace him."

"I'm sorry I missed it." Then, before I could pursue the reason for his obvious dislike of my friend, "So, what's your plan?"

I stared at him.

"I fear I'm a bit out of my element, Jack."

"Really? Well, then, I guess that means I'm in charge."

Something about the way he said it made me exceedingly nervous. It might have been the broad smirk, too. It was that of a man who had waited a long time for revenge and was now holding in his hands the opportunity he wanted.

"I had rather thought something in the way of a partnership..."

Before the last word was completely spoken, he had my arm twisted behind my back and his dagger at my throat. I cursed myself for a fool to have trusted him for a single moment. Clearly, he had taken advantage of my naive willingness to do anything to be free, including the pretense of gratitude and loyalty to our new queen. He would now slit my throat as competently, and likely with less emotion, than he had that of the late jailer.

"I do not take on partners," he hissed in my ear. "And if I were to consider doing so, it would definitely not be a cloud-headed bureaucrat who has never had to wonder whether he would be alive the day after tomorrow."

A moment later, however, I was free; and Dagger Jack leaned negligently against the wall of the building as if he had never moved and the previous few moments of terror had been nothing but a hallucination. He began cleaning his fingernails with the tip of the dagger, seemingly not the least concerned he might lose a fingertip in the process. After a lengthy silence he sheathed the knife and looked at me from under his brow.

"You were saying?"

Dagger Jack Tarragent was a hardened criminal, an outrageously daring thief and a murderer, however justified the death of the jailer might have been. He had promised me nothing, neither help nor safety. I had no more idea of his motives than I did about the process by which bees fly. Yet in that instant I knew without question that if I chose to do so I could leave this alley and he wouldn't stop me. For a moment I entertained doing just that.

"So," I said when that moment had passed, walking over to lean against the wall next to him, "what's your plan?"

Chapter 11

*"**THE FIRST THING WE NEED TO DO**," JACK SAID, THRUST*-ing the dagger into his belt, "is find you some decent clothes."

I looked at him, dressed as he was in a shirt that might once have been white but hadn't a prayer of ever being so again, torn gabardine trousers of uncertain vintage and boots that barely covered his feet the leather was worn so thin.

I, on the other hand, was in my seneschal's uniform—trousers and morning coat of the finest royal-blue broadcloth, ivory linen shirt, pale blue satin vest and formal cravat. My shoes, though certainly not as well-shined as when I put them on that morning, nevertheless were of the very best patent leather.

"I see what you mean," I agreed.

Slipping down the alley to the end, Jack carefully peered up and down the street beyond.

"The brassers will look for us in Riverfront first," he told me, naming the segment of the city where those whose careers leaned toward the nefarious were wont to congregate. "I have a place across the street where we can get a bath and some decent food. You're going to stand out like a whore in a nunnery but there's not much we can do about it. Come."

He strode out onto the sidewalk and started across the busy thoroughfare it fronted, and I followed. We dodged between delivery wagons and foot traffic to a modest tenement on the other side. The front door was locked, but after a few minutes of manipulation with the point of his dagger Jack opened it and gestured me inside.

The interior of the building was much as I had expected. The ground floor had doors to three apartments and the first of a series of stairs leading to the upper floors of which, I soon learned, there were five. The building was redolent of frying meat, strong soap and a myriad of herbs and spices I couldn't begin to identify but which were certainly much more pleasant than the exterior and the location would have led me to expect. Though far from recently constructed, the structure was solid and in excellent repair, the stairs and hallways clean and without any signs of vermin.

As we climbed to the top floor, I heard occasional sounds from within the apartments—crying infants, young children squabbling, a lute played by someone with talent—but there was no question the inhabitants of the place were all simple working people.

There was but one door on the top landing, and when Jack tapped on it once, then three times, then once, then twice it opened. A handsome young woman of about twenty, a brown-eyed beauty with hair the color of fine white wine dressed in a simple gown of good quality material leaped into my escort's arms in tearful joy.

"I knew you'd get out," she cried between the ardent kisses she bestowed. Jack was not reluctant to return her fervor, while I endeavored to find some polite place for my eyes.

Pushing the lady gently back into the apartment, Jack pointed me to the parlor and secured the door.

"We can't stay, Bridgey," he said. "The brassers will be going door-to-door as soon as they can muster the manpower. We'll have a bathe and a bite and then we'll have to scamper." He turned to me. "We're close enough in build you should be able to get by. Bathroom's through there, take what you need from the clothes press."

Bowing to the lady, I moved in the direction he pointed and discovered a sumptuous bathing room equipped, to my further amazement, with running water, abutting an even more sumptuous bedroom. Likely there was a cistern on the roof, connected by a pair of pipes one of which ran first into a large tank that on closer inspection proved to be a boiler. From there, two other pipes ran to the tub and a large sink. Locating a box of matches, I lit the oil-fueled flame to begin the water-heating process.

Going to the aforementioned clothes press, I discovered my host had an exceedingly eclectic wardrobe—everything from complete Court regalia to a set of rags that seemed held together mostly by optimism. I compromised, selecting a sturdy workshirt and trousers, not dissimilar to those I wore when tending my personal garden at the palace, and a pair of riding boots that I could see would be a bit large. Better that than the alternative.

It was but a matter of minutes for me to strip off my own garb, scrub away the memory of the cell in the sink and don my new costume. Although the cuffs of the trousers left a good two hands' gap between hem and instep, that problem was resolved by tucking them into my boots. Confident I would have no further problem blending with the everyday throngs, I started back toward the parlor...and stopped.

The nature of the activity generating the soft sounds drifting down the corridor was unmistakable—and I did not think it wise to interrupt a man like Dagger Jack in the midst of his reunion with the lady. Sighing, I returned to the bathroom, stripped and, as previously ordered, took a bath, instructing myself as I did so to remember in future that Jack's orders were to be followed literally. I did, however, hope the reunion didn't require such time that I would end up pruned from overlong immersion.

Chris followed Ted into the now-noisy camp, and they wove amongst the campsites. Apparently, whatever his friend wanted to talk about required total privacy, as they kept going until they were alone in the trees beyond.

Leaning against a handy trunk, Ted folded his arms over his chest and gave Chris a sharp commandant's look.

"I said earlier that I knew you wouldn't try to pass an impostor off as Edrick's daughter," he said. "But how do you know that's who this woman is? Have you seen her? Is there anything in her face to tell you she's who she says she is?"

"No."

"No what?"

"No, I've never seen her. She's worn veils ever since I first laid eyes on her."

"Then—"

"I just know, Ted." Chris stuck his thumbs in his belt and dug at the ground with one booted toe. "I suppose that sounds crazy, but it's in the way she moves, the way she talks, the tone of her voice. If all I ever did was hear that voice, I'd be willing to swear on my life that was Edrick's daughter."

The newly appointed knight stared at Chris as if the Royal Champion had suddenly turned a peculiar shade of green. Chris understood. He knew he had the reputation of being somewhat unimaginative, demanding hard facts when presented with a question rather than given to leaps of logic or intuition. His training had only stiffened that. Though technically the battles the Royal Champion fought were to the death, that final consummation was, in fact, left to his judgment. If the challenger—and, by symbolic extension, the challenger's master or mistress—would only accept defeat by dying, Chris had to make that choice and be able to live with it afterwards.

Still, his confidence in his own judgment was wavering a bit. What proof did he have that the woman was who she was supposed to be? Hadn't he already wondered how she could have acquired so much poise locked away from human contact? What if she weren't the princess but some Moldori ringer? The tribes had as much to gain from having one of their kind on the throne of Abernal as Benifaz did. Maybe even more.

"Well, there is another way to prove it," Ted mused, interrupting Chris's roiling thoughts.

"And that would be...?"

"If she's really Edrick's daughter, she'll have a birthmark shaped like a soaring hawk."

"And where is this birthmark to be found?"

Ted told him, and Chris stared at him as if it were he turning a peculiar shade of green.

"Let me get this straight. You want me to ask the king's daughter, the Queen of Abernal, to prove her right to the throne by letting me see if she has a hawk-shaped birthmark on her—are you out of your mind?"

Ted's eyebrows lifted so high they nearly vanished into his hairline and his smirk spread so far across his face Chris halfway expected to see his jaw drop off.

"I never said I meant you should ask to see it."

Chris felt the blood flowing into his face and cursed. For as many years as he had tried to school his face and body to hide what he felt, he still couldn't fool people who knew him well. It was as if the part of him that kept his emotions in check went off-duty in the presence of people he trusted. Nor could he hope Ted would overlook that fiery blush. Indeed, he not only noted it with transparent glee but put precisely the worst possible interpretation on it.

"I admire your devotion to your liege lady," he chortled.

"May I remind you, Sir Edgard, that this is not some tavern wench we are discussing?" He put every ounce of Royal Champion command into the words.

It worked. The grin vanished, and this time it was Ted's face that burned. Before he could reply, however, the sharp reports of gunshots from the sentry line sent them both racing back toward the queen. As they ran, a pair of small, compact horses tore past them down the pathway between the tents, where they slid to a stop as their riders, who had been clinging to their sides, leaped to the ground.

Ted had posted sentries outside his tent to guard the queen while Chris was away, and they had their rifles aimed and half-cocked. At that moment Jahmelle emerged and, with a quiet word Chris was too far away to hear, prevented events from escalating any further. The two Moldori warriors, both women, stepped forward and nodded to her.

"Sir Edgard," she said as Chris and Ted came nearer, "please alert your sentries that a small party of Moldori will be arriving shortly and should be permitted passage."

The warriors stood nonchalantly to one side, their tattooed faces neutral. The lack of scarring on those faces said neither had killed yet in battle. Chris knew better than to take any comfort in that knowledge. Just because a wolf hasn't bitten you didn't mean it couldn't. What bothered him even more, however, was whether the queen had known they were coming? If so, why hadn't she said anything?

His suspicions erupted all over again, and he wished he dared reveal them. But what if he was wrong? It had been hard enough working with Edrick, feeling the man's antagonism every day and never knowing what he had done to earn it. The thought of spending another twenty years guarding a queen he had accused of being a fake was not pleasant.

Even so, a glance at Ted told him his old friend was entertaining similar questions. However, Ted was in no position to do anything more than obey unless he planned to switch allegiances at this late date. He clicked his heels and bowed, then strode away shouting for the duty officer.

"Have you finished your talk with Sir Edgard?" the queen asked.

"I'm at your command, Your Grace."

She spoke a brief phrase in Moldori and went back inside the tent. He followed, and the two warriors were right on his heels. He stopped near the entrance, but they continued in to squat on their heels on either side of the chair where Jahmelle sat.

"I'm sure you have questions," she said before he could begin to ask them. "It seems my grandfather desires I have an ehtan of his personal guard for my protection."

The warrior on her left said something in a voice like ground glass.

"He sends his greetings to you as Royal Champion and advises that another hundred ehtana are ready to ride should they be required."

Chris searched his memory for numbers. An ehtan was a score of mounted warriors armed with recurved bows and short lances. Their primitive weapons were more than compensated for, however, by their incomparable riding skills and swift horses that were almost as skilled killers as their riders. The idea of having them to reinforce Ted's men was tempting, but something about the idea didn't feel right. Twenty Moldori weren't enough to defeat the entire Abernali army, and if the High Chief had that in mind wouldn't he have just sent those ninety-nine others along as well? Still, he needed some kind of reasonable excuse for turning down the offer—without one, an outright refusal might cause more trouble than he wanted to deal with.

"I'm honored to have them," he said, touching his clenched right fist to heart and forehead as he met the hard black gaze of the woman who had spoken. She returned the gesture then murmured something else to Jahmelle, who answered her at length.

"Dayahn asked if you have taken a mate," the queen then interpreted, and he had no trouble hearing the laughter she was holding back. For the second time that night he felt heat coloring his face. "I explained you are presently pledged to the crown and so are not free to think of marriage."

"Should I thank her for the thought?"

"Not unless you intend to seek her out when your pledge has been fulfilled."

The pounding of hoofbeats sounded once again outside, and a moment later Chris spun around with hand on hilt as someone pushed into the tent. The two warriors leaped to their feet an instant after Jahmelle, who dashed over to throw herself into the arms of the tall, rawboned newcomer. This woman was no neophyte but a seasoned fighter, her cheeks bearing a dozen of the half-inch slashes that marked her kills. Her skin was burned dark bronze by the sun, and her silver-flecked black hair was trimmed close to her head. A gold-and-ivory torque lay tight around her throat, marking her as not just important but the Moldori equivalent of royalty.

She and Jahmelle talked for a moment, and then she came back to greet Chris with the ritual gesture.

"You are the son of Davvyd," she said with a barely discernable accent.

"I am Christopher, son of Davvyd, son of Harrald."

"I knew your father. He is the reason I am alive."

Chris glanced at Jahmelle, but she was a pillar of mystery in her veils. He thought he knew all his father's adventures during his term as Champion, and he had never heard mention of one that involved saving the life of a Moldori chief.

"I'm sure he would be pleased to know you remember him."

The woman circled him, eyeing him as if he were a prize stallion she was thinking of adding to her stud. She said something in Moldori, and this time Jahmelle didn't bother to control herself. Her laughter pealed out in waves, and even the stern-faced pair standing sentry by her chair grinned. All this female humor was becoming more than a bit irritating, given he—or at least parts of him—was clearly the source of their amusement.

"If Your Grace has no further need of me..." he began, not quite able to completely unclench his jaw.

"I think we've all had sufficient excitement for one day, Sir Christopher," Jahmelle agreed. "Will we be proceeding to the capital in the morning?"

"Ted Truville planned to send for a carriage—"

A sputtering comment from the ehlan leader cut him off. Jahmelle's answer resulted in another sharp comment and a long silence. Then Jahmelle sighed and went to sit on the cot.

"Tell him not to bother," she said. "My grandfather has sent me a horse from the chief's herd so that I may 'enter my camp as a warrior.'"

"But you don't—" know how to ride, he was going to say and then realized that might humiliate her in front of her grandfather's people. She hadn't done too badly during their race for the camp earlier, but that was a far cry from being able to handle a blooded Moldori battle steed. Still, if she wasn't going to protest, he could hardly do it for her. "As you wish, Your Grace."

He bowed and turned to leave, but Jahmelle's voice stopped him.

"Oh, and, Sir Christopher...would you find a place for my mother's *ehlan* to camp?"

Chapter 12

I WAS JUST PULLING MY BOOTS BACK ON WHEN JACK PAD-
ded in wearing only an extremely satisfied smile. Assuming it
was now safe to proceed there, I started toward the parlor
then turned to offer a belated gratitude for his aid.

Jack's back was a mass of healing scabs from neck to
waist, the kind that could only have resulted from severe
flogging. At the sight, I had an inkling as to the reason for
the jailer's death. Flogging prisoners was prohibited—had
been since Chris's grandfather persuaded Edrick Three it too
often resulted in death where none was deserved.

"How long were you there, Jack?" I asked, keeping my
tone neutral. Even so, he stiffened and stood up without
turning to face me.

"Someone in my organization gave me up a month ago
for a hefty reward and a royal pardon. If you hadn't come
along I'd have been hanged, drawn and quartered tomorrow."

"What? Jack, no judge—"

Now he did turn, and the dead look was back in his eyes.

"There was no judge, M'lord Seneschal. No need for
one—I was condemned ten years ago. And it was His Royal
Majesty Edrick the Fourth, may God damn his soul to the

lowest hell available, who issued the sentence the moment he heard he'd trapped me. Only he wanted me to think about it, ponder the approach of my suffering."

"And that?" I tilted my chin up to indicate his back.

"Well, seeing as the king wanted me to suffer, Deck Hallum, the chief jailer, decided he might as well have some fun, too. Had a little problem getting it up, did Deck, unless he was hurting somebody. The street girls wouldn't touch him until he found a way to take care of the problem without leaving them the worse for wear."

"Jack, I—"

He drew in a hissing breath and the look he fired at me killed my words of sympathy in my throat.

"Spare me your apologies, Ruford. They won't fix what's past. You and your kind had the chance to do something and couldn't be bothered. Just get out of here."

Stricken uncharacteristically speechless, I complied and returned to the parlor, where Bridgey, wearing her shift and a smile as satisfied as Jack's, fetched me a glass of decent wine and a tray of cheeses, fruit and fresh bread. Despite the rather upsetting nature of the day my appetite, as always, was sturdy; and I did justice to the offering. Jack tended to what remained when he rejoined us in attire almost identical to mine.

"How soon do you expect the Great White Knight back?" he asked as he refilled our glasses.

"Not before four days, certainly, and likely closer to seven," I replied, opting again not to pursue my curiosity as to his dislike of Chris. "He'll only be able to travel as fast as Her Grace. And that's assuming they are not waylaid en route."

"If they are, they'll know they're going to find a cold welcome when they get here."

I did not fail to notice he had no doubt Chris and the queen would survive any such attempt to apprehend them.

"Right now, I'm more worried about my wife."

Jack nodded. "She'll be the first one they'll go after when word gets back to the palace you've scampered."

He went to an ornate locked cabinet set into one wall of the room and undid the padlock. Inside was an intimidating display of some of the finest weapons I'd seen anywhere. Splendid swords both straight and curved, daggers with beautifully chased hilts and guards and guns. All kinds of guns—pistols and hunting muskets, all perfectly maintained and of the finest manufacture. There was a small fortune in arms in that cabinet, and I admit I was impressed. Clearly, successful outlawry was a lucrative career—provided one didn't get caught.

Jack loaded one of the pistols and holstered it, then tucked it into a pack he took from a drawer under the cabinet. He added a pouch of ammunition, and sufficient powder and shot to replenish what was already made at least once.

"Give me that dagger," he ordered. "It's brasser issue. Might as well wear a sign announcing we stole it."

Removing the weapon from the boot where I'd tucked it into a sheath stitched in the top, I handed it to him; and he replaced it with a much more suitable weapon, a slender stiletto I could tell just by holding it was exquisitely balanced.

"So," I repeated once we were armed, "what is the plan?"

"Simple. We go to the palace and get your lady."

"Simple?" I tried not to gape at him, but it wasn't easy. "There are three garrisons of Royal Guards between us and the palace gates. There are who-knows-how-many City Guard stations, and they will all be looking for us. And even if we manage to bypass all of them, there is still Benifaz's personal contingent, which is firmly ensconced in the palace itself."

"I know. Bridgey, where's that hat?"

"I'll get it."

"Jack, with all due respect..."

"You have no respect for me whatsoever, Ruford. I'm your means to an end. If it weren't for the Ugly Princess, I would have left you in that cell to rot."

It was a bitter thing to say, and he said it with all the acrimony of a man who has lost everything and had to risk his life to reclaim even a part of what was lost. The Jon Tevor Tarragent I remembered had been a courageous, honorable young man; but he was long gone, ground into dust by the greed of his monarch and the exigencies of survival. Dagger Jack Tarragent still had the courage, but he honored no one but himself. What he did now, he did for his own reasons, not mine.

I can't say why that made me trust him even more than I was already inclined to do, but so it was.

"You have a way into the palace."

"I do. And don't tell me you don't know which one I mean."

I did, of course. I only wondered how he had come to know of it. Supposedly, that particular secret of Abernal House was known only to the monarch and the Seneschal. Not even Chris knew of it.

Before I could ask, however, Jack came over and stood in front of me, so close I could feel the heat from his body. He glared into my eyes.

"I'll have your word of honor as Baron Greenwater and Lord Seneschal of House Rediman that once your lady is free you'll never again try to find me or contact me. You will forget you ever knew me."

The assurance he was asking might not seem all that terrible. It was. The honor of the Lords Seneschal was more than a tradition. It was a vital element of who we Rufords are, as necessary to our lives as blood and breath—or as honor and devotion to duty are for the Royal Champion. Once, a younger son of a Ruford Seneschal gave the oath thoughtlessly then was forced to renege through no real fault of his own. Within six months, he fell ill of a fever for which no balm could be found, and in seven months he was dead.

His dying was not, so the histories record, pleasant.

Yet what choice did I have? Having tasted the mercy of Benifaz of Nadwich myself, I shuddered to think what horrors he might perpetrate on Danella. A man who orders small children beaten for no reason save personal pique is not likely to stay his hand—or those of his minions—when the target is the wife of an alleged traitor.

"You have my word of honor, Jack. May death take me if I break it."

"Then let's be about it," he said, and clapped on my head the wide-brimmed farmer's hat Bridgey had fetched. With one last kiss that left her breathless and blurry-eyed, he bade the young woman farewell and led the way to the back of the apartment, where a final flight of stairs led to a small wooden door. Jack leaped to the top and flung the door open, allowing the bright afternoon sun to tumble through.

"Jack," I sighed as I followed him at a much more reluctant pace, "what is it with you and roofs?"

Our journey across the city to the palace was considerably less precipitous than our escape flight, though we did not dawdle. I quickly confirmed my earlier conclusion that Jack was accustomed to using these aerial pathways, as no matter where we went there were sturdy planks available to span the gaps between buildings too broad to jump with any degree of comfort. I can't say I was particularly overjoyed at the seeming convenience the planks provided, however, as they had a tendency to sag just enough midway across to arouse visions of body parts spattered unpleasantly on the cobblestones below.

My companion's earlier reference to an "organization" suggested how the overhead route was maintained, but now we were engaged in rescuing Danella I had no spare energy to ponder how an extensive underworld could operate in a city as closely policed as Registon. Perhaps it was that which also caused the heavy weight of dread clinging to my belly, yet I was certain my dear one's life was already in danger.

We traveled in silence, which given my shortage of breath was not a hardship. It was not until the palace came into view that Jack commented, "Nobody looks there."

I hope I can be forgiven for not immediately grasping the point of this remark. My immediate response, one which was quickly becoming something of an habitual one where Jack was concerned, no doubt reflected badly on my level of intelligence.

"What?"

He swung over the edge of the roof we had just crossed and again used a downspout as a ladder.

"The roofs," he said as I gratefully joined him on the surface of the earth once again. "You asked why I prefer them. When people search, they look down and they look around. Nobody thinks to look up."

We were in a narrow passage between the enclosure walls of two elegant houses of the nobility. When we reached the end that fronted on the palace, I saw we were at the rear of the grounds. What I assumed was our goal lay some thirty paces to our left, where a small copse of ancient nightoaks abutted the fence.

A sentry wearing the gray-and-black uniform of the Army of Nadwich strode past on the inside of the wrought iron fence. I started forward, thinking this was the perfect moment to proceed; but Jack barred my way with a surprisingly strong arm. Not five minutes later, a second sentry passed. Five minutes after that, a third.

"It appears," I sighed, "the news of the jailbreak has been transmitted."

"And they're close enough together that each one is within sight of the man in front of him, and they're going through the trees instead of around them."

When Abernal House was constructed, the king demanded there be a means of fetching in items he desired—items usually of a female persuasion—without anyone else knowing about it. A tunnel was constructed from a point within the grounds into the palace, where it connected to a labyrinth of secret passages. A section of the iron wall was converted to a gate. It was that gate we had hoped to use to gain entry.

I doubted Benifaz knew of the tunnel. This tight security was no doubt the result of his naturally suspicious nature. The reason, however, was unimportant.

"How are we to get in?"

"Same way everyone else does, I suppose. Through the front gate."

I am one who has nothing but admiration for men of daring, and though I cannot say that I truly liked Dagger Jack I had begun to develop a modicum of admiration for his undaunted confidence and obviously strong survival instincts. At least, up to this point, that was how I had seen his behavior. Now, however, it was clear I had been in error. What I had interpreted as courage was simply stark, raving insanity.

Before I could say so, however, the sound of marching feet approaching from the direction of the garrison sent us back into the shadows of the passage. A company of infantry passed, clearly headed in the direction from which we had just come. I was not sanguine they were simply out for a day of maneuvers.

"Slouch," the mad highwayman commanded, and again I involuntarily responded in that less than astute manner.

"What?"

"Slouch. And shuffle your feet when you walk. You're a laborer, not a prince."

I undertook to oblige him, and discovered changing one's mien was not as easy as I had expected. Finally, however, after I had paced most of the length of the alley for what seemed like an hour, Jack was satisfied. After a quick survey of the street in both directions we shuffled out to the walk and crossed the street. Once safely within another passage, we headed toward the main gate of the palace grounds. Per his instructions, I kept my chin tucked into my collar and my hat pulled down as far over my face as possible without totally blocking my vision as we approached the gatehouse.

"Afternoon, Yeoman," Jack said in a backcountry accent so thick I could barely understand even those two simple words. His voice had changed as well, from his normal melodious baritone to a whiny nasal tenor that grated on the ears. "We was told to report to Jenkiss as is putting in waterworks."

"Told by who?" the guard demanded. I could feel him studying me.

"Some coot at the workhouse." At least, that's how I translated "Sa cue oth wargauss."

"If you're from the workhouse, let me see your papers."

Had Jack bothered to ask me I could have told him no one not officially employed at the palace was permitted to enter the grounds without identification papers. I began to consider what other options might allow us to gain entry. I should have known better.

My companion in crime launched a plea for mercy and understanding of which the puling, bootlicking vocabulary was outdone only by the utterly horrendous screech of his voice. He spoke of his starving children and his aged parents and his wife who would be forced to sell herself on the street and...well, I was utterly astounded by the number of helpless dependents whose lives and well-being hung in the balance. He complained that the "cue" had never said "nawtin bawt no papehs" and that Jenkiss was going to be forced to pay a penalty because the waterworks project was supposed to be done today and half his crew were out with the grippe and...

"Shut yer jaw!" the beleaguered guard shouted. He surveyed the grounds, obviously praying devoutly for someone, anyone, with whom he might share the responsibility of allowing us inside.

To his great relief, a short, sturdy man carrying a load of pipe emerged from the hedge disguising a gardener's shed and strolled in the direction of the south gardens where fountains were being installed, ordered by Edrick as a wedding gift for Yolanthe. If all the workmen moved at such a leisurely pace, I could well understand why the unfortunate Jenkiss was falling behind schedule.

"Hey, you!"

The man stopped and turned at the hail.

"Your boss around?" the guard shouted.

"Home for dinner," the other man yelled back.

"He send to workhouse for help?"

"Might have. Probably. Short of hands, I know that."

The guard waved him on then stood aside and gestured for us to proceed. Ten minutes later we were shuffling amiably toward the south gardens. As I myself had drawn up the contract for the work, I knew the project was to be done by sundown today or the contractor—the aforementioned Jenkiss—would be assessed a penalty against his fee. I was also aware that his crew had been shorthanded for the last several days. What I didn't know was how Dagger Jack Tarragent, who had by his own admission been incarcerated for the last month, also knew all of these facts.

I determined that, should I survive my current difficulties, I would institute an in-depth study of palace security procedures with all due dispatch.

Before we arrived at the worksite, however, Jack veered off toward the nightoak grove and quickened his pace to a jog. With each step I expected to hear a shout or, worse, the report of a musket as we were discovered.

But luck—or whatever deity or demon seemed to accompany Dagger Jack—was with us, and I felt at least part of my burden lighten as we stepped into the shadows beneath the branches.

Chapter 13

SILENCE DRAPED OVER THE TENT, AND CHRIS FELT THE HOT blood in his face. He tried to convince himself the queen hadn't played him for a fool, but the evidence suggested otherwise. No wonder she had stayed so calm at the news her mother was dead—she had known all along it wasn't true. So, why hadn't she just said so?

His every instinct screamed for him to attack, that he was in the middle of a Moldori plot just as dangerous as Benifaz's. That such a response would have been total idiocy in a small tent with three armed warriors was the only thing that helped him retain his equilibrium. Best to play along until he could alert Ted.

"I would be honored, Your Grace," he said, bowing formally to her and again to Marvaya. "If you'll permit me?"

Giving the queen one last hug, the Moldori chief strode past him and out into the darkness as he retrieved his sword. He half-expected to get a dagger in his eye before he could reach it, but all the two warriors did was watch him with a lustful glitter in their eyes.

Ted and a squad of his men stood off to one side, blocked from coming any nearer by Moldori lances. Marvaya barked a command, and her riders drew aside and let the soldiers pass.

"What—" Ted began then stopped when Chris held up his hand.

"The ehlan needs a place—"

"We will remain here," Marvaya said. "Your men may go. You are their chief?"

"Cap—uh, Sir Edgard Truville, ma'am." He clicked his heels and saluted smartly, though his eyes were jumping back and forth between the Moldori and Chris. Then he sent the two goggle-eyed sentries who had been guarding the tent off to their platoon.

"Come," Marvaya said, "we will talk."

She led them through the encampment and beyond to a place where the noise of men and mounts was no louder than the slow chirping of the somnolent crickets huddled in the grass. Overhead, the golden disk of the great moon, Sate-hyell, was a celestial grin against the blue-black sky, while her smaller silver sister, Mirdana, was just beginning to peek over the eastern horizon.

"If you'll forgive my saying so," Chris said when his impatience wouldn't wait any longer, "you look quite healthy for a dead woman."

A grim smile carved a slit in the Moldori's scarred face.

"It is not for lack of effort on my late husband's part, young Champion. You did not tell my daughter I was dead?"

"Not until just a little while ago. I—"

"Nor that it was at his wedding feast her slinking weasel of a father died?"

"I came to tell her he was dead and there was a plot afoot to keep her from becoming queen. It seemed...insensitive...to provide too many details all at once. I intended to tell her the rest as we traveled." He paused a moment. "How did you find us?"

"We have...friends...in Registon who have profited much from the treaty that wed me to that lizard. They sent word he was dead, and I thought to protect my daughter, but the Trolls told me it was not necessary. Still, a few more hands can do no harm, true?"

That depends on where those hands aim their weapons, he almost said. Instead, he opted to switch subjects for a moment.

"You said my father once saved your life. He never spoke of that to me—and I was under the impression I knew all the history of the Champions."

A nighthawk screeched overhead, and Marvaya searched until she found it. Silence fell over them again as she watched it soar across the sliver of moon in pursuit of dinner.

"You know my history in your country," she said finally.

"I know what I was told," Chris replied.

She chuckled.

"I see you are a diplomat as well as a soldier, Christopher, son of Davvyd. Well, then, I will tell you what I know, and you can decide how well it fits with what you know.

"When I was a young woman—younger than my daughter is now—I was not content with the way of the Moldori. I hungered to see the parts of the world outside the steppes and the mountains. When the King of Abernal sent his minister to my father seeking a bride for his son to establish a treaty binding our two peoples, I offered myself, thinking it a way to feed my hunger. I had a picture of the prince, and he looked to be a handsome man and such things often sway the mind of foolish girls.

"So, I came to your country to meet my betrothed, who took one look at me and all but spat in my face. I would have left then, except I had sworn the marriage oath and could not betray my honor. So, we were wed, and he came to me to seal our binding." She was talking now through jaws clenched tight, and her voice oozed with loathing.

"He entered the room half-drunk and cursing. He took off his clothes, knocked me to the floor with a single blow and did what needed doing like a boar in rut. I fought him, and though he finished his duty he earned scars for it. He left

106

me, and I dressed to leave only to find my door bolted from the outside. When it was clear there was not yet to be an heir from this performance, he came again, but this time he was prepared. Two of his personal guards tied me across the bed, then watched, laughing and making foul jokes, while he beat me with his belt and then took me. So began my reign as Princess of Abernal."

Chris was already sorry he had asked, but he knew it was too late to tell her he'd changed his mind. He was all too aware of Edrick's preferences, but somehow they sounded even more obscene described in Marvaya's flat, tight voice. He glanced at Ted and wasn't surprised to see his friend's face grim and disgusted.

"He came every night until he knew I was with child. The rest of the time he thought he kept me apart from any who would help me, but he was wrong. There were women in that house who had suffered as I was, and they aided me when they could. Then Jahmelle was born, and she was no more than half a day old when the chief woman of the house came and warned me I was marked for death. I begged her for a weapon, and the next night she came again and your father with her.

"I do not know how they got past the guards at my door, but he brought me a dagger and told me where I would find a horse. When they left, I waited until dark and then feigned illness, screaming in pain. The guards opened the door to see if they needed to call a healer—Edrick would not have wanted to miss the pleasure of killing me himself so my dying of disease could not be permitted. I slit their throats and fled."

She turned to face him, and those hard dark eyes were glistening.

"I did not wish to leave her, not with him; but I prayed to the God of Horses he would decide to let her live until he should get another heir. I knew the cost of divorce was greater than he would be willing to spend, and so as long as I lived she was safe. Yet I could not know for sure, and even as

I rode for my mountains my heart was filled with dread she would be slaughtered like some unwanted kitten."

Clearly, she had a discerning understanding of people to have known it likely Edrick would not kill his only heir. The preservation of the throne of Abernal in the hands of House Rediman was a vital part of their existence, and not even his twisted rage could have made Edrick destroy his family's future. Chris felt his blood turn to ice as he contemplated what might have happened to the princess had Edrick been able to consummate...

But, no. Even had Yolanthe given him a dozen sons not one could have inherited because the marriage was invalid. Only, Edrick hadn't known that. Chris sighed—life just insisted on being confusing.

That thought, however, reminded him of something Marvaya had said.

"You said your being alive wasn't for lack of effort on Edrick's part."

"Edrick tried to assassinate you?" Ted had been silent up to this point, but his tone said he found such an idea all but unbelievable. Chris wished he could say the same.

"Oh, the assassins came from Nadwich, but they had Abernal gold in their pockets. They could not know what I looked like, since no one had seen me for these two ten-years, so they killed the wrong woman, lying in wait like jackals and slaughtering her and her ehlan with guns. They were stupid, too, not even trying to hide their tracks, as if their cowardice had somehow made them invisible. The Dream Dancers sent out word of the assassination, and the ehlans rode in pursuit. By the grace of the gods, it was mine that found them. The one still breathing when we were finished with them told us enough; we could guess the rest."

"He should be brought back here for trial," Ted snapped.

Marvaya smiled again, and this time it was a smile that made Chris's blood congeal to ice.

"Oh," she growled, "he died as well...eventually."

"The silence that followed that revelation—and the ferocious implications attached to it—lasted only a moment.

"What did he tell you?" Chris asked, although he suspected he already knew.

"That a Nadwich rat had hired them to kill me. That my daughter would have been next had they succeeded. Still, we had only the word of a cutthroat, so my father sent a messenger to your outpost to tell them I was dead and we waited. Before Satehyell had died and been reborn once, Nadwich had sold his daughter to Abernal. I knew Jahmelle would not live to see another summer, and I gathered my ehlan to fetch her."

"She is still in grave danger," Chris warned. "Benifaz has named himself regent, it seems, and has issued an order for her arrest and mine. He's bringing troops in to back him and Edrick's council is in league with him."

Marvaya looked at Ted, who interpreted the look correctly and shrugged.

"I don't take orders from Nadwich."

The Moldori laughed, and instantly Chris knew where his queen had acquired hers. Marvaya clapped Ted on the back so hard he nearly fell over, but neither of the two men could resist the urge to grin.

"I watched you before, Truville of Abernal, sending that Nadwich dung off to hunt fish in the trees. You have the look of a warrior. If you knew how to ride a horse, we might make a Moldori of you."

Ted's grin was replaced instantly by a look of total astonishment. He was one of those lucky souls born with a natural affinity for horses and was considered not just an excellent horseman but the finest in the country.

He opened his mouth as if to argue with the woman, but stopped when their eyes met. Suddenly, some other emotion hung on the still night air, part challenge and part the ancient mystery of male and female discovering each other. Chris decided it was time to exercise the diplomacy the queen's mother had credited him with, go back to camp and get some rest.

"We'll want to get an early start," he said as he turned to go, but he might as well have saved his breath. He was the only one listening.

As he strode back to camp, he considered Marvaya's story. It rang true, both because it lacked the melodramatic embellishments of the Abernali version and because he had acquired a fairly reliable depth of knowledge about Edrick the last five years. His suspicions weren't totally banished, but he no longer doubted Jahmelle's identity.

The Dream Dancers sent out word of the assassination...

That was the second time someone had spoken of the mysterious Dream Dancers, and Chris cursed his ignorance. These people were obviously important to the Moldori, and yet he had never heard of them. Who were they? Or should it be what were they? What, if anything, did they have to do with Jahmelle? And why did he suddenly have a sick feeling he didn't really want to know?

Chapter 14

JACK LED THE WAY INTO THE CENTER OF THE COPSE, WHERE a small but elegant gazebo stood in a well-manicured clearing. Striding up the steps to the interior, he knelt on one knee and sharply tapped the near edge of one of the flooring stones with the handle of his dagger. The stone popped up from its setting just far enough for him to slide his fingers underneath and lift it all the way upright to reveal a pitch-dark opening approximately three feet square.

This ingenious trapdoor was not, in fact, solid stone but wood with a very thin layer of stone laminate, hinged and counterweighted for ease of opening. A fine but sturdy chain fastened at the free margin allowed it to be drawn closed from below.

Meantime, Jack had removed the lantern and waterproof tin of matches from their hidden niche under one of the benches in the gazebo. Lighting the lamp, he used the cord attached to its handle to lower it into the opening, revealing a column of sturdy metal rungs fastened to a wood-paneled shaft. Once settled on the floor below, the lantern provided sufficient light to illuminate our way as we climbed down to a narrow, low-ceilinged tunnel. Jack closed the trapdoor and unfastened the lamp from the cord, then set off at a steady jog.

I had been in the tunnel the previous year to tend to routine maintenance, and the place clearly was due for another visit. Edrick had rarely used it, employing members of his personal bodyguard to deal with whatever cleaning up was required after one of his indulgences.

We came to the flight of stone stairs at the palace end. At the top was a plain heavy wooden door with a well-oiled iron latch and hinges. *How many times*, I wondered as Jack opened it and stepped beyond, *has this passage given him entry to the palace?* And, again, how had he come to know of it at all?

Harlon Ruford, the first Ruford Seneschal, had supposedly obtained our family's present position in exchange for the destruction of the plans to this tunnel and the passages within the walls. As we Rufords are a prolific tribe, it wasn't within the then king's purview to simply make my ancestor disappear, so the bargain was struck. That everyone else involved in the construction was, after being very handsomely paid, sent on a long journey from which he never returned, is a matter not discussed. We prefer to think our ethics have improved significantly for the better compared to old Hary's.

Jack and I were now in a small alcove off the palace wine cellar that was never visited for the simple reason there was never anything in it. The official reason was that it was infested with some species of mold that ruined the wine. We crossed to the far side of the wine cellar, where a rack of wines so old they surely must have long since turned into vinegar was flush against the wall. Clutching the neck of an ancient stoneware jug jutting from the third shelf from the top, Jack pulled it halfway out of its cradle. With a soft rumble, the rack swung out to reveal another flight of stairs, this time built of wood.

Dust lay heavily on the treads, except where it had been scuffed away. Jack stood to one side of the opening and with a mocking grin made an elegant bow.

"After you, Milord Baron," he said.

He was on my heels as I moved inside, and he quickly pulled shut the secret door. I was already at the small space beneath the stairs, lighting another lamp. Thus equipped, we began our climb to the third floor.

The staircase and the passageway that opened at the top were unpleasantly cluttered with soft, sticky spiderwebs that clung tenaciously to everything. The dust we stirred up as we walked evoked a sneeze.

"I would suggest you keep those to yourself," Jack muttered.

"Have I ever mentioned just how helpful I find this constant stream of advice you provide?" I replied just as quietly.

"We might get lucky, and your wife will simply have been confined to your quarters. At any rate, that seems the logical place to start, wouldn't you say?"

I wished I could be confident that was the case, but my belly told me Danella was in serious danger.

We wended our way through passages so narrow we were forced to shuffle sideways. At various places I could hear barely audible voices coming from the other side of one wall or the other, and at intervals a narrow lance of light would stab through to reveal a spyhole. Had our errand been less pressing, I would have taken the time to peer through some to see if I could learn anything useful.

Two more staircases and another passage later Jack stopped and hung his lamp on a peg near one such opening. Shading his eyes with one hand, he peered through.

"Well?" I whispered, restraining myself with only the greatest effort from shoving him out of the way so I could see for myself.

"The good news is...she's there."

"And the not-so-good news?"

"There's a pair of guards with her—and His Serene Highness King Ratface."

"That would be just like Benifaz. He would want to observe whatever ill-treatment she was subjected to." I uttered an entirely out of character oath. "Let me see." He obliged, and I shaded my eyes as he had to block the lantern's glare.

This particular spyhole was the one located in the carved wainscoting beside the bed. Danella sat firmly upright in a wooden chair, a Nadwickian thug on either side. She was trying very hard not to show fear, but I knew her face as I knew my own. Her terror was obvious to me even had I not been able to see the hands she clenched white-knuckled in her lap.

What turned my anxiety into seething rage, however, were the bruises already darkening on her face and the blood trickling from her split and swollen lip.

Benifaz stood directly in front of her not a half-pace, his hands clasped behind his back, his feet apart as if he were bracing himself on a tossing deck. His face was beet-red and his beady black eyes glittered.

"I have been patient with you, madam," he snarled. "I can accept you would not know specifically where your traitorous husband has gone, but I will not believe you have no idea as to where he might possibly have fled."

"Your Majesty," my beloved replied in a voice so close to tears it made my own eyes burn, "I swear to you I have no notion where my husband is. We have no other house in the city, and the only other place he might go is Greenwater. I have nothing else to offer."

At that moment Jack tapped on my shoulder, then gestured for me to move some distance back down the passageway. He snatched his lamp from its hanger and followed until we were at one of the points where the hidden ways crossed and there was room for us to stand face-to-face.

"How many guards did you see?" he demanded.

"Just the two in the bedroom. The door was open but I couldn't see if there were any more in the sitting room."

"How well does your lady follow orders when she's surprised?"

"Danella is never surprised."

I could tell he didn't believe me, but he opted not to argue the point. Instead, he turned left into the cross path and traveled three paces, then set his lamp on the floor and peered through another spyhole.

"It looks clear, but keep your eyes and ears open," he ordered, and then tapped lightly at three points on the wall. At the third blow, the wall swung outward and we stepped into the small hallway that connected the main wing where my chambers were located with the stairway to the servants' quarters on the topmost floor. Drawing his dagger, Jack crept silently down to the intersection and peered around the corner.

"I was afraid of that."

He stepped back so I could replace him. Two more guards flanked the entrance to my quarters.

"Now what?" I whispered after we had retreated a distance back down the hall.

"You'll know what to do when the time comes. Just let me do the talking."

With that he strode down the hall and around the corner to the door of my chambers, and I followed. At our approach, the guards raised their weapons and trained them on us. Without even slowing down, Jack bent, snatched the knife from his boot and threw it. I had to pause briefly to accomplish the same maneuver but within a second of each other the two lay dying on the floor.

"Now to see how many more there are," Jack muttered. We retrieved our blades, and he pounded on the door.

"I ordered we were not to be disturbed," Benifaz shouted.

"The traitor has been retaken, Your Majesty," Jack shouted in return then motioned for me to flatten myself against the wall. A moment later the door began to open, and in that instant Jack launched himself at it, knocking that man off his feet. Without a pause, he leaped over the prostrate soldier, spun and knocked him out with a kick on the point of the chin.

The two in the bedroom dashed through the door, pistols drawn. They fired, and I felt the ball clip my cheek as I dove to the side. Jumping to my feet, I launched myself at the one nearest me, noting peripherally that Jack had his pack open and was drawing out his own gun.

I hit my target, and we tumbled to the floor. His breath whooshed out as I fell on him, but he recovered quickly and landed a punch to my ear. I heard a pistol and hoped that meant Jack had succeeded in eliminating his opponent. I was preparing to pound my own in the belly when Benifaz's razor voice slashed the air.

"Stand up, both of you, and place your hands on your heads or I will scatter this woman's brains from here to the front gate."

All combat ceased, and I raised my head to discover the King of Nadwich just inside the door from the bedroom. He held my wife with one arm bent agonizingly behind her back and a loaded pistol to her head.

Slowly, carefully, lest the tyrant misinterpret my motions, I climbed to my feet and did as commanded. From the corner of my eye I saw Jack, who had wounded the second guard, hesitate.

"For God's sake, Jack..." I pleaded.

Never taking his eyes from the king, he laid the spent weapon on the floor and stood up.

My opponent also stood, and I braced for the blow his face told me he intended to throw. However, at a sharp word from Benifaz he instead went to retrieve a pair of muskets from the bedroom. Although clearly in pain from the wound in his shoulder, the other man accepted his weapon.

Danella looked from me to Jack, and as I watched a look of resolution replaced the fear in her eyes. With just the barest of nods, she suddenly raised her foot and brought it down full-force on Benifaz's instep.

The pistol went off, the barrel having thankfully been thrown off dead aim at Danella's skull, the king howled with anger and pain and Jack and I attacked. I knocked the musket barrel to the side just as it was fired and sank the blade of my stiletto into the man's belly, angled up to penetrate the heart. He howled and sank, and I let his weight free the knife. I then turned toward the bedroom door.

Danella, a stain of blood on her bright hair, lay on the floor. As I took the first step toward her, Benifaz seized her by the collar of her dress, raised her and backhanded her across the face.

It was as though the entire universe contracted to a narrow tunnel with myself at one end and Danella at the other. I have no memory of taking the two strides that carried me to within reach of the villain who had so abused her, but I clearly recall the immense satisfaction I had in sinking my fist in his belly, then cracking his jaw with my knee as he bent double from the force of the first blow. He sank to his knees, struggling to breathe.

"A bit of haste, if you please, Milord Baron," Jack suggested as I prepared to continue exacting my revenge, and I forced my rage down to a manageable level. Gently, I gathered Danella into my arms and started for the door.

Despite his obvious discomfort, Benifaz was glaring at me with utter hatred. The feeling, I'm sure I needn't add, was one I returned in full measure.

"I'll have you all hanged, drawn and quartered for this," he snarled.

"In that case," Jack said, going to where the man knelt in a single stride, "I might as well make it worth my while."

And then he sent His Grace of Nadwich the rest of the way to the floor with a single, very satisfying blow to his receding royal jaw. He strode past, and we started back the way we had come.

Chapter 15

TED TRUVILLE ORDERED THE COMPANY TO BREAK CAMP as soon as they had eaten the next morning. Chris, who had slept in a borrowed blanket on the floor of the tent he'd shared with Ted and his second-in-command, was forcibly reminded why he hated sleeping on the ground by his sore back.

Though his impulse was to dress and go immediately to the queen's tent, he forced himself to work the kinks out by running through his sword forms instead. The Moldori would make sure nothing happened to her, and she likely needed some extra sleep after all the unaccustomed exercise—not to mention excitement—she'd had.

The chill morning air on his bare chest and back felt quite pleasant by the time he was halfway through his drill. Though being surrounded by a large body of armed men packing to move on offered all sorts of distractions, he applied the kind of focus to the movements they demanded if they were to be done correctly; and the noises and smells and sights of the bustling encampment disappeared. He was one with his blade—until some sense of intrusion broke through his concentration and alerted him he was being watched.

He spun around. Queen Jahmelle, flanked by the two Moldori who had arrived first the night before, stood silently under the pink glow of the dawning sun. The light breeze ruffled her veils and the folds of her skirt. Her escorts were gazing at him with undisguised appreciation, their eyes traveling all over his bare chest and down to his boots. They exchanged a glance and a grin. He felt like a side of beef being considered for dinner.

Suddenly remembering his manners, he dropped to his knee. He'd had the etiquette of his office drummed into him practically from birth, and the monarch's being a woman just made them all the more important.

"Your Grace," he said. "I didn't think you'd be awake yet, or I'd have—"

"Sir Christopher, I appreciate your devotion to duty," she interrupted, "but I really don't think you need hover quite so much under present circumstances."

It would have sounded like criticism if he hadn't heard the laughter in her voice. She was right, of course. There were certain to be times in the coming days when he would need to be her shadow, and likely her patience would wear thin at his constant presence very quickly. It would do them both good to take advantage of any chance to be apart. He did wish those bloody women would stop licking their lips, though.

He got up and put on his shirt and arming doublet, uncomfortable to be half-naked in front of his monarch and beginning to feel the chill now he'd stopped working. Just then Ted returned from whatever commander's errand he had been on, leading his mount and followed by Marvaya and the ehlan. The chieftain led a gorgeous dappled Moldori mare in addition to her own traditional black.

"Come, daughter," she said. "Take horse, and we will go."

Chris sighed softly. He had anticipated this and before falling asleep had wrestled with how he would deal with it. In the end, the direct approach was his preference, as usual. He hoped his assessment the queen's mother would appreciate honesty was correct.

"Honored Marvaya, I really think that would be a bad idea."

Immediately, the air took on a flavor of hostility, and the glitter he saw in the Moldoris' eyes did not bode well for his future health. Even Ted was looking at him as if he'd lost his mind. At the moment, this single company was all he had to protect the Queen. For all he knew, the rest of the army had defected to Benifaz. To someone thinking strictly in military terms, an ehlan of Moldori could only be an asset. However, despite the martial nature of his primary job, the Royal Champion had to think in broader terms.

"You would keep us from protecting my daughter?"

"I would keep the Queen of Abernal from meeting her people surrounded by folk those people consider...would resent as intruders in Abernal's affairs." Good job, Evergild. Just spit it out that her people are likely to cause trouble rather than prevent it because your people consider them thieves and savages.

Marvaya's eyes narrowed, and he could see the muscles of her jaw rippling. The resentment and outrage coming from the ehlan were colder than the wind.

"I believe Sir Christopher has a point, Mother," Jahmelle said softly as she stepped to his side and rested one hand on his arm. He started—she moved like a Moldori, noiseless and quick; and he hadn't been aware of her approach.

"You expect these..." Marvaya swept her arm to indicate the soldiers around them. "...to be sufficient?"

"My people don't know me, Mother," the queen explained. "All they know is that I have been hidden in the mountains all my life because I was too frightful for my father to look upon, and that I am half-Moldori. They will wonder if I am truly Abernali, or if I will seek vengeance by turning the country into a Moldori holding. I believe I will have a better chance of convincing them I will not do so if there is nothing to suggest otherwise."

She stepped forward and into her mother's arms; Marvaya dropped the reins and enfolded her. Her face said she

120

saw the logic in the words, but the chieftain's eyes said her heart quivered with fear for her child's safety. They fixed on Chris's, those eyes. They demanded he swear he would die before he let harm come to her and vowed that if he failed he, too, would die...eventually.

Then Marvaya dropped her arms and barked something in gutteral Moldori. Retrieving the reins of the gray, she handed them to Jahmelle.

"This is Cloudskimmer. She is a coronation gift from the Moldori to the Queen of Abernal, and of the finest blood of the herds."

Jahmelle took the reins and curtseyed to the fine-limbed mare, who nodded her head as if acknowledging the gesture. Chris felt a shiver up his spine that had nothing to do with the autumn breeze and the sweat drying on his skin. It was said Moldori horses had the intelligence of humans, that they were not beasts of burden but equal partners in Moldori life. Now, as he looked into Cloudskimmer's dark eyes he could swear she was laughing at him.

It made him feel half-sick, and in the back of his brain a dark voice began to whisper that perhaps the Nadwich Lump might be a better choice for the throne after all. He squelched it. He wasn't a child to be frightened by things that on the surface seemed unexplainable. He knew what real fear of the dark powers felt like—and the evil stink of magic that engendered it.

Shaking off such ridiculous fancies, he finished dressing with the help of Sergeant-major Carpent, who had serendipitously arrived with his and Ted's horses. The Moldori were already mounted and turned like a flock of birds to follow Marvaya as she sped out of the camp. Jahmelle stood beside the mare, stroking the satiny arched neck and watching until there was not even dust left to mark the passage of the ehlan. He didn't interrupt.

She sighed and said something to the mare in a voice too low for him to hear. Then she swung into the saddle as if she'd been doing it all her life. There was nothing for it but to do the same, and he and Ted flanked her as she rode down the hoof-beaten path toward the highway. The rest of the troops fell in behind with disciplined precision.

By midmorning they would reach Norburgh, the first town of any significant size between the capital and the mountains. The garrison was located just beyond, with the rest of Ted's battalion and two others besides. It would be their first encounter with their own forces, which might even now be preparing to prevent Chris and "the impostor" from reaching Registon...and very possibly their last.

"Thank you, Sir Christopher," Jahmelle said after they had ridden for one hour and most of another.

"For what, Your Grace?"

"For saving me from having to be the one to tell my mother I couldn't accept her help. To be honest, I'm not sure she would have listened to me."

"She wasn't going to listen to me, either. In fact, I wasn't sure how much longer I had to live just for suggesting it."

Dammit, he hadn't meant to say that! What was the matter with him? Every time he opened his mouth lately he was blurting out things he shouldn't. It was hardly diplomatic to suggest your queen's mother was a murderous savage who slit throats rather than listen to reason.

"Probably not long," Jahmelle chuckled, and from her other side Ted grinned over at him. "My mother's temper is rather easily ignited. However, it seems that together we are sufficiently persuasive she accepted the truth of the situation." She patted Cloudskimmer's neck. "However, I doubt she'll keep her distance once this issue of my accession is decided."

"There is no issue, Your Grace. You are Edrick's sole legitimate heir." At least he hadn't babbled the doubts he'd entertained the night before.

"You know that, and I know that. But what of the people, Sir Christopher? Might they not prefer someone they know to...a monster so ugly she had to be sealed in a tower?"

This time the look Ted tossed him was grim. There was that, wasn't there—the old "better the evil we know" business? That the evil in question was likely to be little more than a pawn of Nadwich might not make any difference to the people, who knew this woman he already admired greatly as The Ugly Princess, fit only for the company of Trolls.

Nor had he missed the careful neutrality of her voice. She hid it well, but he had become familiar with that voice in their short acquaintance; and he knew the knowledge of her reputation hurt.

Ted responded before Chris could think of what to say.

"Abernali are a stubborn lot, Your Grace," he said thoughtfully. "I've listened to my men since we ran into you yesterday, and I won't say I haven't heard a few wondering. Even so, not one of them said he favored the L—uh, Your Grace's cousin; and I think you'll discover that goes for most of the rest of the people. They might not like the way their monarchs behave, but they are dedicated to the fact those are their monarchs.

"Your family has ruled this country in a direct line from parent to child for longer than any other in history—or in any other country, for that matter. They're proud of that. They also don't like the idea of foreigners telling them what to think.

"With all due respect, ma'am, I think you could have two heads and eat live chickens and your people would still welcome you with open arms because you're Edrick's daughter."

The sound of hoofbeats from ahead signaled the return of the scout, whom Ted had sent out to see what might be lurking in wait for them. The column halted until the man arrived.

"Report!" Ted commanded after answering the soldier's salute.

"Sir, I saw no sign the garrison has been mobilized, and there are no indications of the presence of Nadwickians. I talked to a couple of innkeepers, and they said a troop passed through yesterday—probably the one we ran into—and announced a reward for anyone who turned in Sir Christopher and the queen."

"And?"

"None of the ones I talked to seemed happy about it, sir. They asked if I had any news—"

"You didn't tell them we were coming." Chris interrupted, then watched with despair as the man's face flushed. "Damn—by now they've had time to alert the garrison."

"I think you and Her Grace should stay here until I have time to ride in and see what's happened," Ted stated, and Chris was about to agree when the one person they couldn't argue with took the decision out of their hands.

"No, gentlemen, I think not," Jahmelle said, her voice ringing with determination. "I will not spend the rest of my days hiding and running. If you are correct in your assessment of the people, Sir Edgard, then we are in no danger. If you are wrong, then it's better we have this over and done."

Without waiting for them to reply, she spoke to her horse and set off down the road at a brisk canter. The rest of them had no choice but to follow.

Chapter 16

TO MY CONSIDERABLE RELIEF, DANELLA, WHO HAD BEEN unconscious when I picked her up, began to come around as Jack and I sped down the hallway toward the hidden door.

"Bart..." she murmured.

"Shhh, darling," I whispered in her ear. "In a moment."

Behind us I could hear uneven footsteps. Apparently, the one guard we'd left alive had regained consciousness, and Benifaz had dispatched him to stop us. He rounded the corner into the hall just as we reached the section of wall that held the entrance to the passages and shouted. Jack reached into his pack, pulled out his second pistol and cut the shout off in the middle with a ball right between the man's eyes.

Moments later the entry swung open, we stepped inside; and he pulled it shut behind us.

I set my wife on her feet, but she leaned against me, her arms still around my neck. It frightened me to see her like this. What had that miserable Nadwickian done to her?

Jack started for the stairs leading to the wine cellar, but I stopped him.

"Danella's bleeding, and so am I," I whispered. "And she can barely walk."

He retraced his steps and held the lamp up to see.

"So, what do you suggest? You need somewhere to hole up until after dark. Maybe even longer."

"This way—and bring the other lamp." Lifting Danella once again, I started in the opposite direction until we came to another staircase, then a second. The second climb ended in a room under the eaves, lit by a single window.

Jack was right, of course. We could hardly leave the palace grounds the same way we had entered, spattered with blood and accompanied by a woman whose battered face was known to every guardsman who had ever stood sentry at the gates. By now Benifaz had likely commanded every available man to search palace and grounds for us. I wouldn't be surprised if the perimeter guard was doubled.

"Bart, I can walk now," Danella said, and I saw that much of the animation had returned to her eyes. Her head wound was still bleeding but not at an alarming rate. The ball had barely grazed the scalp.

Still, we made a rather gory pair, the cut on my cheek having soaked my collar.

I led her to a wooden storage chest at the foot of the bed. A small table flanked with ladderback chairs sat under the window on the left side of the room and a washstand with a bowl and pitcher occupied the side opposite. A narrow wardrobe stood behind the door, and a dusty braided rug covered the center of the unvarnished plank floor.

The bed should have been bare; and, given it had been a year since Danella and I had cleaned here the dust should have been deep enough to leave tracks. Instead, the mattress was covered in decent linen and a thick down comforter, and the furniture bore only a thin coating. As much, perhaps, as might have accumulated had the occupant been absent for a month.

"Jack, just how long have you been sneaking in and out of the palace? And how did you know about the passages?"

He set one lamp on the table and blew it out. For a long moment I thought he was not going to answer as he stared through the window. Then, with a shrug of his shoulders, he slumped into a chair and stretched his legs out in front of him.

"Did you ever wonder how I escaped?"

Danella had taken off one of her petticoats, and we were tearing it into strips for use as bandages.

"Everyone wondered how you escaped, Jack."

As a member of the nobility, Jack and his grandfather had been imprisoned in chambers in the east wing of the palace that had been especially constructed for highborn prisoners. The windows were covered with heavy, if decorative, iron grilles, the door reinforced with steel. When the death sentence was passed, guards were posted at both door and windows for additional security.

Yet the seventeen-year-old condemned had vanished as if he'd somehow turned to smoke and drifted up the flue.

Of course, I knew there was a hidden door to the passages in the chamber, but no one else should have. Unless...

"Are you saying my father...?"

"And Sir Davvyd. They smuggled me off the grounds, put me on a horse with enough food to get me to the mountains and told me to find the Moldori." He stood up and started for the door, taking the lamp with him. "I'll fetch food and water. Then, when I can, I'll slip out and get something a little less conspicuous for the two of you to wear."

Without waiting for a response, he vanished down the stairs.

I turned back to Danella to find her weeping soundlessly. I sat next to her and pulled her into my arms.

"It will be all right, my love. Jack is very resourceful and—"

"I tried to be brave," she sobbed, as if deaf to my attempt to soothe her. "I couldn't. He kept demanding to know where you were and then he told the others to hit me and I couldn't help it. I begged him to stop. I groveled in front of him. I'm so ashamed."

"Danella, you were wonderful."

127

"I thought I could do this," she went on, still oblivious to me. "I thought I could manage to behave like a born lady, but I couldn't. I could see them all staring at me, wondering how I dare to pretend to be one of them; and I—"

"Danella, dearest, hush. It's all right. Really. You have more nobility and courage than any of them. Do you think any of those high-nosed snobs could have risked death to do what you just did?"

I had been aware all along that being amongst those she had been taught were superior to her by accident of birth made her uncomfortable. I had also seen that discomfort growing less as she discovered the titled had all the same flaws and virtues as any other. She tilted her tearstained face up, and I realized only then she had spoken in the past tense.

"I was afraid he would kill you," she said, cupping my undamaged cheek with her hand and smiling tremulously. "And in that very instant I realized he was nothing more than a nasty old man, just like every other nasty, bullying old man I ever encountered in Father's shops."

I used one of our rags to clean her face a bit and then bent to kiss her.

"And you handled him beautifully."

"Who is that other man?" she wondered, taking the cloth from me and beginning her own repairs. "He looks familiar, somehow."

Jack returned with a loaf of bread, a small wheel of cheese and a bottle of wine tucked in his pack by the time I provided her with a brief synopsis of his personal history and events since we had last been together. He also had a jug of water, which we immediately put to use cleaning away the rest of the blood as well as we could.

The cheese and wine he had no doubt abstracted from the cellar, but the bread was still warm from the oven. He had a handful of matches as well so I could relight my lamp when darkness arrived. Before I could express my amazement, however, he saluted Danella and was gone.

"Is he always so abrupt?" she wondered.

"He's a strange man with a sad history."

"I gathered that from what you were talking about before. But I'm sure I've seen him somewhere."

As we ate I considered the surprising information that my father and Chris's were responsible for the young count's escape. It made me wonder what other secrets those two might have harbored over the years, and how many other times they had committed treason to save the innocent from Edrick's savage hand.

I also tried to remember details of the charges levied against Jack and his grandfather, but between the years that had passed and my having been more interested in girls than politics at the time I finally had to give it up.

King Edrick's funeral was held the next day, the third following his demise, as tradition required. The Nadwickian hypocrite gave the eulogy, lamenting that his dear "brother" should be so insulted in death as to have some impostor passed off as his daughter and heir. Standing at his side was his nephew, the vacant-eyed young man of sixteen his parents named Demtri but who quickly and sadly became known as "the Lump." Benifaz planned to see him crowned as soon as good taste allowed.

We learned all this from Jack, who as promised returned with fresh clothing and additional food that afternoon. I had spent the morning in the passages, hoping I might overhear something about Chris and the queen, but except for the staff everyone in a position to have such knowledge had either attended the funeral or pretended to.

"Ratface is telling everyone he tripped on a wrinkled rug," he snorted after giving us a detailed recounting of the ceremonies over a cup of wine.

"Is there any news yet of Chris or the queen?"

Jack grimaced. "There are soldiers all over the countryside looking for them, and Overlack just issued a proclamation officially naming the Lump Edrick's heir."

"And was this announcement well-received?"

"About as if the entire country was just diagnosed with terminal brain rot," Jack snorted. "Still, nobody's going to do anything at this stage to irritate Ratface, so we need to get you two out of here and tucked away somewhere safer."

"Why can't we just stay here?" Danella asked. She had been surreptitiously studying him all along, but I could tell by the way she nipped her lower lip she was no closer to solving the mystery of where she had seen him.

"Because it's too dangerous for me to keep sneaking onto the grounds with every soldier in the place on high alert." He opened the second pack he had brought and handed her a stack of clothes. "Nothing suitable in the wardrobe, Ruford?"

"I was fortunate to find something of yours to fit reasonably well the first time, Jack. I trust you brought something for me, as well."

He had, of course, and after handing it to me bowed to Danella and withdrew so she could change.

"I would have preferred women's clothing," she muttered as she pulled on the coarse wool trousers.

"But they won't be looking for a lad."

Which only earned me a look that advised she was well aware of the necessity of the disguise and didn't need me to insult her intelligence by suggesting otherwise. It also conveyed she didn't feel the need to pretend to be happy about it.

A half-hour passed before Jack tapped lightly on the door and let himself in. He scrutinized both of us closely before nodding his approval.

"Let's go." He snatched up his packs and headed back to the door.

"Now?" I protested. "In broad daylight?"

"Now, in broad daylight, while everybody is in the Great Hall reminiscing about the good old days under Edrick and licking the boots of Ratface and his stupid nephew. There are delivery wagons arriving regularly to make sure there's enough food for the mob. One of them is taking us out of here."

We hurried down the stairs and through the passages, Jack and I with lanterns and Danella between us. We returned to the cellar, where Jack left us to ascend to the kitchen. Moments later, he whistled the first bar of a popular tavern song as a sign the way was clear.

Upstairs, a grocer's wagon with a canvas cover stood outside the delivery door; and we slid in amongst the empty crates, carefully arranging them over us as the driver snapped his whip. With a jolt, our conveyance started for the rear gate of the palace grounds.

"Hold!"

I believe my heart skipped a beat at the sound of that single word spoken in a Nadwickian accent. I know I held my breath. Would they search the wagon?

"Afternoon, soldier," I heard Jack say, and his accent was just as Nadwickian. "Hot for this time of yar, ain't?"

"Aye, so," the unseen guard replied. "Druther be home."

"'Tis cooler there, no arguing. Be going back m'self oncet I make enough to buy me a wife."

"Need to see in the wagon, brother—king's orders. Got escaped prisoners to catch."

Jack snorted.

"Long gone from here, I'd wager."

"Not a bet I'd take, but orders is orders.

By now I had no choice but to take a breath. At the same time, I heard Jack leap down from the wagon seat and walk to the rear of the bed in the company of another man—presumably the guard. Still chatting, comparing the skills of the occupants of various Nadwickian brothels with his companion, Jack untied the canvas and started to lift it. A stack of crates he had strategically piled at the tail of the bed tumbled to the ground the moment the cloth that had been supporting them was gone. One of them contained a layer of rotted potatoes.

Cursing, the soldier ordered Jack to replace the crates and be on his way. Even so, I lay with every muscle tight as bowstrings until our vehicle stopped again and Jack slapped the canvas above my head to signal we had arrived at our destination.

We were in the courtyard of a smithy. The shop was closed, as were all places of business, to show respect for the deceased Edrick. However, as I helped Danella down, the door swung open slightly, although no one emerged.

"This place belongs to a friend of mine," Jack said as we started for it. "You'll be here for two days unless something happens that you need to move sooner."

We stepped into the dim workshop, kept reasonably warm by the banked fire of the forge. On the left a ladder disappeared into what turned out to be a loft filled with sacks of charcoal. On the side facing the courtyard, a small space had been cleared and two pallets arranged. A chamber pot and a jug were the only other furnishings.

"Hom will see you're fed and supplied with water, the forge will keep you warm enough and you can tidy up at night after he closes. On the off chance Ratface finds out you're here..." He climbed atop the stack of bags nearest the wall and fiddled with a bolt before pushing a trapdoor up. "...you can get out this way."

"Why does that fail to surprise me?"

Jack only grinned while Danella looked from one of us to the other with a look that asked what she was missing.

"Our new friend has a serious affection for rooftops, Nell," I explained.

"Of course," she said, her look of confusion transforming to one of comprehension. "That's very smart—nobody ever looks up when they're hunting someone."

Jack snickered, and disappeared through the trapdoor.

Chapter 17

LIKE MOST OF THE OLD CITIES ESTABLISHED AROUND THE first royal outposts, Norburgh had long ago exploded beyond the limits of its original walls. The old keep had been built where the early roads from the Deciron Empire and Nadwich joined to form the Great Seaward Highway. It was now, as it had been for as long as history was recorded, a city of traders and bankers and men who used money to make money.

Jahmelle slowed her mare to a walk as she neared the outskirts, allowing her escort to assemble in parade formation. Here, the buildings were mainly dwellings, with a few shops catering to the necessities of food, clothing and after-work entertainment. The occupants were used to having troops pass their doors, so very few paid more than passing attention to them until that point.

Then, the veiled woman riding at the head of the soldiers attracted notice. The presence of the Royal Champion was all the additional information need for the passing interest to become total attention. Neighbors were alerted, doors and windows opened and taverns emptied as the news spread that the Queen of Abernal had arrived.

Ted Truville rode on her left, half a length back. Chris rode the same distance behind on her right. The troops formed a sharp-edged block three wide. They proceeded into the city.

Even if they hadn't heard the announcement from the Nadwickian intruders, the Norburgians would have had no problem recognizing the Ugly Princess. Had her distant prison not been provisioned by local businesses for the last twenty years? Had those doing the provisioning not spoken in the last few years of occasionally having glimpsed a veiled figure walking the parapets? Had they and their associates not wondered frequently over mugs of ale what horrors lurked under those shimmering coverings?

So, as her entourage passed through the ever-more-crowded streets toward the Norburgh Tower, citizens fell into step behind until, by the time the gates of the ancient keep gaped before them, it seemed half the city trailed in their wake. Even so, they were a quiet and orderly group, and after some initial concern for Jamelle's safety Chris relaxed and focused on the more dangerous confrontation ahead.

The commandant of the garrison awaited their arrival in the forecourt of the gates, in full dress uniform and mounted. The duty company stood in three lines behind him, their weapons at port-arms.

Jahmelle halted just inside the limits of the enclosure, and Chris moved up to her side. It was now the commandant's decision to make whether to accept her as his queen or obey the dictates of Nadwich and order her arrest.

Long, quiet moments passed—astounding, considering the size of the mob spread out across and along the street behind. It was so quiet that clicks of the hooves of nervous horses and the soft jingle of harness was all that could be heard.

"Sir Champion," the commandant called in the parade ground voice that was almost as much the reason for his rank as his skills as a soldier, "what is the word?"

"The king is dead!" Christopher replied in the same tone and volume. "Long live Queen Jahmelle of Abernal!"

The commandant urged his mount forward until he reached the midpoint of the forecourt. It was almost possible to feel the collectively held breath of the people. Then, without any further hesitation, the commandant swung from his saddle, strode to within three paces of Jahmelle, doffed his hat and sank to one knee. A moment later, he lifted his head and shouted, "God save the Queen!"

The roar of approbation that followed was enough to shake bricks from the buildings. Pigeons took wing in droves, and the bells in the great cathedral across the court from the keep began to ring. Rising to his feet, the commandant stepped forward and took Cloudskimmer's bridle, then led Jahmelle within the walls of the keep between ranks of cheering soldiers.

Each royal keep had quarters reserved for the ruling monarch. Chris escorted the queen there as soon as the requisite formalities had been observed and Ted's company dismissed.

"This seems to have gone well," she commented. Chris heard the slight tremor of relief in her voice.

"I think it might be wise for you to stay here while I take a company to Registon. Once it's clear his nephew has no support, Benifaz might just decide to give up and return to Nadwich."

He opened the door to her chambers and waited for her to go inside. She crossed to the narrow window, looking out across the rooftops.

"He might also decide he has sufficient military support to quell this 'uprising' and meet force with force," she said after several minutes. "I prefer my reign not start with bloodshed, if it can be avoided. We wouldn't want the people of Abernal to decide their half-Moldori queen is not only ugly but as uncivilized as the rest of her mother's tribe."

Chris knew he should say something. Despite her level tone he had in their short time of acquaintance become quite sensitive to the nuances in her voice. Perhaps it was the veils, forcing him to listen more closely, since he had no expressions to read. He was certain his father would have known what words were appropriate for this sort of moment when what he really wanted to do was put his arms around her and just offer comfort.

"No," she went on after the silence had acquired much too much weight, "we will continue tomorrow as we did today, and pray Sir Edgard is correct and that the King of Nadwich has no real taste for a battle there's a chance he will lose."

There was a light rap on the door, and when Chris opened it a pair of serving girls hustled in with hot water for bathing and fresh linens for the bed. He didn't miss the glances of burning curiosity they tossed at the woman by the window. Not far behind them came the commandant's wife with a tray of food and the information a reception was already set up for that evening. It seemed as good a time as any to take his paralyzed tongue and go.

Jahmelle requested Truville's company as her royal escort, and early the following morning the procession set off for Hartshill, the next municipality of significant size on the highway. There, and in all the towns and villages through which they passed, they were met with the same joy and enthusiasm. Mayors and townspeople alike presented their new queen with gifts—unique tapestries, exquisite jewelry, bolts of rare fabric, baskets of fruit and bottles of their best wines—so many they needed a convoy of wagons to carry them.

In each place Jahmelle stopped long enough to thank them and speak briefly with those who requested it. Chris had no doubt they would have progressed even slower than they did had he not reminded her their enemies were abroad.

On the evening of the seventh day after Norburgh they reached the city of Riverbend and were welcomed into the royal quarters of the garrison there. Jahmelle greeted the men then retreated to change into fresh clothing in preparation for a dinner with the local nobles and city officials.

She was finally able to discard her riding clothes altogether rather than simply sending them off to be cleaned. Her trunks and bags had traveled at a better pace and arrived at the garrison just that afternoon and been placed in her quarters in anticipation of her arrival. When she emerged for Chris and the garrison commander to escort her to the town hall for the banquet she wore a gown of salmon pink and veils that shimmered and changed color like mother-of-pearl. The royal signet gleamed on her thumb, and she seemed to float over the floor to meet them.

For the next three hours, she was the center of all eyes as the meal and a variety of entertainment was followed by the now-familiar lengthy presentation of gifts. Not one guest was overlooked, and several times she had Chris or the commander escort her amongst the tables so she could speak to those who lacked the courage to come to her.

In time, however, the festivities ended, and the queen and her escort took their leave and returned to the garrison. The commander bid them goodnight at the hall leading to his own quarters, and Chris started to lead Jahmelle to hers.

She stumbled and would have fallen had he not moved quickly to catch her by waist and knees and lift her into his arms. She draped one arm around his neck and leaned her head against his shoulder.

"Your Grace, you're exhausted," he scolded, though with all due courtesy, as he strode down the hall carrying her. "And you didn't eat anything at the banquet. Tell me you had something beforehand."

"I'm afraid I fell asleep in the bath and there wasn't time," she admitted. "It was just a momentary dizziness, Sir Christopher. Really, I can walk."

"We're almost there." Nor did he set her down even to open the door, though he told himself it was only because he feared she would faint again and not because the weight of her against him was a pleasure he wasn't willing to give up any sooner than he had to.

The three noblemen's daughters who had been sent to act as her ladies-in-waiting jumped up from the chairs where they'd been working on embroidery and hurried over as he settled Jahmelle onto a divan in front of the hearth.

"Lady Antona, would you fetch Her Grace some warm milk and something to eat," he ordered.

"I really detest warm milk," Jahmelle said with a smile in her voice. "Would it be all right if I had a pot of herb tea instead, Sir Christopher?"

The young women were staring at them, their wide eyes going from the woman on the divan to the tall man in antique chain mail standing over her with arms akimbo. Although all three had been wisely kept away from court, they had heard enough gossip about Edrick's personality to expect the queen to shortly be demanding Chris's head. As he felt the blood transfusing his face he considered she might just as well take it, because it certainly wasn't doing him much good lately.

"Forgive me, Your Grace," he said, drawing to attention. "I forgot my place."

"Lady Antona, would you and the other girls please fetch me something to nibble before bedtime?"

Sweeping curtseys, and glancing over their shoulders with undisguised curiosity as they departed, the girls obeyed.

"Sir Christopher," Jahmelle said, patting the seat beside her, "would you mind sitting down so I needn't crane my neck?"

He could hardly refuse, although once he was seated he regretted he hadn't simply pulled over another chair. The divan was not large, and when she turned to face him the edge of her veil skimmed over the back of his hand. The airsoft touch sent a tingle along his arm, and he could feel her eyes meeting his through the opalescent fabric. It was ridiculous, but he couldn't shake the sensation no matter how much he told himself he was being ridiculous.

"Your Grace, I—"

"What is the duty of the Royal Champion?"

"To defend the monarch from harm and the country from its enemies." That was an easy question—his father had made him learn it before he was old enough to talk without a lisp.

"Which you have just done." She leaned forward and took his hand between both of hers, and the tingle paled beside the jolt he experienced at her warm touch. "Sir Christopher, while I have no doubt I will have need of a champion, there is something I will need even more in the coming days—a friend. Someone whose advice I can respect and whose purposes I can trust. Will you be my friend as well as my champion?"

Chris opened his mouth to answer, but his throat had gone dry. The aura of her scent—vanilla and cinnamon and musk—surrounded him and made it hard for him to breathe. It took every ounce of will he had to push aside the reaction of his senses and engage his brain.

"I'd be honored, Your Grace," he finally managed, and then he lifted her hand and pressed his lips to it...just a bit too long for politeness. *What the hell is wrong with me?* he wondered. *This is the queen, my queen. I'm acting like an idiot.*

What might have happened next he was destined not to learn, for the sound of soft giggles from the hall outside signaled the return of the ladies with Jahmelle's bedtime snack. Setting her hand down, he stood and bowed, then started for the door. Then, realizing they hadn't decided what time to leave for Registon the next morning, he turned back just in time to see the Ugly Princess softly trail the tips of her fingers over the back of the hand that still carried the sensation of his kiss.

Chapter 18

THE DAY AFTER EDRICK'S FUNERAL QUEEN BARBA WAS packed off to Nadwich. According to Jack, who dropped in—literally, through the trapdoor—that night, she had attended draped in dense black veils, not as a sign of respect for the departed Edrick but because her loving spouse had blackened both her eyes when she protested his plan to keep Yolanthe in Abernal and wed her to Demtri.

While our sojourn in the smithy was hardly comfortable, Danella and I were grateful. Earlier that afternoon we were able to overhear a conversation our host had with one of his customers during which we learned Benifaz had placed a substantial reward on both our heads. Sufficiently substantial I myself might have been tempted. A slightly smaller amount was offered for the unknown individual believed to be aiding and abetting us in our nefarious plot against the integrity of the crown. The irony of our having to depend on the criminal underworld for safety from the upstanding citizenry was one I preferred not to dwell on.

Late the following night we bundled our few belongings and followed Jack across the rooftops to another bolt hole, this one in the garret of a house of ill repute. Our new location inevitably led Danella to ask questions I would rather not have had to answer, as there was always the risk of her inquiring how I came to be so knowledgeable on the subject.

I awoke the morning of the sixth day to discover I was alone, and to say I nearly choked on my terror is to far understate the level of emotion involved. I was fastening my trousers, preparing to risk discovery by undertaking a search, when the door leading to the rooms below opened and Danella, clad only in one of my shirts, padded into the room carrying a laden breakfast tray.

"Where in the hell have you been?" I roared, my relief expressing itself in the form of an urgent desire to turn her over my knee.

If she sensed this, Danella chose to ignore it.

"I woke up and smelled the most wonderful aromas," she said, setting the tray on a rickety table in one corner. "I tried to resist, but then I thought it must be the...ladies...having breakfast and decided I should be able to blend in. Jack did say they all know we're here."

I had to admit, my shock was rapidly dissipating under the onslaught of those very aromas, emanating from under a crisp, clean napkin covering the tray. She removed it, revealing hot coffee, fresh eggs and sausages, crisp rolls and a small dish of cherry jam. Given we had been subsisting on warm water, bread and cheese to this point, I could well understand her inability to resist this particular temptation.

She turned back to face me, looking up at me through her lashes in a way she had never used before.

"I do apologize if I frightened you, my love," she said, and crossed the few feet separating us with a most decided sway of her hips to run her finger over my lips. "I promise I'll make it up to you...after we eat."

She did—quite nicely.

That night when Jack arrived, this time using the door for a pleasant change of pace, he had wonderful news. The queen, accompanied by Chris and a contingent of troops, had made a triumphal entry into Norburgh.

"I'm not surprised," Danella said. "And I'll be very glad when they reach here and we can go home."

Unfortunately, the only place we went over the following week were to three more hidey-holes of varying degrees of comfort. Finally, he brought news that gave life to our flagging spirits. Chris, with the Ugly Princess and an entire company of dragoons, was in Riverbend and preparing to advance on Registon the following morning. Her Grace, whose name we at last learned was Jahmelle, had traveled from her place of lifelong confinement with the unequivocal support of her army and her people.

That same afternoon the King of Nadwich departed. He did not take his nephew or his daughter with him. Instead, he ordered the boy to "behave like a king," placed him in the hands of the Spiders and trotted east as fast as his horse could travel.

The citizens of Registon wasted no time preparing for their queen's arrival, and even with the short notice they managed to give the city a festive air. Great banners were strung across the streets, garlands of autumn flowers and leaves adorned the lampposts, flags flew, fireworks sparkled and popped. Mounted lookouts were posted on the road to Riverbend, and before dawn people began to line the thoroughfare that ran from the highway to Abernal House.

"I won't stay cooped up here and miss this, Bartrim," Danella said.

"Nor will I, love. Jack said he'd come by at noon, and the queen's party is expected at three."

"I just wish I had something decent to wear," she complained, glaring at her trousers and boots.

"By sundown we'll be back in our own rooms, my dearest, and you may dress any way you please." I honestly failed to understand her severe distaste for her current attire, as I found the way the trousers in particular fit rather fetching. I had, however, learned early on that mentioning this was not the way to make her feel better.

Jack arrived as promised, and the three of us struggled through the ever-increasing crowds to the waterfront. The river Woodrath flows between that city and Registon. It widens here just below a wide stone bridge with a gate on the city end. Using one of Jack's rooftop routes, we finally found a viewpoint from atop a tall warehouse from which we could observe.

The Spiders had announced they would greet the princess in the name of King Demtri, as they declared they were now convinced she was, indeed, Edrick's daughter, although illegitimate. What defect of judgment led them to continue their by this time clearly fruitless plan I have no idea. Perhaps Benifaz had convinced them his retreat was merely to arrange military support, and they actually believed him.

Whatever their reasoning—or lack thereof—when the lookout galloped to the palace with word that Queen Jahmelle was approaching, the Spiders, accompanied by a half-company of the Royal Guard, rode out to meet her.

The royal entourage reached the far side of the bridge just as the Spiders reached the gate. Without hesitation Christopher led the procession onto the bridge floor. There was a tense moment as they reached the midpoint. Overlack, Entreput and Settleson, clad in their traditional accoutrements, shifted in their saddles and looked at one another as if they had forgotten whose turn it was to be in charge.

The moment ended when a tall figure clad head-to-toe in shimmering silvery veils and mounted on a magnificent Moldori mare rode up beside Christopher. The late afternoon sun sparked off the great diamond in the royal signet and the contingent of fifty royal guards accompanying the First Minister quietly broke ranks, rode forward and reformed in disciplined style on either side of their new ruler.

"Jack," I said as the royal party passed below us, "we need to get to the palace. I refuse to miss the confrontation between Christopher and the Lump."

143

"Then we'd best hurry," he replied, clearly as eager as I to observe the event, although he tried not to let it show. We set off across the rooftops for the secret entrance onto the palace grounds. By the time the royal party reached the front of the palace we three were safely ensconced in the minstrel gallery over looking the Great Hall.

The room was nearly empty. A half-dozen Nadwickian soldiers, part of a platoon Benifaz had left behind as a token of his affection, stood around the high seat. Demtri, seemingly oblivious to what was happening, sat on the throne with a large bowl of grapes on his lap, tossing them in the air and attempting to catch them in his mouth. His aim was not particularly commendable.

There was a sudden influx of light as the great bronze doors opened. Christopher strode to stand before the throne, and I expected him to challenge the young man on it at once. Instead, he turned and watched, along with those few of the nobility who had opted to remain after the funeral, as the tall, stately lady in the veils seemed to glide across the floor. Demtri stared at her, his jaw nearly touching his chest.

"Cousin," the Ugly Princess said in a voice that rang through the hall, "I believe you are in my chair."

The silence dragged on and on as the pathetic young man's eyes leapt from one person to another, clearly begging for help. One of the Nadwickians made a move toward his sword, only to freeze immobile when Chris drew his first. Slowly, Demtri the Nadwich Lump set aside his bowl and stood then descended the steps. He paused on the bottom one then shivered and ran from the room.

Sheathing his sword, Chris stepped to the queen's side and placed her hand atop his then escorted her to the throne as the Nadwickians spun on their heels and marched away. He stopped two stairs below, and she completed the climb, then turned and faced the staring assemblage as he did the same.

"I name this lady Jahmelle Alliya Dihan of House Rediman, trueborn daughter of Edrick Rediman and the Lady Marvaya of Moldor and by right of blood Queen of Abernal," he called in a voice that rang off the walls. "Who challenges this, challenges me."

But, of course, no one did.

"Come, love, we must greet our new lady," I said, starting for the stairs that led down to the hall. I was halfway there before I noticed she had not followed. Rather, she stood in the center of the gallery, hands on hips and foot tapping. Jack leaned against the wall, cleaning his fingernails with his dagger. "Is something amiss, my dear?"

"Bartrim Ruford, do you really expect me to greet the new queen dressed like this?"

"I understand your objections, my sweet, but you know the law. Until the Seneschal acknowledges the new monarch, he or she is still subject to challenge, and protocol requires that the Seneschal's lady accompany him."

She turned to Jack, as if planning to enlist his aid in arguing her point—a rather fruitless exercise, I thought, given he was the one who had dressed her so in the first place. Nor had I missed his admiring glances at the way her trousers fit. Indeed, had I not by now been completely convinced of Jack's underlying integrity, I might have taken offense.

However, instead of continuing her protest Danella merely stared openmouthed, first at Jack and then over his head at the wall where hung one of the many portraits of scions of House Rediman. The next instant Jack looked up from his engrossing endeavor, saw her expression and straightened. His own face took on that icy hardness I had seen less and less over the last week as he stepped far enough away from the wall to look at the painting—from where I stood, I couldn't be certain which one. He flushed dark, spun on his heel and strode to the railing.

To my surprise, Danella abandoned her argument and swiftly came to join me, though her face was deeply thoughtful. Together, we descended the stairs and crossed the rapidly filling floor of the hall to stand in front of the throne.

"Your Grace, I am Bartrim Ruford, Baron Greenwater—"

"So, you are the famous Ruford Seneschal I've heard so much about," the queen interrupted. When she didn't need to shout, her voice had an intriguing huskiness.

"Hardly famous, Your Grace," I protested, giving my tall, imposing friend in shining armor a rather sharp look. Just what had he been telling her?

"You seem to be out of uniform, Milord Baron," she noted.

"Matters became somewhat...complicated, Your Grace. May I present my wife, the Lady Danella?"

Danella curtseyed as gracefully as one can clad in thick-soled work boots, and I suspected I would pay dearly later for adhering so closely to proper protocol. I could have requested leave for us to retire to our rooms and return properly attired before introducing her. Still, best to get things over with.

"I'm delighted to meet you, Lady Danella," Queen Jahmelle said. "Perhaps you will enlighten me about these 'complicated matters' later this evening."

"Your Grace, there is one other you should meet," I said, although we had clearly been politely dismissed to put ourselves to rights.

I turned to call Jack down for introduction, but the gallery was empty. I can't say I was surprised—indeed, what surprised me was that he had stayed with us as long as he had. Still, I had hoped to be able to find some way to repay him for all he had done, whether he liked it or not. I was fairly certain I could find that apartment house in the butcher's quarter if I tried. So long as I assigned the search and reward to someone else, I would not violate the deadly oath he had made me give.

"Well," I continued lamely, "another time, perhaps."

"I believe we could all do with a bit of rest," the queen said, getting to her feet. I took a step forward to escort her to her quarters, but Chris had already moved to her side. Together they left the Great Hall for the Queen's Tower.

Danella was quiet as we went to our quarters. Baths were already being prepared when we entered, and I was anticipating immersion with considerable pleasure when I noticed the frown darkening my dear one's brow. Recalling her reaction on the minstrel gallery, I was about to ask her what had caused it.

"I'm worried about Chris," she said before I could voice my curiosity.

"Chris? Why? He seemed perfectly fine to me."

If I say that at this point she gave me a look only married men are able to interpret, those of you who share that happy state with me will understand the chill that afflicted my spine.

"He's not fine," she informed me softly. "He's in love… with the queen."

Chapter 19

ALTHOUGH ROYAL CORONATIONS ARE GENERALLY HELD IN the spring to allow ease of travel for nobles and other invited guests who lived in outlying areas, Chris insisted Queen Jahmelle's should be held as quickly as could be managed. She concurred, so Danella and I were immersed in preparations within days of the queen's entry into Registon.

Despite the weight of my duties, however, I used every opportunity to observe Chris's behavior when he attended Her Grace, and even with my dull wits I quickly realized my wife was correct. The Royal Champion's attachment to his monarch went well beyond the call of duty. This, naturally, led me to wonder whether she was also aware of it, and what her own feelings in the matter might be.

Before I'm condemned as a busybody, bear in mind that Christopher Evergild and I had been raised together since the age of five when, as tradition required, I was fostered with Earl Davvyd and Countess Milena. As my only siblings are sisters, he is my brother in all but blood. So, knowing as I do the history of House Rediman and the disastrous consequences that arose in the past when the Champion and a reigning queen fell in love, my interest was much more than simple curiosity.

One might think it impossible to gauge the emotions of a woman draped in veils. However, there are subtle movements and tones of voice that can tell an intelligent observer much. It seemed to me that Queen Jahmelle did know how Chris felt—and was not inclined to encourage it. While she enjoyed his company when he was present, she rarely required him to be so if he had other business, which made me suspect I was not the only one knowledgeable in her family's history.

So focused was I on this matter and the coronation that I completely forgot the queen had expressed interest in hearing more about Dagger Jack. When a page brought word Her Grace desired to see me in her private office a week following her arrival, I assumed it was to discuss some aspect of the upcoming ceremonies. I had just knocked and been bidden to enter when Danella also arrived, and we entered together.

Her Grace was alone, and immediately led us to a small conversation area near the fireplace.

"Now," she said once we were all comfortable, "tell me about this man who saved your lives."

"His name is Jon Tarragent, Your Grace, and he is by right Count of Montrivert," I began, prepared to provide Jack's complete history.

"Do you mean Lady Olivia's grandson? Then he did survive—I'm so pleased."

Danella was, of course, at a loss, as I had also neglected to share the details of my sojourn in the jail with her. She didn't know about the princess's kindness toward Jack's grandmother all those years ago.

"But why didn't he stay?" the queen continued. "Surely, he knows I would never enforce that outrageous death warrant."

"Alas, Your Grace, that undeserved original has been replaced several times over by others that have been well-earned.

Perhaps you've heard of the infamous highwayman, Dagger Jack?"

"Ah."

I still marveled at the queen's breadth of knowledge, even knowing as I did her educational background and, through Chris, that the Moldori had not felt compelled to obey Edrick's edict of isolation.

"Tell me, Ruford, do you think you might be able to find...Dagger Jack...and persuade him to meet with me here on my word he will not be arrested?"

Frankly, my feeling was that I had as much chance of finding Jack as I did growing a second head, but I could continue to try. I said as much and was getting up to take leave when Danella stopped me.

"Wait, Bartrim, there was something I meant to tell you about Jack, and in all the confusion it slipped my mind. Do you remember when we were all up in the gallery?"

Indeed, I did, and I sank back into my chair, explaining briefly to Her Grace how we had observed her arrival.

"He was leaning against the wall under one of the portraits there," Danella said as soon as I had finished. "I happened to glance up and that was when I realized why he had always looked so familiar. I must pass those paintings half a dozen times a day and..."

She paused, not for dramatic effect but because she was clearly recalling her reaction to the discovery she was about to share.

"I remembered that when you told me about Jack's past you said you could never understand why the king and the three ministers had wanted to kill him."

"Death did seem a bit drastic, given his age and the overall lack of any evidence tying him to treason," I agreed. From the corner of my eye, I saw the queen was leaning forward, clearly as interested as I was.

"You also told me you overheard the ministers saying Overlack had convinced the king he should...eliminate all his...illegitimate children. That day, Jack was standing under the coronation portrait of King Edrick," Danella said. "And he looked just like him."

As he strode through the halls toward the Royal Council Chamber, Chris had to more than once dodge some precipitous serving lad or lass, all of whom seemed incapable of completing their errands at anything less than a dead run.

One of them had brought the message the queen needed to speak to him immediately, interrupting his observation of the newly organized Queen's Own Royals as they drilled. Jahmelle had rewarded both Ted Truville's troops and the fifty guardsmen who had so unhesitatingly declared their loyalty by commissioning them her personal guard under the command of Sir Ted. Since the palace guard had not received the intensive military training of the dragoons, and the dragoons knew little of palace etiquette, both he and Ted had spent most of the last two weeks developing and implementing a training program. If this morning's drill were any indication, it was working.

The difference in the palace atmosphere was amazing. Maids now went about their work without constantly glancing over their shoulder. Other members of the staff, including Danella Ruford, were often heard cheerfully humming. In the city, toasts to the Ugly Princess were heard on a regular basis, and Jahmelle had ordered no one was to be chastised for referring to her so.

She had also prevented Chris from taking any action against the Spiders, which he didn't understand. She hadn't explained, just asked him to humor her for a bit. Now, two weeks after her arrival, he suspected he was about to learn just what she had in mind for them.

The Spiders' story had taken a twist, now that the queen had arrived. It seemed they had been helpless victims, forced to do the will of Benifaz or suffer dire consequences. They swore their undying devotion and loyalty and spoke of their eagerness to assist Her Grace in learning the ins and outs of government. It had taken all of his control to keep a straight face as they slowly convinced themselves they had outwitted the lady and secured their former places. He didn't know what Jahmelle had planned for them, but he was definitely going to enjoy watching it.

The queen had this morning called the first meeting of her new Council of Ministers. She had filled the three long-empty seats with a noted woman scholar, a retired general recommended by Chris's father and the leader of the Loom-weaver's Guild, a successful businesswoman noted for her generosity to ambitious young women desiring to follow in her footsteps. Although women had always been eligible for the council, none had been appointed in so long that the impact of Jahmelle's naming two had shocked some, appalled a few and delighted most of the women.

All three of the new appointees were already seated when Chris strode to take his place next to the queen's chair. Moments later the Spiders entered, paused when they saw their usual places directly on either side of the royal chair were occupied then accepted the situation and took the three that remained.

Comfortable in both their chairs and their belief the silly girl had accepted their tale of having been victims of Beni-faz's greed, they were completely astounded when the silly girl's first order of business was to suggest they were all deserving of relief from the stresses of their many years of serving the crown. At a gesture, a scrivener placed in front of each man an official resignation from the council, already bearing the queen's signature and seal.

They protested that the honor of serving Her Grace far outweighed the burdens of office. That they had nothing but her best interests at heart and were certain she understood the necessity for maintaining some degree of continuity with the previous regime. That there were powerful enemies surrounding Abernal who might look askance at the abrupt departure of those whom they had learned to trust.

The meeting was interrupted at that point by the entrance of a dozen very large and beautifully decorated Moldori warriors. The group of silent, unsmiling men, not one less than seven feet tall and proportionately well-muscled, casually dispersed about the room, hands resting lightly on the hilts of their double-edged swords.

These were the fabled Pillars of Moldor, personal bodyguard of the High Chief, and their reputation as fighting men gave even Chris nightmares. A half-dozen had been sent by the High Chief to ensure the safety of his granddaughter until her coronation in another four weeks. While their presence gave him more time to focus on training the Royals, Chris couldn't help feeling it implied the Moldori didn't trust him to do his job.

Now, their arrival put an abrupt end to the babbling protests of the traitors.

"I'm sure all three of you gentleman will enjoy your years of leisure," Queen Jahmelle said as Overlack, Settleson and Entreput picked up their pens and signed the documents before them. "Thank you for joining us this morning. We wish you a pleasant journey home."

With no other pressing business, the council adjourned; and Chris walked Jahmelle back to the Lady's Nest. He fought to suppress it, but he was profoundly annoyed. Even granted that his political skills were weak, he could see the contradiction between refusing a Moldori escort on the way to Norburgh only to intimidate the Spiders with Moldori warriors. With an effort, he kept his voice level.

"You might better have used the Royals just now."

"I had intended to," she said. "Then Grandfather sent the contingent of the Pillars, and Mistress Hammet felt they would make a...deeper impression. Professor Preton and General Drelpot agreed, to my great surprise."

Well, Chris thought, not missing the hesitation as she tried to spare his feelings, *that's what Ministers of Council are for, I suppose.* They should have let him handle the situation, since that was why he was always in the council chamber during meetings in the first place. Would they, he wondered, have felt the need of the Pillars had his father been standing beside the queen instead of him?

"I still think it's dangerous to just let them go," he said. At least he didn't have to dance around something that bothered him with diplomatic language. Jahmelle had asked him to be her friend, and friends didn't prevaricate.

"If we had any solid proof they were guilty of treason, I wouldn't. But we don't, Christopher, not enough to satisfy any real sense of justice. I'll just have to hope the fact they no longer have any connection with the government will make them uninteresting to those who might be tempted to use them."

"You could have offered them a chance to face me and clear their reputations. That's what I'm here for, among other things."

They were outside the door to her sitting room, and she stopped and turned to face him.

"Despite the Moldori half of my heritage, Sir Christopher, I take no pleasure in bloodshed."

Her voice was soft and gentle, but it jabbed his chest like a thrown spear. Was that how she saw him—as savage in his own way as the Moldori? Didn't she understand that was his job, to be the last bastion of justice when all other avenues failed?

"Nor do I, Your Grace," he said, hearing the tight resentment in his tone but unable to do anything about it. "I apologize if I've given you the impression otherwise. By your leave?"

Only, he didn't wait for her to give it, just bowed and walked away, feeling her veiled eyes on him until he turned the corner to descend the stairs. He'd go back to the practice grounds and work with the Royals. At least there nobody questioned his motivations—or his competence.

Chapter 20

MY SEARCH FOR DAGGER JACK BEGAN THE EVENING AFTER the queen's request with the simple expedient of my climbing to the room under the eaves in hopes he might be there. I need no longer fear the repercussions of my oath. It was superceded by the one I took to serve and defend House Rediman. Legitimate or not, Jack was a member of that house.

I saw I was doomed to disappointment at first glance by the layer of dust that lay over everything in the hidden chamber. Still, I left a note.

The next day I rode to the Butcher's Quarter and located the tenement, only to find the apartment there just as empty. Questioning the other tenants was useless—they all swore no one had lived there for months. As the looks I received as I continued to inquire became steadily less friendly, I soon abandoned that search.

Hom the Blacksmith pretended he'd never seen me before in his life. The ladies at the bordello were more pleasant. They, at least, recalled Danella with considerable pleasure, asking after her as though she were an old friend. However, their faces went blank at the mention of Jack's name nor would they agree to pass along the message should he chance to visit. I spent what time I dared for two weeks looking for him and finally had to confess to the queen that I had failed.

So, it is not difficult to imagine with what considerable surprise it was that I looked up from my account books one late afternoon in mid-November to see none other than Dagger Jack leaning casually against the doorframe. Despite his relaxed posture, however, his face was as hard as steel.

"I've been looking for you," I announced, starting to my feet intending to escort him to the queen's office. "Or, rather, Her Grace—"

"She found me. I'd like to know how."

"I'm sure I have no idea. I know I couldn't. Still, it hardly seems something to complain of. A full pardon and complete rehabilitation. For which, by the way, congratulations, M'lord Count."

He made a deep courtier's bow that was as rancid with mockery as it was saturated with elegance.

"Perhaps I'll even survive to enjoy it."

"Beg pardon?

"Her Grace thinks I'd be bored playing lord of the manor after my exciting life as a criminal, so she offered me a job. I'm her new spymaster." He tried to maintain his dour tone but he couldn't, and when our eyes met he broke into a wicked grin. "So, I go from Dagger Jack to cloak-and-dagger and am still likely to make intimate acquaintance with a noose. Or worse."

"I should think Her Grace rather intended your part to be more of an executive position."

"It may well be, once I've had a chance to train a few people. Right now I'm not only the spymaster but the master spy, and you may be sure there's more than a little plotting afoot in several quarters. So, this is as far as the information I just gave you can travel. I'm only telling you because you know about the passages, which I'll likely be using more frequently in future. I'd rather not arrive some night in the wee hours and have you shoot me for a thief."

"I make no promises," I replied, though my own grin matched his. His only response was a snort, and then he was gone.

Jahmelle completed her new council—three men and three women. They began by instituting a number of changes or reversing earlier rulings that had been less targeted at justice than at filling the pockets of the Spiders and the royal treasury.

Despite the general support the Ugly Princess had from the populace, there were still some who felt otherwise. Three days before her coronation, an assassin somehow inserted in a group of temporary employees hired to help with the preparations managed to hide in an alcove outside the royal bedchamber. What remained after her Moldori bodyguards were finished questioning him fit easily into a small box. Unfortunately, he had never seen the one who hired him—the entire transaction took place in unlit alleys and his contacts had been swathed in cloaks and used disguised voices—and could provide no information.

One day a fortnight before the turn of the year, Chris approached the polished double doors of the queen's private aerie. The two Royals on duty snapped to attention and saluted. He returned it and tapped on the door, which swung open almost immediately. Chris bowed to Princess Yolanthe, who smiled and stepped aside to let him pass.

Benifaz's daughter had resumed her original title, since she had not been formally crowned queen consort. Yolanthe had pleasant quarters near the queen's, and the two young women had quickly become fast friends. To no one's surprise, a rather rude letter from her father had arrived a week after his precipitous departure demanding the lady's immediate return. Benifaz had wasted no time in finding a new buyer and clearly felt certain his veiled threats would be amply intimidating to the inexperienced young woman on the throne of Abernal.

Without even pausing for breath, Queen Jahmelle dictated a reply advising her esteemed neighbor and fellow monarch that her former stepmother had become a citizen of Abernal at the time and by virtue of her marriage. By law, though that particular law had been long ignored, she had the freedom to choose to remain in her new home and enjoy all the honors due a deceased king's consort. Lady Yolanthe, he was informed politely, had chosen to do so. Other than Benifaz, only Chris, Jahmelle and Ted knew the marriage was totally invalid.

"Good morning, Sir Christopher," the queen called.

She sat in a windowseat where the bright morning sunlight cascaded over her shimmering veils and made them sparkle. She was surrounded by a dozen young women of all shapes, sizes and coloring, maids of honor chosen not for their family background or their beauty but for their intelligence and common sense. Some were working on exquisite needlework. Two sat at a small table in the corner absorbed in a close-fought game of chess. Lady Kerri of Brunsmere was at the desk, her forehead creased with concentration as she wrote in a small bound journal, no doubt composing another of her excellent poems.

The two women on either side of the queen stood and moved away as Chris approached, and after he had made his bow Jahmelle patted the seat beside her. He sighed inwardly. Sitting beside her made him uncomfortable, and not all of the discomfort resulted from her ignoring the difference in their station in front of her women. Nonetheless, he sat, and was immediately much too aware of the soft drift of her veils and her subtle scent.

"We have had another letter from King Benifaz," Jahmelle said without preamble and handed it to him.

The thwarted tyrant had not been impressed by her response to his previous demands. He now threatened to remove his daughter by force of arms.

"I will not begin my reign with a war, Sir Christopher. I would appreciate hearing your thoughts on how we might deal with this situation and avoid unnecessary bloodshed. Other than compelling Yolanthe to return to Nadwich, of course."

"That option wouldn't even have crossed my mind, Your Grace. As for this," he gestured with the letter, "Benifaz is a bully. I think we can manage to call his bluff without anyone's getting hurt."

"Then I'll leave this in your capable hands. However, that wasn't the only reason I sent for you." She took the letter and handed it to Yolanthe, who carried it to the hearth and tossed it onto the fire. "I know that as Champion you are officially the head of the armies of Abernal after me. However, I feel that should be recognized formally. So, after conferring with my council, I now name you Earl Marshall of Abernal."

As ceremony required, Chris slid to one knee on the floor and laid his hands between hers.

"It is my honor to serve thee as thou dost command," he recited.

"As it is my honor to accept thy service," she responded in the soft, husky tone that always made him want to shiver. Had she been an ordinary woman, he would have suspected she used it on purpose, well aware of the effect it would have on any normal, red-blooded male. "And, in addition, I've prepared a small gift in commemoration of this event that I hope will please you. Lady Danah?"

As Chris stood up, the lady summoned, a short, stout, dark-haired woman with a knowing twinkle in her eye, stepped forward with arms extended. Across them lay a uniform, dark gold tunic with black piping, black trousers with a dark gold stripe and a white peaked cap trimmed with gold and black.

"Again, with the concurrence of the council, the rule that the Champion must wear armor has been rescinded," Jahmelle explained. "I've had this made to replace it. This, of course, is the parade uniform. The one for everyday wear is less conspicuous and there is another for formal occasions. They've been delivered to your quarters. I trust it will suit?"

"Yes, of course, Your Grace," he said as he took the handsome garments.

"I think Sir Christopher should try it on so we can see if it fits," Lady Danah said with a smirk he saw echoed in more than one pair of feminine eyes.

"I should see to taking care of Benifaz," he countered, feeling the blood color his face at the thought of stripping down to try on the uniform with this bunch snickering in the next room.

"Yes, of course, Sir Christopher," Jahmelle agreed, but the way she did it, using his own words, told him she understood his excuse for what it was.

With a hasty bow, he escaped the room as quickly as courtesy allowed, sent the uniform to his chambers with the first servant he came on and headed down to the practice yard.

Three days after issuing his warning, Benifaz sent an army westward to retrieve his daughter. At the border, however, they encountered Sir Christopher Evergild, dressed in the royal blue-and-buff working uniform of the Earl Marshall of Abernal, supervising a brigade of the Royal Army of Abernal engaged in military maneuvers. After a polite exchange of courtesies, the Nadwickian general led his men back the way they had come.

As soon as scouts confirmed the would-be enemy was returning home, Chris ordered the troops back to their garrison and returned to Registon. News of the outcome of the confrontation preceded him; and the city, looking for any reason to celebrate, welcomed him with enthusiasm. An invitation to dine with Jahmelle awaited him in his quarters, so he wore his black-and-gold formal uniform to the admiring looks of the rest of the dinner guests.

When the meal ended he made to leave along with the others but Jahmelle stopped him. Once they were alone, except for the lads clearing the table, she tucked her arm through his and strolled out into the garden. His breath made clouds in the chill late-autumn air, and the frost-stiffened grass crunched softly under their feet. Overhead, stars glittered in the cloudless sky and a waxing moon hung low on the horizon.

"We have won this battle," she said finally. "I suppose it is too much to hope for that it will be the only one."

"I wish I could tell you otherwise, Your Grace."

She stopped and turned to face him. They were in a shadowed part of the grounds where there was only starlight, and as he looked at her he thought he could see a dim outline under the curtain of her veils. In that moment he was not the Earl Marshall and she was not the Queen of Abernal. For a breath's time, he was aware of her in a way that made his heart pound and his blood burn, aware that a woman was beneath the silken barriers.

He clenched his hands into fists to prevent them from reaching out and stripping away the concealment.

"Thank you, Christopher, for your never-failing honesty," she said softly. "I wish you a good night."

He bowed and strode away, cursing himself for a fool. She was his queen and as far beyond his reach as those stars. Kings could wed the daughters of lesser nobles without approbation, but those few times a ruling queen had done the same had been disastrous enough subsequent Royal Councils and Consortiums had refused to permit it.

No, Jahmelle of Abernal would wed a prince or a grand duke or a king, not her Earl Marshall; and he was mad to think that, for that moment, she had been as aware of him as he was of her, that the tremor he saw brush over her was anything other than the cold touch of the night wind.

※※

As the months passed, I feared Chris would be the exception to the series of happy outcomes resulting from Queen Jahmelle's accession. I saw the pain he suffered as the inevitable royal suitors began to arrive. Abernal was a prize coveted by many, and the queen was wise enough to know a kind of peace would continue as long as all those who sought her hand could hope to succeed in attaining it.

Of necessity, of course, she must appear to enjoy the attentions they lavished on her, some of which barely remained within the bounds of courtesy.

The most persistent of the pack was the younger brother of the Emperor of Decir, Grand Duke Niklaes. On the surface, the man seemed a fine catch—handsome as an angel with liquid dark-blue eyes and a riotous tumble of blond hair, broad of shoulder and narrow of hip. He wooed the queen with all the ardent passion of a man truly in love, pressing fevered kisses to her hands, gazing soulfully at her veiled countenance as if he could see past the shimmering shield to the woman beneath.

That he made my flesh crawl and filled me with an overwhelming urge to infest his sheets with vermin were of no import.

The Deciron Empire encompasses most of the northern quarter of the continent on our side of the Great Forest, the vast ocean of ancient trees that splits Karlathia in two. It is sprawling, decadent and, if the tales carried by those merchants who traded there are true, hungry for new sources of the revenues necessary to support its increasingly useless and bloated upper class. In addition, with only one year-round port, Decir might—and did—look greedily on Abernal's two bustling harbor cities.

Benifaz, too, seemed to have overcome his objection to Her Grace and offered his son and heir, Nortend. Alas, poor Prince Nortend was the spitting image of his father, although rather more of a mouse than a rat, and abominably stupid. Nevertheless, the queen treated him with the same mixture of teasing and admiration she lavished on Niklaes and the others.

And there were others—princes and dukes and chiefs' sons, all pledging their undying devotion and pleading for a lifetime to shower it on the Ugly Princess. All the while the Queen's Champion, Lord Earl Marshall Christopher Evergild, was forced to stand in his assigned post, unmoving and stone-faced in her shadow, his fists white-knuckled with the effort he expended not to tear the slavering pack into fish bait. When the queen retired, so did Chris—straight to the training yard to destroy some poor practice dummy.

So, leaving the queen in the capable hands of her Royals, he took leave and went home to visit his parents then sent word he would make an inspection tour of the garrisons before returning to Registon. His behavior was perfectly normal, yet I could not escape a constant feeling of dread. My friend was a strong man with a powerful will, but his feelings for his monarch were an enemy he had no previous experience in combating. Inevitably, he must return to his primary duty. Just as inevitably, the queen must choose a consort. It was a situation that did not bode well.

The new year arrived, and with it another influx of eager princelings. Her Grace arranged balls and masques and theatricals to keep the mob entertained, and rumors she had finally selected this one or that one rose and fell like the sun.

One unseasonably warm February morning Grand Duke Niklaes suggested a ride outside the city to shake off the confinement of winter. He had presented Her Grace with a blooded Deciron stallion, an elegant creature with the grace of a unicorn and the golden coat and silvery mane and tail that characterized the breed. Accompanied by Lady Yolanthe, Sir Ted Truville and a hand of the Royals, Queen Jahmelle and the Deciron prince set off to enjoy the sun. They had not been gone an hour when who should dash into my office but Dagger Jack, and it was clear he was not there for tea.

"Where is the queen?" he demanded.

"Gone riding with the grand duke and Lady Yolanthe."

Jack spat out a curse so vile it nearly took the paint from the walls then spun on his heel and dashed away. Needless to say, his obvious concern aroused my own; and I was right behind him as he ran for the barracks where the Royals were housed. A shout brought Captain Hegver, Sir Ted's second-in-command.

"Get these men mounted," Jack ordered. "The queen is in danger."

The captain had opened his mouth to argue, but Jack's final words sent his jaw shut with a snap. At his nod the sergeant-major bellowed out the command and the guardsmen hastened to obey.

"Jack, what—"

"Benifaz and the Emperor have colluded to kidnap the queen and force her to marry Niklaes. I'd have been here sooner, but one of my informants was playing a double game and the Imperial Police nearly had me. I came as soon as I could—but obviously not soon enough. Damn it!"

"I'll send for Chris." By some foresight for which I was now eternally grateful, Chris had ordered a cote of carrier pigeons added to the Royals' barracks, so it was only a matter of minutes before birds were winging for the garrisons. Even so, the entire company of Royals thundered through the gates before the last message was sent.

Filled with trepidation, I returned to the palace. My first impulse was to inform Danella, who was supervising a crew cleaning one of the many attics, but I opted to wait. Despite Jack's apparent confidence in the accuracy of his information, it was yet possible this was nothing more than a false alarm and that the queen and her party would return unharmed.

That hope dimmed as the hours passed. A pigeon brought back a message from Chris stating he was already en route to the palace and would arrive the next day. By then it was clear I had to say something, for the abrupt departure of the queen's personal guard had not gone unnoticed.

I summoned several of the lads and had them spread the word that the entire staff was to assemble in the Great Hall in an hour then went to find Danella. She found me as I was about to begin my search.

"Bartrim, what is wrong?" she demanded, pulling off the kerchief with which she had covered her hair. "Where is the queen? She should have been back—"

"Yes, I know. Jack uncovered a plot, and the Royals went to fetch her. I fear—"

The sound of hooves outside interrupted. Hoping against hope for good news, we hurried to the front doors and stepped out into the gathering twilight.

Jack and Major Hegver dismounted, their faces grim. Behind them, six guardsmen held the reins of six horses bearing chilling burdens. Danella slid her arm around my waist, and I put mine about her shoulders and held her close as Jack climbed the steps as if his shoes were cast of lead.

"We were too late," he said. "The queen is gone, and we couldn't find a trace of where they've taken her.

Chapter 21

THE WINDED CAVALRY MOUNT HADN'T EVEN COME TO A complete stop before Chris leaped from the saddle and raced up the stairs into the palace. He had been riding for the last fourteen hours, cursing himself every minute.

Someone must have alerted Bart and Danella to his arrival. They reached the Great Hall only minutes after he did, followed by a familiar-looking dark, lean man with an aura of wolf about him. There were a dozen or so courtiers clustered about, and the eyes they all turned on him seemed to accuse. *You are supposed to defend her. Where were you?*

Hiding, that's where he'd been—hiding behind the legitimate excuse of the Champion's semiannual inspection tour. It was either that or twist the neck of the strutting Grand Duke Niklaes of Deciron until it snapped like a twig.

Standing beside her whenever there was a social occasion, watching him paw at her and drool on her, had been almost more than he could bear; and he had known if he didn't put some space between himself and the Deciron one of them would end up dead.

Or at least very, very battered.

It was no consolation that his well-honed instincts had warned him Niklaes was trouble from the moment the arrogant fop had arrived. When the trouble struck, he hadn't been here.

Without discussion the four of them went into the queen's private office. The stranger locked the door and leaned against it. His eyes didn't just accuse—they glittered with mayhem.

"Tell me."

To his surprise, both Bart and Danella turned to look at the stranger.

"It was a trick. There was an ambush near the standing stones. All six of the Royals were shot, and the two women have vanished."

"And you are...?"

"Her Grace's chief of intelligence," Bart interjected, "Dag —er, Jon Tarragent, Count of Montrivert."

"I'll need a fresh horse and—"

"Don't waste your time, Lord Earl Marshall," sneered Dagger Jack—Chris knew who he now was despite Bart's effort to cover it up. "There are no tracks, no signs of which way they went."

Chris had only met Jon Tarragent once. It had been just before Jack and his grandfather were arrested for treason, and he had admired the quick skill the older boy had with a rapier and dagger. He had admired Jack's skill with women even more.

Then came the arrest and the trial and the escape, though how Jack had managed it Chris still couldn't understand. For three years it seemed the young traitor had simply vanished—was, perhaps, even dead. Then the raids began, and the robberies. Again and again money and jewels intended for the royal treasury were taken, by a thief who always left his calling card: a thank-you note on fine vellum with the Montrivert crest stuck to the empty transport with a dagger. Jon Tevor Tarragent, born with blood bluer than just about any in Abernal, had become a common thief.

Now, for some reason, this thief seemed to think he was in charge.

"The ground is muddy," Chris said. "There have to be tracks."

"Are you saying I'm a liar or just incompetent?"

He snarled like a wolf, too, one that was just this side of tearing out someone's throat. Chris's dislike flared into instantaneous and profound outrage. It didn't help that until this moment he hadn't known there was such a thing as a "chief of intelligence." Bad enough he had failed to protect the queen. Learning she apparently didn't trust him enough to share this bit of information just made it worse.

"Whichever fits," he snapped, in no mood to coddle a highwayman, no matter what his title or his alleged governmental function.

"At least I was doing my job."

"That's enough!"

They stared at Danella Ruford, standing with face flushed and arms akimbo. In all the years Chris had known her, he had never heard her raise her voice. Now she looked ready to smack both of them. Bart merely leaned against the wall and looked smug.

"Our queen has been kidnapped by a devious scoundrel at the behest of two conniving tyrants. What is needed is some intelligent discussion of how to go about finding her, not engagement in a pissing contest."

Bart's smirk vanished, and his jaw dropped. Danella's opposition to crude language was legendary.

"Christopher," she continued in her normal serene tone, "how long has it been since you've eaten and rested?"

"Danella, I appreciate—"

"That's what I thought. Jack says there are no tracks. There are, therefore, no tracks. I see no reason why you can't bathe and eat while we consider the next step in the search." She paused, and tears welled into her eyes. "And we have six good men who deserve at least a moment's mourning."

Chris didn't need to ask—in *his* absence, Ted would have led the contingent guarding the queen. So, Niklaes had that to answer for as well, and so did his puppetmasters.

The weariness he had been trying to ignore settled over him all at once, and he knew Danella was right. With it came grief for Ted and an ache in his chest that made it hard for him to breathe. It was more than just his fear that his monarch was in danger. His woman was in the hands of murderers—his woman, even if he could never be more to her than he was now. As for his old friends' surprising loyalty to this newcomer, that was something to be studied later—after the queen was safe at home.

Nodding, he bowed to Danella and left the palace for his new quarters in the Royals' barracks. En route, he paused in the chapel, guarded by a pair of grim-faced guards, and knelt for a time in prayer beside the bier of his other old friend. I should have been here. It should have been me, not you, Ted. I'm sorry.

With the efficiency he had come to expect from Bart and Danella, there was a bath waiting; and he stripped off his dirty, sweat-stiffened uniform and sank gratefully into it. He had intended to think about the next step in the search, but the combination of hot, herb-scented water, fatigue and worry proved stronger than his determination and he slid into sleep.

And dreamed.

He stood in the center of a valley surrounded by ancient, rounded mountains. Grassland spread out in all directions, and the cloudless sky overhead was a deep azure lit not by the sun but as if from behind, like a celestial lampshade.

"Christopher."

He spun around, knowing that rich velvet voice as well as he did his own, expecting to see the familiar iridescent veils. What he did see was a young woman, tall and graceful, with skin the same exquisite shade of gold as summer wheat, waist-length hair of glimmering silver and dark-chocolate eyes.

"Jahmelle?"

"You must hurry, Christopher. They have sent for a priest, since the way to both Decir and Nadwich is closed, and have threatened to kill Yolanthe if I do not take the vows."

Chris knew the way of dreams. His shame and anxiety had clearly formed this one and combined with his longing to know what lay beneath her silken barrier to produce this vision. In a moment she would disappear, just as she had in reality.

But she didn't disappear. She stood, waiting, her moonlight eyes seeking...something.

"We don't know how to find you," he cried, allowing his despair to show in dreams where he would never do so awake.

"I know that, Christopher." Her face registered relief, as if she wouldn't have been able to speak again had he not done so first. "That's why I've come...to show you."

That's why I've come. That was an odd thing for a dream image to say.

"This is not a dream, Christopher. You must believe that. What you see here is real. I told you my veils were those worn by the Moldori Dream Dancers. I did not tell you they are forbidden to anyone else, even the granddaughter of the High Chief."

"Magic," Chris spat, and every ounce of his distaste for both the word and what it meant saturated his tone.

"You do not care for magic." Her voice was carefully neutral.

"To meddle with the laws of God and nature? It is an abomination."

"And will you for that reason reject my help and leave me to those who hold me captive?"

She had him—and he could tell by the gentle understanding in her eyes that she knew it and regretted using emotional extortion to win his cooperation. She held out her hand and he took it, reluctantly, and in that instant he saw a place, and a way to the place, and the precautions that had been taken to guard the place...

Chris awoke in lukewarm water, every image from his dream-vision clear and sharp. He knew where to find her, and he knew how he could rescue her. The way he had learned it made him sick to his stomach.

He climbed from the tub and wrapped in a towel, then yanked the bell cord to summon his valet. He still felt uncomfortable having a body servant, but Bart had insisted what would do for the royal champion would not for Earl Marshall of the Realm. Now he was glad he had someone to dispatch to the commander of the Royals and the Rufords. The man had already laid out one of his uniforms, but when he was ready to put it on Chris stood for a long moment staring at it.

He remembered vividly the day she told him he no longer had to wear the antiquated chain mail. He had wrestled a long time with the unacceptable feeling her gesture aroused that she had made it for reasons other than simply wanting to ease his discomfort. Had that been the moment when he began to lose sight of his place, of his duty? How many times had the Ugly Princess used her witch's power to spy on his dreams?

Turning his back on the garments so carefully laid out on the bed, Chris strode to a wardrobe in one corner of the room and flung open the doors. His combat shirt of chain mail hung there, carefully tended and polished to a soft gleam. The metal greaves, the studded gloves—all were meticulously preserved. He began to put them on.

Along with the images of where she was, Jahmelle had communicated the information the priest was expected to arrive within three days. If they left within the hour, they could have the kidnappers' lair surrounded by late the following morning.

As he strode through the garden toward the door to the kitchen, the image of Jahmelle flashed in his mind's eye. At least he no longer need wonder what the Ugly Princess was hiding. She was not a beauty, like Yolanthe, but the face in his dream had been appealing as much for its clear strength and character as for any classical element of feminine attractiveness. Something about it bothered him, however.

Dagger Jack Tarragent—he'd be damned if he'd address the man as "Count"—paced like a caged panther in Bart's office until he saw Chris.

"Where is she?" he demanded. "And how do you know?"

"She's being held in Overlack's hunting lodge. It's in a small clearing in the Kingswood."

By now Bart and Danella had joined them, and Bart was dressed in his uniform and armed. Chris almost forbade him to come, having already lost one friend; but he held his tongue. Until Ted was officially replaced, Bart was head of the Royals by virtue of his Seneschal's position. He chose to ignore the look the Rufords exchanged at sight of what he was wearing.

"Is she unharmed?" Bart asked.

"For now. The blockade I ordered has forced them to change plans. They've sent for a priest—and the law requires a royal marriage be performed by a bishop, so they had to send a fair distance. They plan to force her to marry as soon as he arrives. Then the emperor gets Yolanthe, and he and Benifaz are one big happy family."

He had hoped Dagger Jack would forget his second question; but, as he was soon to learn, Dagger Jack never forgot anything.

"And you know this how?" he repeated.

"She told me. In a dream."

Chris waited for the derision he expected that confession to elicit, but to his astonishment none of the others so much as raised an eyebrow.

"You knew."

"That she was a Dream Dancer?" Danella asked. "Yes."

"You didn't tell me. She didn't tell me."

"She was going to tell you," Bart admitted. "However, knowing your feelings regarding things magical and given the talent had little to do with daily events—"

"He knew," Chris snapped, tilting his head at Jack.

"I spent three years with the Moldori after Edrick murdered my grandfather."

Sudden rage burned through Chris, an anger more deep and engulfing than he had ever felt in his life. His friends, people he had trusted implicitly, had lied by omission. Worse, they had advised his queen, the woman whose protection was his foremost duty, to do so as well. He felt betrayed and manipulated. "I prefer honest answers," she had told him, but she had not been honest.

That memory triggered another, and he realized what it was about Jahmelle's dream image that had bothered him. The warm golden bronze of her skin that had captured his eye that night in Ted's tent was nothing like that of the woman in his dream, though he didn't doubt her identity. The Ugly Princess had doffed her veils only to don a disguise. Perhaps that ability to appear however she wanted was another manifestation of her magic. Another lie.

Abomination.

Chapter 22

I DID NOT NEED TO BE A MIND READER TO KNOW DANELLA'S thoughts when we entered the kitchen to find Chris wearing the antiquated chain mail he so much detested. The excitement that had claimed us when his valet brought the message Chris knew where the queen was vanished, even before he turned and we saw the hard grim lines on a face not suitable to them.

The mystery was solved in moments when he told us the source of his knowledge, and I understood. Christopher's antipathy toward all things magical was one of those few aspects of his character I had never been able to understand. Granted, he was by nature a formidably pragmatic man more comfortable with the concrete and physical than the ethereal and metaphysical. Yet he respected both religion and philosophy despite their lack of appeal to him.

Nor had he shown he had any concern for magic one way or another until the summer of our twelfth year, nearly erupting into violence when an innocent palm reader at a local Faire snatched his hand and offered to tell his fortune. When I requested an explanation, he evaded me, insisting he had just overreacted to being unexpectedly touched.

For that reason, I had counseled Her Grace that unless there was need it would be best if my friend were not aware of her...special talents. I had also cautioned Danella not to mention them, should occasion arise. I felt the look of betrayal Chris gave me like a knife in my chest—and I would have done no differently had I known we would come to this pass.

"If we leave within the hour, we'll reach the lodge by midday tomorrow," Chris said at last, his voice that of my commander rather than my friend. I saw Danella open her mouth to remonstrate with him and cut her off with a quick squeeze of the hand.

"The wagons are loading as we speak, and the Royals will be ready to ride within the hour," I assured him, allowing no whisper of my concern in my voice.

He said nothing more, only nodded, tossed his napkin on the table and left us. The door had no sooner closed at his back than both Danella and Jack started to demand an explanation. I had none.

"Should I be worried?" Jack wanted to know, and I squelched the reflexive outrage his question inspired. One would have to have been blind and demented not to see his antagonism for Chris was reciprocated, but this was hardly the time to explore it.

"Sir Christopher Evergild is the Royal Champion," I told him sternly. "His duty is to protect the monarch and he will do so because his breeding and training—not to mention his personal sense of honor—will not allow him to do otherwise."

Jack's grimace said he thought little of either breeding or training and placed even less faith in the concept of personal honor, but he let the subject go and followed Chris.

"Be careful, my love," Danella said, trying hard not to reveal her fear.

"Count on it," I said, and sealed the bargain with a kiss.

"And watch out for Chris," she added when she was at last able. "He worries me, the way he is."

I gave her another last brief kiss, preferring that to telling her I was just as concerned, and went to find my horse.

The troop of twenty-five Royals selected for the expedition rode through the gate of Abernal House thirty minutes later as the quartermaster signaled his drivers to pull out. The barrier Chris had erected between us had grown denser rather than otherwise, and I saw Jack watching him with a distrustful gleam in his eyes.

The Kingswood, which lies half a day's ride to the east of the city, is a vast range of virgin forest, a spur of the Great Forest that has been carefully managed as a retreat and hunting preserve for as long as there has been an Abernal. It flows over the low ridges where the mountains slope off toward the sea.

Over the centuries, various rulers have given favored courtiers permission to use certain of the half-score of royal hunting lodges within it as their own. Edrick had done so with all three of his ministerial cronies, but only Overlack had accepted. It was rumored dark deeds were committed under its mossy slate roof, but no one had ever procured evidence of such. The privacy of the lodges was sacrosanct. They were also, for obvious reasons, set up so that guarding the safety of the inhabitants was easily done and not so easily circumvented.

Although I'm certain every man would have gladly ridden through the night, common sense insisted well-fed, rested warriors would be more efficacious. For that reason, I ordered the troop to a primitive camping site a half-mile off the road two leagues into the forest. The region was used for military training as well as for royal amusement, so there was a path into the area sufficient for the supply wagons to use. I didn't notice the absence of both Chris and Dagger Jack until the tents were up and the cookfires blazing.

Chris returned just after dark, entering the command tent and tossing his sword onto the cot where I'd placed his gear. For want of anything more useful to do, I was reading; but I set the book aside and left to fetch him something to eat from the mess tent as he poured a mug of ale from the pitcher on the table. I returned to my reading while he ate, although I saw not a word on the page as the silence dragged on.

Finally, when it became apparent he was not going to pursue the issue, I did.

"Do you plan to sulk about this the rest of your life?"

He looked up from the empty plate he had been staring at for the last quarter-hour and glared at me.

"You lied to me, all of you."

"We chose not to share irrelevant information we knew would upset you deeply."

"Spare me your convoluted justifications, Bart. An omission is a lie no matter how you try to dress it up. And true friends don't lie to each other."

"Good gods, Chris," I sputtered, tossing the book aside, "of course, they do! I can't imagine how any close relationship could survive in an atmosphere of total, unremitting honesty."

"I have never—"

"Kerin Allemont."

He had the decency to blush, as well he should. In our fifteenth year, I was smitten with typical adolescent obsession with the nubile blond daughter of a local mercer. For months I filled Chris's ears with paeans to the glistening platinum locks and the melting violet eyes of the incomparable Kerin. I will not embarrass you with what filled my nights. To my naive adoration, she was the pure embodiment of womanhood.

What I didn't know—and what Chris chose not to tell me until long after dreams of the lovely Kerin had become distant memories—was that he was enjoying all the benefits of those luscious charms on a regular basis. Rather, when I waxed eloquent about my plans to seek her favor and pondered if the look she had given me as I passed her father's shop should be interpreted as a hopeful sign, he listened to my dreams of conquest and commiserated with my frustration.

After I had learned the truth, of course, I realized his support had never gone as far as to actively encourage me to pursue the wench.

"We aren't talking about some backstreet roundskirt," Chris snapped. "We're talking about the Queen of Abernal, whose life I'm pledged to defend."

"And how does your not knowing Her Grace has the capability of visiting those who request it in their dreams interfere with that?"

"I—" He stopped, whatever self-justifying quibble he'd been going to offer freezing on his lips, and sat frowning for a long moment. "Request?"

Aha! I thought. *So,* that's *the problem.* It hadn't occurred to me until that moment there was any more than his hatred of things magical involved in his reaction, which was really rather stupid of me. What man in love doesn't dream of the object of his affection—and not always in ways suitable for said object to share?

"Except in emergencies, such as our current situation, when they may use their abilities to advise of danger, Moldori Dream Dancers are prohibited from entering the dreams of others unless their presence is specifically requested."

He tried to hide it, but Chris's relief peeked out nonetheless. For a moment.

"How do you know?" he demanded.

"Jack told you he lived with the tribes. He likely knows more about them than anyone except the queen."

I realized only after I said it that it might be a bad idea to cite Jack as the source of my knowledge. Still, Chris appeared to accept at least the hope the information was correct, and it seemed a good time to change the subject. Well, slightly.

"Where is Jack, by the way?"

"Most likely dead," Chris replied coldly. "The crazy fool thought he could get into the lodge and let the queen know help is on the way."

"And you approved?

"He didn't ask my permission. We were just supposed to slip close to the place together for a look."

"His idea or yours?"

"His."

"And he invited..."

"He told me what he planned and I told him he went nowhere without me." Both his tone and his expression said Milord Earl Marshall had yet to gain any real faith in either the skills or the integrity of Dagger Jack Tarragent. "We hadn't gone more than halfway to the sentry line when he said he had to...well, I waited twice as long as he should have taken before I knew the only thing he'd needed to eliminate was my company."

He glared at me, as if I were somehow to blame for Jack's preference for solitary ventures. Fortunately, I was saved from having to respond by the call of the bugle signaling lights out.

It was Chris's custom on any bivouac to travel the camp at this time in case any of the troops wished to speak to him. Tossing back the last of his ale, he stood and strode out of the tent with plate and cup, and I decided I would most definitely be asleep by the time he returned.

After cleaning his eating utensils and leaving them in the mess tent, Christopher strolled along the narrow lanes between the tent blocks. Knowing his presence was informal, those troopers not already in bed nodded or gave a casual salute if they caught his eye.

He wanted to believe Bart was telling the truth about the queen's ability to invade his dreams. His gut told him it was the truth, and it had always been an unfailingly dependable advisor. The relief he got from knowing his offensive and possibly treasonous dreams were still his own, however, didn't extend to the sick horror he felt at just the thought of magic.

That had begun back nearly twenty years, to a dark night when a curious boy slipped out of the warm safety of his bed and followed a kitchen girl to a grove of ancient oaks.

He was nine years old, full of the conviction he knew right from wrong and just beginning to chafe under the strict rules that bound his days. He yearned for adventure and he missed Bart, who had gone home to Greenwater for his mother's birthday. He heard the girl—Hilka—telling another of the serving women she was going to a secret meeting that night of the full moon, where she would acquire the power to escape her servitude for a life of wealth and pleasure.

So, eager to observe this mysterious gathering, he had forced himself to stay awake; and when the tall clock in the great hall rang eleven he used the downspout outside the window as a ladder and waited by the door of the servants' barracks. Not long after, Hilka emerged, wrapped in a full-length cloak. Silently, she and her unsuspected shadow trotted through the postern gate and across the fields to an ancient grove where shattered remnants of walls surrounded a stone altar.

Fearful of getting too close and risking discovery, Chris found a tree by a small outcrop of jumbled rocks nearby and climbed up. Torches thrust into the ground at the four corners of the ruins made eerie shadows dance among the dozen black-cloaked shapes encircling the altar. They waited without sound or motion for what seemed hours, and he was on the verge of dozing off when the torches suddenly flared with a roar. The cloaks fell, and the naked men and women –six of each—sank to their knees chanting in a guttural language that made his hair rise on the back of his neck.

A red-robed figure wearing a hideous bronze mask strode into their circle, and their voices fell to murmurs. He raised his arms to shoulder level and began to chant a counterpoint, his voice amplified by his mask to quiet thunder. His companions stood and began to dance, slowly at first, in time with his chant. He spoke faster and faster, louder and louder; and their eldritch ballet kept pace until he gave one great shout and silence fell. The dancers fell on their faces, arms outstretched, fingertips touching.

The man in the mask turned to the gap in the shattered walls through which he had entered, and Hilka stepped into the torchlight. She, too, was naked, her long, rust-colored hair falling to her knees. She stepped over the ring of worshipers, knelt before him and kissed his feet.

Four of the six men stepped forward and lifted her, then laid her on the altar and bound her wrist-and-ankle to the corners. They rejoined the circle and began their eerie recitation, repeating the same unidentifiable phrase over and over.

The masked man glided to the altar and trailed his left hand along Hilka's body, ending his travels by thrusting below the dark triangle where her thighs joined. She moaned and lifted her hips, tossing her head back and forth. The circle danced and chanted as their master dropped his robe and stepped onto the stone, then knelt between her widespread thighs and jammed his rampant phallus into her secret place.

For a brief moment, Hilka seemed lost in a world of pleasure, writhing and moaning and pleading for more. Then something happened...something changed. As the copulation rhythm increased, the shape of the man in the mask blurred and shifted and grew. The mask, too, transformed, the hideous casting becoming instead an even more hideous face.

Hilka began to scream, first in terror and then in appalling agony was the organ invading her swelled to the size of a man's forearm. The dancers shrieked with mad joy and collapsed into an orgiastic mass as the screaming died on one last, tearing note and the beast roared with triumph. It leaped off the sundered corpse and stood, its gore-smeared phallus thrusting obscenely toward the sky.

Terrified to near hysteria, Chris buried his face in his lap, certain he would be discovered and torn to pieces by the demon below. He stayed there, shivering uncontrollably on a night warm as fresh milk until the gray light of early dawn and the first challenges of awakening birds gave him courage to look again.

The tumbled walls were empty, the torches gone. Only drying red-brown stains on the rough-carved stone block remained to remind him of what he had seen. Scrambling from his perch, he raced as fast as exhausted legs could carry him to the manor, uncaring whether his forbidden excursion was revealed.

As, of course, it was.

Standing before his father's wide rosewood desk, ordered to tell where he had been all night, he babbled the entire story in a barely coherent rush. His father listened, his already stern face somehow becoming more so. When Chris was done, Davvyd rang for a footman and sent for Hilka. It took only moments for the man to return, Hilka walking humbly behind him.

He'd known it wasn't really the maid, known what curtseyed modestly wasn't even human, though he couldn't have offered one reason for his knowledge. Yet there, it seemed, she was, making him either a liar or fabulist, neither of which carried any weight with the Royal Champion. He apologized as ordered and took his whipping in silence and never spoke of it again, even when the nightmares woke him screaming. Nor would he explain why from that day forward his flesh crawled at even the thought of occult ceremonies and mystical powers.

Yanking back from that memory, which rose in his mind's eye two decades later as clearly as it had his physical ones then, Chris shuddered and had to force his meal to stay where it belonged. His queen, the woman he was sworn to give his life to defend, was one of them.

Abomination.

When he was old enough, he had quietly sought out as many of those whose faces and bodies were stamped indelibly on his memory as he could. Hilka was first, and the image of her inhuman body dissolving after he removed its head also remained clear and ineradicable. There were four more like her; the demon-priest he never found. The others he allowed to live, but using the excuse it fostered vermin he razed their unholy temple and had the altar stone smashed to sand.

"Getting lost in thought can get you dead."

Chapter 23

TRAINING SO INGRAINED IT WAS ALL BUT INSTINCT SPUN him around; and had the owner of the soft voice, indeed, been standing directly behind him the infamous career of Dagger Jack Tarragent would have ended abruptly on the blade he was named for.

Jack, however, was off to his right in the deep shadow under a tall maple, leaning with deceptive nonchalance against the broad trunk. Shoving the knife back in its sheath, Chris stuck his thumbs in his belt. It was the quickest way to refrain from wrapping his hands around the other man's throat.

"A little trick I learned from a traveling player once. I'd be happy to teach it to you."

"The last thing I need is help from you."

"Just what is it you have against me, Evergild?"

"You mean besides your having managed a full pardon from the crown you've been robbing for ten years, refusing to follow orders and basically acting as if rules apply to everyone but you?"

"Really? Or is it more that I knew something about the queen you didn't? Do you wonder what other secrets she shared with me and not you?"

It took all of Chris's self-control not to respond to the taunt. That, and a small, sane voice that murmured there was more than a dribble of truth in what he said.

"Since you're all in one piece, I take it your little excursion wasn't a success," he said instead.

"You take it wrong, Milord Earl Marshall. While the task was a touch more complicated than expected, I spoke with the queen and Lady Yolanthe both. They're unharmed—so far."

That "so far" sent a chill through Chris's blood.

"I should have gone with you."

Jack snorted as he straightened and sauntered into the dim moonlight.

"I'm a thief, remember? Of course, you do. I used to make my living getting into places people wanted to keep me out of and living to do it again." He stopped outside the range of Chris's blade. "You'd have gotten us both killed, clomping around in all those reconstructed pots and pans."

"Don't push me too far, Tarragent," Chris growled through clenched jaws.

"I'd be careful with my threats if I were you," Jack retorted. "You're the one whose job became obsolete the minute Benifaz tried to usurp the throne. The queen is going to have a lot more use for a spymaster from now on than she will for a diplomatic anachronism."

For a long moment it seemed as if the two of them might yet come to blows, and then Jack grimaced.

"Look, Evergild, I know you think I'm lower than a snake's cock and totally undeserving of the good wishes of any decent human being, but the reality is that however much it offends your concept of justice the queen has given me a full pardon for past offenses, and we are going to have to work together whether we like it or not."

There was no question the man was right. Chris had learned enough about Jahmelle in these last months to know she didn't make decisions impulsively. Whatever she saw in this man that he didn't, it was certain to be a stronger argument for keeping him around than Chris could muster for getting rid of him.

"I can see where you might have acquired some useful skills," he admitted with stern reluctance. "So, did you actually learn anything of value on your excursion, or did you just pick up some loose coin?"

Jack snorted.

"Only one with any coin in that lot is Niklaes, and I wouldn't touch anything of his without gloves. But I do have an idea how we might manage to get out of this with a minimum of blood loss, if you're interested."

"I would be interested, yes," Chris said. "Why don't we adjourn to the mess tent, and you can tell me about it?"

I cannot say concern for the queen was the only cause of the tense silence that prevailed the following morning as we prepared to continue our rescue journey. After a short meeting with his commanders and squad leaders, Christopher ordered the troops underway then rode well to the fore.

Jack, too, seemed to have been stung by whatever bug infected Chris. Although he and I rode side-by-side, only his horse was actually present; and after a half-dozen attempts to initiate conversation I decided his horse was likely to be the better companion.

I suspected there was more to the escalated bad feeling between the two than Jack's having eluded Chris's company the previous day, but without any information I couldn't fathom what lay at the bottom of the situation. That the two men most responsible for Her Grace's safety should be so totally antagonistic to one another did not bode well for a smooth rescue operation.

Nor was this kind of childish behavior typical of Chris. Although inclined to be a bit narrow-minded where issues of right and wrong were concerned, he had always before managed to accept those with differing viewpoints with at least a vestige of courtesy. Then a thought struck me. Was it possible he saw Jack as a rival, not an unrepentant felon but another man encroaching on the queen's affections?

In all the excitement, neither Danella or I had thought to tell Chris about Jack's relationship to the queen, and he was certainly in no state of mind to notice the strong resemblance between Jack and the young Edrick.

I resolved to correct this unfortunate omission as soon as possible, if only so I might have someone to talk to.

Our horses' hooves and our tack were muffled so as not to alert the grand duke's sentries, whom Jack had reported were stationed where they could observe while they avoided detection. They were posted in pairs no more than four paces from each other in a tight circle around the lodge. Eliminating them was going to be a challenge.

We reached the camp just after midmorning and picketed the horses. Silently, the troop of Royals, which now seemed rather too small a force for the task at hand, disbursed into the surrounding forest. Jack sat with his back against a tree and his eyes closed, though I doubted he slept. On the opposite side of the slightly overgrown clearing Chris practiced his sword forms, sweat quickly forming on his face despite the relative chill. He had let me wear his mail once—not this set but another made for him when we were in our mid-teens—and I quickly abandoned any envy I had entertained of his future. Frankly, it made me itch just watching him.

Major Hegver stood with stalwart patience at parade rest near the picket line, staring into the trees as he waited for the runner who would bring the news the enemy sentries had been subdued. Thus, having nothing better to do, I began composing a stern letter to a local greengrocer whose produce had shown a serious decline in quality in recent weeks. The crown annually contracts with local businesses for its needs, with payment made quarterly; I suspected this particular individual, having acquired his contract, had immediately abandoned his original suppliers for lower-priced ones.

I had mentally rewritten the missive several times when the messenger brought word the perimeter was secure.

"Bart, you're with me," Chris ordered, striding for his horse. "Hegver, you and the corporal wait on the road to head off the bishop."

"But what about—" *Jack*, I meant to say but discovered he had already vanished. I had no idea what part he was to play; perhaps Chris had not deigned to give him one. In any case, I had no time to comment because Chris was already mounted and riding toward the path. I followed suit as quickly as I could and caught up.

Some fifty yards from where we had waited an access road angled off to the left toward the lodge. The brush on either side had been recently cleared, providing a clear line of sight from the front door of the building for the last segment of the approach. I had assumed we would dismount and make our way surreptitiously to a point where we could reconnoiter and determine the best method to proceed. However, to my shock and dismay, we made no effort to conceal our arrival. Instead, we simply rode up to the lodge as if we were just dropping by for tea.

The clearing was much larger than I expected, at least an acre and possibly more. The house, a single story with a gambrel roof wrapped on three sides by a broad open porch, must have contained fifteen or twenty rooms within its walls of dressed fieldstone. A small barn and a paddock with a half-dozen horses, including the golden stallion that had been Niklaes's bait, were located behind and to the left of the house.

The grand duke emerged from the building as we approached and awaited us on the veranda, leaning quite casually, with arms folded, against a porch post at the top of the short flight of stairs. Clearly unaware his circle of protection was gone, he smirked with all the confidence of a man in total control of his destiny—and of those around him.

"Come to rescue the fair maidens?" he asked when we drew rein several paces from him.

Without answering the taunt, Chris dismounted, after tossing me a look that ordered me not to do likewise. Striding to the foot of the stairs, he drew his sword, the one crafted for the Champions' official battles. He was an impressive sight—blade and armor glittering in the late winter sun, his face no softer than the granite paving stone on which he stood.

"Give me the queen and Lady Yolanthe, and you can go back to your brother in one piece."

Nicklaes snorted.

"Oh, please, Evergild, one would think someone in your position would have better things to do than posture like some character in a fairy tale. There are six men inside with orders to kill the women if I so much as twitch. I suggest you be a good boy and go play knight in shining armor somewhere else."

"If you had wanted Her Grace dead, she would be."

"It's my darling brother who wants her—or, rather, her seaports. I personally have no interest whatever in either of them. By the way, would you like to know what she really looks like, your Ugly Princess?"

I imagined I could hear Chris's teeth grinding.

"Your lack of interest won't keep you alive if anything happens to her."

"No," Niklaes agreed, "but they will."

He pointed upward. Two musket barrels protruded over the peak of the roof. The grand duke whistled as if calling a dog, and the snipers moved to become more visible as they aimed at me.

"You didn't really think I'd engage you in a sword battle, did you, Evergild? I would suggest that if you have any feelings for your friend the Seneschal you'll put that thing back where it belongs."

"Ambushes seem to be your specialty," Chris sneered, making no move to do as he'd been ordered. I can't say I welcomed his intransigence, under the circumstances.

"So much less hazardous to the health, and they do get the job done. Now, will you put your toy away and move along or shall my men add some unattractive holes to Baron Greenwater?"

Chris still hesitated, and I could see his fist clench on the hilt of his weapon. Then he put it back in the scabbard and waited.

"Now, I presume you have men all around who are quite capable of eliminating my people aloft," Niklaes continued, as if discussing the weather, "but one of them will surely take you and your chum with him before he goes. At the same time, those inside will dispatch your queen. Will your handsome Royals risk that?"

At this point I struggled not to draw my pistol and punctuate Niklaes's arrogance with a lead period. Almost as the thought crossed my mind his smug leer froze, and he stiffened. Carefully, slowly, he dropped his hands and stood erect, holding them away from his sides in plain view.

"Ladies, if you please," I heard Jack say from behind him, and a moment later the queen and Princess Yolanthe stepped one after the other around the now-glaring Deciron. Their clothes were soiled and rumpled, and Yolanthe's hair showed the lack of a comb, but they appeared otherwise unharmed.

I dismounted and made my bow as they approached then offered an arm to each and escorted them swiftly toward the shelter of the trees, following a zigzag course. I earnestly prayed Niklaes had neglected to instruct his snipers to shoot the queen should his plan go awry. It was a prayer in vain.

Bullets whined past us, and I thanked all and sundry deities that the snipers were apparently less skilled at hitting a moving target than a stationary one. A few hasty steps and we were out of sight, if not range; and the three of us dove for shelter behind a giant fallen oak.

I heard the pop of distant guns, and chancing a look over our shelter I saw the two rifle barrels on the roof disappeared.

Niklaes lay facedown on the veranda, either dead or unconscious. My preference was for the former.

However, next instant Jack shouted to someone inside and was thrown a length of rope, with which he bound the grand duke like a chicken trussed for market. Chris had vanished, but as Niklaes began to stir he rounded the corner of the house farthest from the stables sheathing his blade.

I was unaware the queen had moved until I saw her crossing to meet him. He stopped, waiting until she was near enough to touch him, her veils shimmering and drifting. For one dreadful, eternal moment I feared his peculiar obsession with magic would overrule his honor; and that he might turn his back to her.

His eyes never left her concealed face as she confronted him, tall and steady. Did he wonder, as I confess I did, whether Niklaes had, in fact, seen her face?

Slowly, he pushed back his mail coif and sank to one knee at her feet. Taking her hand, he pressed his lips to it. He said something—I was too far away to hear—and she shook her head slightly. Then he bowed his head.

The queen raised her free hand and made as if to lay it on his shoulder, then hesitated. For another long moment neither of them moved, and it seemed as if the entire world held its breath. She gently combed back a lock of hair that had fallen forward and tucked it behind his ear. I saw him tremble just before he rose again to his feet, laid her hand atop his and led her back toward the lodge.

Chapter 24

CHRIS ESCORTED JAHMELLE BACK TO WHERE DAGGER JACK waited. A handful of scruffy thugs gathered on the porch watched them approach with snakes' eyes, and it took all his self-control not to toss her over his shoulder and run for the sheltering forest. Niklaes's erstwhile minions were all armed, and he trusted them about as far as the end of his nose; but Jahmelle had said she needed to speak to them.

"Gentlemen, the crown of Abernal is in your debt," she said, sounding as if she were comfortably on her throne in the Great Hall.

Chris could hear Niklaes quietly cursing in a hard, steady voice. Already the Royals were marching the grand duke's captured sentries into the open, and that many soldiers clearly made Jack's companions nervous.

"We'll get our horses and meet ya," the short, heavyset one muttered, and all five—hadn't Niklaes said there were six?—slithered toward the stable.

"Thank you as well, Jon," the queen continued. "Please carry on—I wish to speak with Lady Yolanthe."

She started toward Bart, who had reappeared with the Nadwickian princess on his arm, as the Royals herded the captives into the stables.

"An excellent plan, Count Montrivert," Chris commented in the same sedate tone the queen had used.

"I'm glad you appreciated it, M'lord Earl Marshall," Jack said, and then flashed a wicked grin. "You see now there are advantages to having friends in low places."

"Traitors!" Niklaes snarled. "I'll see every damned one of them dismembered inch by—"

Jack interrupted what would likely have been a tirade with the toe of his boot in the grand duke's ribs.

"When you hire killers," he said as Niklaes wheezed for breath, "you should make sure they're selling their loyalty as well as their blades."

He looked up at Chris and grinned again. Chris grinned back. He was beginning to understand just what made this rogue so attractive to Bart and Danella—yes, and to Jahmelle. He resisted the reaction that thought aroused.

He'd had doubts when Jack outlined this plan the night before, but the compelling argument that it was likely the safest way to rescue the women far outweighed them. Jack had recognized Niklaes's "guards" as mercenaries, as were the men he'd hired as sentries. Their loyalty, he insisted was only as enduring as the amount in their purses. Offer them double what Niklaes was paying, and he had no doubt at all they would turn on the grand duke in a breath.

"It went pretty much as I expected," Jack said. "Ebner and his men were getting a little tired of his royal highness's attitude, anyway, so when I named our price they did in the one real guard and that was it. Oh..." He turned back and leaned over the glaring, gasping prince. "...it also helps if you pay a decent fee. You might want to pass that along to your tightfisted brother. He's obviously spending way too much time with Benifaz."

As if the small clearing around the hunting lodge weren't crowded enough, at that moment the bishop's coach rolled off the road and stopped beside the queen. Major Hegver sat beside the Royal corporal, who was driving in place of the trussed-up Deciron Hegver rolled to the ground from the baggage carrier. Bart addressed the vehicle's occupant, then opened the door and lent his shoulder to the elderly man who emerged.

"Ah, Sir Christopher," the Archbishop of Castelmoor said as Chris and Jack joined them, "congratulations on a most daring rescue. Major Hegver has apprised me of the situation." The old man's eyes fell on Jack and widened as his eyebrows rose to where his hairline had once been.

"It was a joint effort, Your Reverence." He registered that look of astonishment. Jahmelle had deliberately not announced Jack's pardon at his request, something else Chris had learned during last night's strategy session. Being a wanted outlaw got him into the places he needed to be, he said. No doubt the bishop was wondering what Dagger Jack Tarragent was doing here without being in chains.

"It was a most satisfactory blending of talents," Bart said smoothly, his eyebrow quirked in the way that always annoyed Chris. It was a warning, that eyebrow, that explanations would be demanded. "Sir Christopher's distraction enabled C—uh, Dagger Jack to subvert the grand duke's men and all was achieved with only a few casualties."

"It is always best when bloodshed is kept to a minimum," Queen Jahmelle added, and Chris could feel her eyes locked on him.

He was beginning to feel uncomfortable. His role in this had been minor, the plan Jack's. He could hardly take credit for a rescue that wouldn't even have been necessary had he been by her side where he belonged.

Maybe Jack was right. He was an anachronism, a man whose main purpose no longer applied. The time when matters of state conflict could be decided by a sword fight were done, and he had no more interest in the kind of covert machinations that marked the new era than he did in making pottery. If he hadn't been there, Bart or even Hegver could probably have done just as well as he had. The worst, though, was that he had failed in the one part of his job that still had relevance, and all because of unseemly jealousy.

"It's done," he managed to say, though his throat ached and his voice rasped. "The Royals will see you back to your palace, Milord Archbishop, when they escort the grand duke back to Decir." He turned to the queen, focusing his eyes where the breeze pressed her veil against the line of her chin. "If Your Grace agrees, I think it's time we went home."

Rumors that something had happened to the queen had spread throughout the city, and although he would have preferred otherwise Chris knew the only way to end them was to return in full view of the citizenry. Jack, to preserve his anonymity, stayed behind to ride in with the mercenaries.

The rest—the queen, Yolanthe, Bart, himself and a half-dozen Royals—reached the city by late evening. As they rode slowly down the main concourse, where shopkeepers were closing their doors and the night population had just begun to emerge, all activity stopped. Moments later, cheering began. Jahmelle acknowledged it by waving, although he suspected she was more exhausted than she allowed any of them to see.

He left her in Bart's talented hands and went to his quarters. His able valet had anticipated him—a hot bath was once again waiting, and a full set of clean clothes. He took off the chain mail, the symbol of his purpose however burdensome he had always considered it, and tossed it into a distant corner. The clink and clang as the other pieces landed atop it stabbed his heart more painfully than a blade.

But he had no time to brood. He had no doubt the armies of Decir and Nadwich would be alerted not long after Nicklaes returned home; and that job, at least, he could still do. That the preparations for war would give him an excuse to beg off the inevitable invitations the queen would send for him to join her for dinner was just an added benefit.

He suspected he knew where the conversation at such a dinner would go, and he was not prepared to travel in that direction. Not now. Perhaps not ever. The reason for his aversion to magic was his own business. He hoped the dire necessity for war planning would prevent her from insisting.

He was wrong.

After a week in which he buried himself in troop counts and weapons inventories and map studies, Sir Christopher Evergild was summoned to an audience with his queen in her salon. Wearing his formal uniform of white and gold, he approached the heavy wooden doors that stood ajar under the watchful icy eyes of two Pillars of Moldor. The High Chief had once again dispatched six of the giants as bodyguards, another reminder to Chris of how dismally he had failed.

The Moldori, however, saluted the Earl Marshall respectfully, one warrior to another, as a ripple of laughter wafted from the room beyond. That merry laugh, like clear crystal water chiming over sun-washed stones, did to his knees what the queen's velvet voice did to his spine; and he had to make himself remember she was not what he had thought her to be.

Queen Jahmelle sat on the windowseat, her ladies around her like a garden of exotic flowers against the murk of her veiling. Since her abduction, she wore black, as if mourning the short moment of peace she had enjoyed.

He crossed the room to where she perched like a morbid crow in a flock of brilliantly feathered finches. Somehow, being with her gave even the plainer ones a special glow. Or was that just another example of magic at work?

She laughed again at some quip by one of the young women; and despite his ambivalence, Chris stopped to enjoy the sound. As he did, Yolanthe noticed him and brought him to the queen's attention. Then the princess quickly shooed the bevy of blossoms from the room, closing the door firmly behind.

As befitted the informal location of the audience, he bowed and kissed the hand Jahmelle extended.

"Please, my lord Earl Marshall," she said, moving aside slightly to make room. "Sit here with me."

As he obeyed he noticed she wore a different scent than usual, a light one in which roses and lavender predominated. He waited for her to speak so he might enjoy the dark softness of her voice, but she remained silent for almost longer than was comfortable.

"It seems we must, after all, go to war," she said finally, just before his urge to fidget became unbearable.

"And I think we can safely assume both Benifaz and the emperor have received full reports of our troop strength and resources from the former Ministers of Council," he said, careful to keep "I told you so" out of his tone.

"So, we will fight; and my people will die because I am a woman."

The pain in her voice made him want to put his arms around her, to hold her and tell her it was more complicated than that, tell her it was only men's greed that had created this mess. Except, she was right. Had she been a man, likely none of it would be happening. Benifaz would have simply married his daughter to the new king, issues of consanguinity conveniently overlooked; and all would have lived happily ever after.

"So, Sir Christopher, what would you advise?"

"You could marry."

She turned her veiled face toward him, and he could feel her invisible gaze burn his.

"You confuse me, Christopher. How will my marriage prevent us from going to war?"

"It won't," he admitted. "But from what I've heard from Jack, the whole point of all this has been to give the emperor access to our ports. If the L—uh, Prince Demtri had been allowed to retain the throne, he would simply have signed a treaty in perpetuity allowing Decir to use them without tariff. When that didn't work, the next plan was to force you to marry Niklaes, who would have arranged to have Abernal annexed to the empire. I'm sure Benifaz made sure he would receive ample reward for conceding his own claim to the throne."

"Then, what—"

"Bear with me, Your Grace. We know the size of the armies of both Nadwich and Decir, and in a fight we have a better than good chance of defeating them. As long as you're unwed, though, the problem remains. Who's to say that even with the Pillars the emperor or Benifaz won't find a way to kidnap you again—and take you to where we can't reach you in time? Nor do I think they would be willing to fight a battle on two fronts, since if you are wed any attack on Abernal would be an attack on the Prince Consort's land as well."

"And who among those not massing an army on our borders do you think could be bribed to wed the ugliest queen in this or any other generation?" she asked.

He opened his mouth to protest there were any number of men who would do so, then closed it. Now that he thought about it, the only two of that rash of suitors who had actually proffered marriage had been the Nadwich heir and Niklaes.

He had even overheard conversations where the idea of marriage to the Ugly Princess led to shudders and threats of suicide should it ever be required. Had he held any respect for the people holding the conversations he might have been tempted at the time to wring a few necks.

It was so awfully unfair. She was intelligent, literate, kind and devoted to justice, yet she was condemned to live behind a silken curtain lest the sight of her offend or disgust those very people who benefited from her kindness.

Then he remembered the magic.

"Never mind, Sir Christopher," she said when he had no answer for her. "I wanted to speak to you about...the dream."

Ice clogged his belly, and he wondered if she was able to read his mind as well as invade his dreams.

"I would rather not—"

"I know. I think, though, that we must. I am ashamed I allowed myself to be persuaded not to speak of it to you. It was the same as lying, and I cannot abide liars. Can you forgive me?"

Forgive her? He couldn't even look at her. He had rehearsed again and again a scene in which he confronted her with her deception, had envisioned her over and over making excuses, wielding her royal prerogative as her main defense. Not once had he pictured her simply admitting she was wrong and asking his pardon. Magic users were evil; they never pled for forgiveness.

"I don't...It's just..." He was babbling, his mind racing in all directions trying to collect all the thoughts that now ran scattered. And, abruptly, he was telling her the secret he had never told another living soul in twenty years. He shivered like a child—like the child he had been—as he recounted that night of terror, and when he was done he wanted nothing more than to curl up and disappear.

Jahmelle was silent for another long moment, and he wasn't sure if he expected her to deny the truth of his story, as his father had, or destroy him for knowing too much.

"And you believe there are others—other demons masquerading as human?"

"Yes."

She stood and strode to the far side of the room then spun back.

"I would never have thought Abernal could be home to such an...an abomination."

The word seemed to echo. It rattled in his skull and dislodged the roots of his old terror. Yes, the creatures were an abomination. The magic the demon-worshippers created to bring them was an abomination. But was magic itself evil? Or was it the way in which it was used that made it so?

Moldori Dream Dancers, he had learned after a long talk with Jack, helped those whose minds were troubled. They were, in fact, healers of the mind, using their power to enter dreams to find the causes and determine the cure. Some had the Sight and acted as advisors when needed. They went always veiled, so that those who consulted them were not distracted by their appearance. It was convenient for Jahmelle that she was able to use that custom to her advantage.

She misread his silence.

"I understand," she said. "I would find it hard to trust someone who deceived me again as well."

"No, Your Grace...I was thinking about your earlier question." He stood, his knees watery and his belly twitching. He'd fought battles with less fear.

There was no logic to it. It wouldn't strengthen her position or provide her with the resources Abernal might come to need desperately if its enemies refused to accept defeat. He only knew that some force he couldn't interpret gripped him and insisted this was what had to be done.

"And you have an answer?"

"I...would be honored if you would consider...being my wife."

There was no question he was suitable. A Royal Champion had married a Rediman king's niece three generations back so his blood was sufficiently royal to be acceptable save to the most conservative of those responsible for approving the monarch's consort. Countering that, however, was the too-well-remembered time when another Royal Champion had loved and wed another queen and learned passion and measured justice were not compatible.

Jahmelle knew this as well. She came to him slowly, her hidden eyes never leaving his face. She came so close to him her veils brushed his chest and her scent was a heady cloud around them. Now the quivering in his belly had nothing to do with nerves, at least not the kind related to courage.

"Your oath in my service does not demand that great a sacrifice," she said, and the deep huskiness had a soft edge that made his blood heat.

"It is my honor, not a sacrifice."

He tried to see past the draperies, but when he lifted his hand to touch the shroud she moved swiftly back out of reach. No doubt his own feelings were making him read more into her voice than was really there. Already, second thoughts were clouding the exhilaration that had swept over him when the words finally were said, the offer made.

This was insane. She needed a husband who could provide her with the protection of his armies and his treasury. Love had no place in the world of royalty, yet here he was offering her nothing else—and he hadn't even told her. He had made his offer so it sounded like charity, and if she had the sense he gave her credit for she would order him out of her quarters and her life forever.

"I will accept your offer," was all she said, and then she was gone.

Chapter 25

I WILL ADMIT I RECEIVED THE ANNOUNCEMENT CHRIS AND the queen were to wed with mixed emotions. The weeks that followed did more to increase my apprehension than to relieve it.

Following the kidnapping, my friend had buried himself in preparations for war, spending his days meeting with garrison commanders, his nights poring over reams of materiel reports, troop counts, reserve rosters and weapons inventories. He ate in his room or in the Royals' mess, avoiding the palace except when he was required by his office to attend Her Grace.

This hardly seemed the sort of behavior of a man in love who had proposed marriage—and I had no doubt he had. Although I saw in that one instant following her rescue when Queen Jahmelle caressed his hair that she reciprocated his love, she would not have initiated the idea. Even on short acquaintance she understood his devotion to duty would have prevented him from refusing, no matter his feelings or the unfortunate facts of history.

Yet, when I looked into Chris's eyes as the queen discussed with Danella the details of a wedding appropriate to current circumstances I did observe that the stunned look of betrayal was gone.

"It's all right, Bart," he said, knowing as only an old friend could what was going through my mind. "I understand now, about the magic."

"I'm delighted, of course, but—"

With a glance at his betrothed, he stepped far enough away from her that we could speak privately.

"The summer we were nine, when you went home that midsummer, I...saw something."

As he described his experience, I explored my memories and unearthed one from that year of waking in the dark hours of a winter morning and, at first, not knowing why. Then, I realized Chris lay on his side facing away from me shuddering with sufficient violence to make the entire bed quiver as he muffled wrenching sobs.

In the four years I had fostered with the Royal Champion, I had never known Chris to suffer a single nightmare, nor had anything other than his father's rare spankings ever brought tears to his eyes. To see him stricken so with terror triggered my own. The part of me that loved my friend desired to offer comfort, but the main part was a small boy filled with dread and words frozen in his throat, not wanting to know the depths of horror that could trigger such a response.

Chris's tale explained much, and even hearing about it chilled me. It did not, however, quell the peculiar knot in my belly whose warnings I had learned to respect. Though breaking his long silence had relieved some of the dark aura that surrounded him, I sensed a shadow still remained.

"Dear God, Chris, no wonder fortunetellers give you megrims," I said when he was done, wondering as I did when I had become so inane. Chris was courteous enough to respond with a wry smirk that didn't reach his eyes.

"I've heard you do a better comeback than that in your sleep."

Fortunately, I was rescued from the necessity of overcoming my own megrims to offer a suitable retort by Danella's calling me. As if to reinforce my concern, Chris only bowed to the queen, mumbled something about mortar shells and left.

A small royal wedding being something of an oxymoron, I had no time to contemplate my forebodings. Like much of the royal life, there were necessary steps prescribed by law that could not be avoided. First, the proposed match must be presented to the full assembly of royal ministers. As several of them were not in the city, messengers were dispatched requesting their immediate return. I admit I had hopes they would refuse to permit the match, though I could still not articulate why it troubled me so. Queen Jahmelle shared nothing other than genealogy with that historical royal whose twisted character had forced her Royal Champion mate to a horrendous decision. It was the Royal Champion, in this instance, whose behavior troubled me.

The process of collecting the council consumed a week, after which the ministers, apparently not troubled by history, enthusiastically approved the marriage.

Next came an announcement of the nuptials to the Consortium of Guilds that necessitated collecting all the heads of all the trade and craft guilds for a banquet. As we made these arrangements during the week we awaited the arrival of the ministers, some time was saved. The invitations went out the moment the ministers gave their approbation to the match.

This did not stop some of the subtler of the Queen's enemies from attempting to bribe her servants to add a bit of special seasoning to her food or wine or that of her intended. According to the method we had agreed on, I left a note for Jack in the secret room that I required his advice; and we devised a method of screening potential employees we hoped would eliminate most, if not all, of the would-be spies and assassins.

I would like to say my reservations evaporated with the passage of time and the untrammeled enthusiasm with which the majority of the populace received the proposed wedding of the Champion and his lady, but I saw nothing in Chris's demeanor to alleviate them. Though as fond of praise as any other man, he was uncomfortable with the adulation that inevitably accompanied the Champion's position. He didn't mind acting like a hero, but he hated being treated like one and always had.

Still, even his modesty didn't quite explain his clear effort to avoid spending time alone with his prospective bride. Except that now he dined nightly with her, his routine did not change. It is true that, as Jack brought news that both Nadwich and Decir were mustering armies of unexpected size, the burden of preparing to meet those forces lay on Chris's shoulders. Still, how difficult would it have been for him to linger for even an hour after those dinners in the gardens with his lady?

The Guilds banquet proceeded without flaw, and the wedding announcement was received with a standing ovation. When the pleased guildsmen were once again seated, Chris leaned toward Her Grace and spoke then left the high table. I caught up as he was crossing the kitchen.

"Practicing evasive maneuvers?" I inquired as we dodged bustling cooks and servitors to emerge into the blessed quiet of the kitchen gardens.

"Don't you have a feast to manage?"

"Don't you have one to attend? Besides, management, if done properly, occurs prior to an event if the event is to be successful."

"Then you'll excuse me—I have a war to manage."

"And a wedding."

He stopped and turned to confront me. Save for well-trained reflexes, I would have stunned myself banging my head on his medals.

"I would think someone with your great responsibilities would have better things to do than meddle in other people's affairs," he snapped.

"Not people—friends. I assume we still share that designation."

"For the moment."

"And my responsibilities are somewhat lighter than anticipated, as the Lord Earl Marshall has opted to usurp a large portion of them."

The telltale blush he hated proved my arrow had struck. Provisioning the army was my purview, but he had added that task to all the others without so much as a warning.

"For a man in love," I continued, "you go to great lengths to avoid the company—"

"My marriage to the queen is a matter of state."

"Oh, for God's sake, Chris, who do you think you're talking to? Look me in the eye and tell me you don't love her."

He couldn't, of course, and after a moment's struggle his composure crumpled and he presented me a face of abject misery.

"I should never have offered to wed her, Bart. But I knew it was what she wanted and, God, I wanted to so badly the words came out before I could stop them."

"What's wrong with loving her?"

"Nothing. But marrying her could destroy her. She needs to marry some prince with the power to protect her, not an—never mind. Just plan the wedding. I'll be there."

He started away, but I stepped in front of him.

"'Not an' what?"

"Leave it be, Bart, or I swear I'll knock you into the basil."

He meant it, too. Even best friends fight, and I recognized the icy glint in his dark eyes that said I was on the brink of overstepped bounds. On the other hand, so was he.

"I don't know what's gnawing your ass, old friend, but don't think this is the end."

We stood for an interminable moment, eyes locked and jaws twitching.

"Don't count on it," Chris growled, and shoved past me to disappear into the shadows.

As angry as I was, the import of that last remark slipped past me and vanished into a dark drawer in the basement of my memory. I stormed back to the Great Hall calling him every kind of addlepated fool. Worse, in my frustration, I am ashamed to say, I was unnecessarily abrupt with my people for the time required for it to abate.

For the next fortnight Danella and I were too busy to think about anything other than the wedding details. We ordered the necessary supplies for the wedding dinner, which would be a mere shadow of the feast at which Edrick had died, summoned seamstresses and tailors to create the wedding garments, cleaned the palace from roof to cellar, set up quarters for those of the nobility without houses in the capital and dropped nightly into bed near midnight to grab enough sleep to begin at dawn the next day.

We did manage to share meals with Jack, who was now forced to rely on reports from agents rather than take the field himself. With the queen's permission he shared those reports with Danella and I, although after hearing them we came to a new appreciation for secrecy.

Benifaz of Nadwick had, it seemed, already had designs on Abernal long before Edrick married his daughter. He had been conscripting and training troops in secret locations for at least three years. His commander was a disaffected former Abernali officer who thought himself Chris's equal if not his superior and resented that the leadership of the army was part of the Royal Champion's inheritance. In fact, the man was quite brilliant and had used everything he learned from Davvyd Evergild to create a military force across the mountains that was far better than any Nadwich had previously fielded.

The Deciron Emperor had always wielded enormous military power. In addition, however, he had acquired a school of scientists and engineers and ordered them to focus all their attention on a logistical problem—moving his troops across the defensive wall of mountains. They had begun expanding one of the narrow trade roads into a broad highway the previous year, and the Deciron Army was massed to march.

Benifaz fielded five thousand well-trained, professional troops, the Emperor double that. We had, at most, half their numbers and no time to train conscripts. We were unprepared. We'd had no reason to be otherwise, and a prosperous population resents mightily paying taxes to feed and clothe soldiers for which they see no need. So, the monarchs of Abernal had maintained only sufficient army and navy to patrol the borders and coasts and offer the appearance of safety. Taxes were thus kept reasonable, and the people were pleased.

As a result, we were now staring the Beast of Conquest right in its foul-breathed, slavering jaws.

The day of the wedding arrived, and despite the threat of war the cathedral was packed. I knew why, and it had nothing to do with respect for the crown. The nobles and merchants and city officials who jammed the nave were there for the moment when the ceremony ended and Sir Christopher Evergild lifted his bride's veil for the ritual kiss.

He stood before the altar, resplendent in his white-and-gold formal uniform, glittering with his medals and honors, a cloth-of-gold knee-length cape draped on his right shoulder. Sunlight streaming through the great stained glass windows sparked on the diamonds and sapphires of the Champion's coronet and glistened gold in the tumbling waves of his hair. He was every inch a prince, and the ceremony that would officially endow him with that title was a mere formality.

A fanfare brought the assembly to its collective feet as the first of the queen's Flowers—the Princess Yolanthe—began her progress toward the front. She wore bright sky blue to symbolize the element of water, and was followed in orderly succession by three more ladies in ivory, green and red.

When they stood two on either side of the aisle below the altar, a second fanfare rang, and the great pipe organ pealed with the opening chord of the royal anthem. The queen stepped through the doors, then two more paces into the nave to where a shaft of golden light slanted from a great rose window. She wore white, the color that contains all others, but her flowing gown was sewn from a silk cousin to that of her Dream Dancer's veils. Under the sun, it shimmered like nacre, rainbow shades moving over it in waves so it almost appeared to be a living thing. A soft sigh rose from the crowd.

A moment later there was a rush of indrawn breath as two others entered and took places on either side of the queen, the ones reserved for the bride's parents. The silver-haired man on her right wore the flowing black-and-violet robes of the Moldori High Chieftain, there as Her Grace's supposed only living direct male relative.

It was the woman on her left who was the focus of all those eyes, however. Clad in the tight leather breeches and sleeveless vest of a Moldori warrior, her scarred face immobile as stone, she seemed to radiate an energy that reeked of danger. Her tight cap of blue-black hair bore a gold-and-ruby circlet that had been missing from the royal treasury for two decades—the ancient crown of the queens consort of Abernal. She had surrendered all of her weapons to Danella's safekeeping just before her entrance, save for a black-handled dagger with a gleaming silver falcon's head capping the pommel. No one old enough to remember that far back could fail to recognize it: Davvyd Evergild's heirloom dagger, which he claimed to have lost.

While the nave buzzed, the queen, her mother and her grandfather advanced to the altar, and the ceremony began. The whispering tapered off as the Ugly Princess and her Champion pledged eternal love and fidelity and the day's first shock was replaced by the former eager anticipation. Soon, all those morbidly curious wedding guests were sure, they would be privy to the hideous deformity that had led their late king to banish his daughter from human sight.

The pledge was sealed, the marriage complete. Queen and Consort turned to each other, and they were likely two of the very few still breathing regularly. Then, gracefully, Chris sank to one knee, still holding his bride's hand. He moved it so they were palm to palm then placed his free hand atop the other. I never learned whether she had known he would do this, but Queen Jahmelle unhesitatingly clasped his hands between hers.

In a voice that rang from one wall of the cathedral to the other Sir Christopher Evergild repeated his oath of fealty. Finished, he pressed his lips to her hand, then stood, slid her arm through his and escorted his wife from the church, her intact veils refracting the light in a hundred shades of color.

Chapter 26

THIS WEDDING FEAST, LIKE THE ONE BEFORE IT, WAS doomed to interruption. I had just completed the initial toast to the royal couple when the doors flew open and a dust-encrusted messenger strode into the hall. I doubt anyone was ignorant of what his message must be, and the joyous chatter stopped as if some bellicose concertmaster had cued for a pause.

Chris and the queen both stood and went to her private study, followed by myself and the grim young soldier. We were accompanied by Her Grace's mother and grandfather, and I caught the trooper flicking his eyes back and forth between the two Moldori with mingled curiosity and trepidation.

The invasion, of course, had begun. Nadwich had crossed the mountains, and its army was encamped below the foothills that marked Abernal's northern boundary. Observers Chris stationed where the highway from Decir opened onto the plain reported the Emperor's forces were no more than a day behind. The majority of our own troops were already in place, positioned according to Chris's orders as strategically as possible given the vast difference in numbers.

After thanking the man and sending him to the kitchen for food and rest, the queen clasped Chris's hands and the connection between their eyes was almost visible.

"We will be going, daughter," Chief Marvaya said, and Queen Jahmelle released her husband to follow her mother and grandfather back to the Great Hall.

"I'll see to your gear, Chris," I told him, though my now ever-present sense of impending doom screamed at the inanity. How I wished I might join him, confront these enemies who had stolen our peace and disrupted our lives. I suppose if I had pleaded he would have allowed it.

But my true task was to remain to command the last bastion of defense for the queen should the unthinkable happen, and I knew expressing my concern that Chris's mind was not wholly on the coming battle would earn me no thanks. Besides, what could I do about it?

"It's ready." Then, before I could utter so much as a farewell, he strode past me and was gone.

To say I was shocked at this abrupt departure, without even a goodbye kiss for his bride, would be totally inadequate to describe what I felt. I stared at the closed door, my mind a blank, as if the span of carved nightoak might offer an explanation of what had so changed my friend.

However, all it did was swing shut, and even the queen's veils were insufficient to mask her astonishment at finding her bridegroom already gone. For one long moment I felt a powerful urge to ignore my station and my training and take her in my arms to offer comfort. Then the moment passed, and she seemed somehow to pull herself even more erect than usual.

"We must return to the hall," she said in a voice with only the barest hint of a tremble. "Some of the guests will want to leave as soon as possible."

Queens don't weep in front of their subjects.

I escorted her back to her place at the high table and stood behind her in Chris's place as she verified everyone's suspicions. Those with properties in the north wasted no time bidding farewell. The rest left more slowly, but not by much; and when the last had presented her courtesies the queen and her four maids of honor went back to the Lady's Nest.

The confrontation between the Royal Army of Abernal and the aggressors, now known as the Battle of the Champion's Plain, was engaged two days later. Chris ran three mounts into the ground to reach our lines and arrived as the last of the Deciron artillery poured out of the pass. The sight of the guns, larger and, based on their placement, with greater range than anything in our own arsenal, laid an even greater pall over the situation.

Yet veterans of the battle have told me since that the heavy weight of dread the great mass of men and guns created lifted noticeably when the Earl Marshall's gleaming white-and-gold banner with its sigil of a sword with the scales of justice for a hilt was lifted over the command tent. Chris had that effect on those he commanded, and though he was aware of it I never really thought he understood its depth. He surveyed the enemy's lines then, despite his exhaustion, walked through the camp with his commanders, offering a joke here, a compliment there.

Had our enemies chosen to launch their attack that day, it is likely they would have won easily. The Emperor's general, however, supremely confident that the outcome of battle was a foregone conclusion, decided his men deserved a night's rest so they could better enjoy the coming slaughter.

Dawn was ushered in by the sound of drums as the enemy armies moved into position. Simultaneously, the Deciron cannon began to roar as soon as there was sufficient light to aim. Though our troops held the high ground, that advantage served mainly to delay matters and allow them to take a toll of the advancing infantry. Inevitably, the guns found the range and rained destruction on the embrasures and defensive walls our side had constructed. Chris had only two choices then: pull back and accept defeat, or order the charge.

What followed is described by honest historians as "a brave and hopeless massacre." Within two hours fewer than half the

Abernali troops still fought. Ammunition exhausted, they battled hand to hand, and the Earl Marshall's banner flew from one end of the front to the other as Chris rallied them with shout and sword. Musket balls flew past him like a swarm of lethal insects, yet some power seemed to protect him.

Then, suddenly, the eastern flank of the Nadwickians staggered. Word spread through the Abernalis that help had arrived—and, indeed, it had. Out of a half-dozen pathways only they knew, one hundred Moldori ehlana poured onto the plain, their powerful bows flinging shaft after shaft, and for each arrow a Nadwickian fell. It was eerie, that unrelenting accuracy; and it added the element of superstitious fear to the attack.

At the same time, the bombardment that had still been decimating our lines began to slow and then stopped altogether. Chris and his commanders immediately set to work pulling their shattered army together for one final, desperate assault; and he was about to order the charge when someone shouted, "Trolls, milord! They've taken out the guns and are advancing."

Rising in his stirrups, Chris looked to the east. Like reapers mowing a field, the Trolls moved through the ranks of the Decirons, and those of the emperor's soldiers who did not run died. He could not see what weapons they used, but there was no questioning their effectiveness.

It was those same veterans who told me what happened next. The battle was not won, but it was now clearly not lost. It was the proper time for Chris to pull back to his command post and leave the final fighting in the hands of his commanders. Fired by hope and the sort of courage only those who have regained it can truly understand, the remnants of the Army of Abernal threw themselves against the enemy as the Moldori slaughtered Nadwickians and the Trolls slashed the stunned Decirons to ribbons.

There was one pocket of the Emperor's forces holed up in a trench that had for some reason withheld their fire through the hours of battle. Sword gleaming, his banner resplendent,

Christopher Evergild rode to the front of the platoon readying an attack on the position and led the charge with a rousing, "For Jahmelle and Abernal!"

Only then did he learn the full extent of the advances our imperial enemy had made.

A gun unlike anything ever seen before began spitting ball after ball in a fusillade that would have torn the advancing forces to ribbons had it been more accurate. Chris ordered his men dismounted and prone while he stood in his stirrups and told them where to fire. He kept his mount in motion, surmising quickly that the weapon was difficult to aim; and of the six soldiers holding the emplacement all but one had been killed when the bullet slammed into his thigh, shattering the bone and knocking him to the ground.

"Jahmelle!" he murmured one more time as the gunner fell and his own men lifted him, blood pulsing to stain the brilliant white that had made him a conspicuous target, to carry him at a run back to the medical tent. I suspect, based on what subsequently occurred, that he regretted, as he sank into unconsciousness, that the man who shot him wasn't accurate enough to have done the job right.

"How is he?"

Jack leaned against the doorframe to my office, and I detected more than simple polite inquiry in his voice.

"Dying."

"That makes no sense." He came in and slumped into a chair. "The wound was nasty, yes, but not fatal. They stopped the bleeding right away."

I sighed and rubbed my face with my hands. He was only repeating my own thoughts, and hearing them no more inspired an answer than thinking them.

"The doctors believe perhaps the wound wasn't cleaned properly."

"It's gangrene, then? Can't they just take the leg?"

"It's not gangrene. There's no sign of infection. In fact, the wound itself is healing well, although he'll have a slight limp.

However, they suggest there might be a poison in the blood that's causing his fever and coma." I got up and poured us each a healthy dollop of brandy, even though the noon meal was still being prepared. "I don't think he wants to live."

Jack took his glass, but he didn't drink. Instead, he gazed into the amber-red depths, his mouth a tight line.

"It's my fault," he said abruptly.

"That's ridiculous, Jack. You—"

"When we went to rescue the queen, I taunted him. He was always so sure he knew exactly how things ought to be done, that his was the only way. I could see him wishing he could hold his nose every time he looked at me—the thief who dared to look at his queen. And there he was in that stupid chain mail like some gallant knight in a fairy tale, even though I could tell it made him itch." He stopped and emptied his glass in one gulp.

"And...?" I prompted when the silence went on too long.

"I told him he was useless, obsolete, an anachronism. I meant to apologize later, but everything happened so fast I never got around to it. And it didn't really seem to bother him, so..."

She needs to marry some prince with the power to protect her, not an—

An anachronism? Was that what Chris had started to say, only to decide it was no one's business but his?

Then the rest of that conversation came back, leaping into my mind with the sharp chill of a midwinter blizzard.

Don't think this is the end, I had warned him, and he had growled, *Don't count on it.*

I felt sick, and part of me wanted to slam my fist into Jack Tarragent's brooding, contrite face.

Christopher Evergild had trained from the time he could toddle to do one thing, to be one thing—the Royal Champion. He had grown up knowing the fate of the kingdom rested in his hands and mind and skill. It wasn't what he did, it was quite literally who he was. He had been forced to assume that responsibility at a younger age than any of his predecessors for reasons he had not understood until he learned the truth of Queen Marvaya's and Jack's escapes. Lacking proof of Davvyd's intervention, Edrick could only make the man's life as miserable as possible, something he was very good at. Driven to the point of considering regicide, Davvyd retired and the burden fell on Chris.

But the world where one man could be the main bastion of his country was gone, lost in the inevitable changes that new ideas and new ways of doing things create. Christopher Evergild was an honest, straightforward man who believed passionately in justice and honor and who had discovered he was in a minority. Then he had failed the one responsibility that remained to him. He had allowed his queen—the woman he loved—to be placed in dire danger because of what he would see as his own weakness. He had allowed personal jealousy to overwhelm his duty.

I should have known. Hadn't I watched him sit up at night until his eyes burned studying when some aspect of his lessons wouldn't sink in? Hadn't I practiced swords with him until I could no longer raise my arm and knew he was in no better shape, only to have him call for another opponent? Christopher Evergild had never, ever, accepted failure; and so he had never experienced it.

Perhaps, given time to think about the way the world was changing, he might have found a way to adjust, to adapt his knowledge and training and find a new niche for himself. But the new era had arisen almost overnight. Granted, his skills as a commander were sufficient for that position to offer satisfaction and purpose, but that wasn't the same. Chris's life had been focused on a centuries-old tradition; and his identity with it, an identity that no longer existed.

Although he was never an arrogant man, Chris had accepted that his life's work was to do what no other could: defend crown and country single-handedly. That responsibility, that thing that had made him who and what he was, was gone, and...

Snatching Jack's glass, I seized his arm and half-dragged him toward the door to the main palace.

"What the hell...?" he sputtered.

"You have to tell the queen. She may know some way to fix it."

Though he had the decency to look ashamed at having to confess his cruelty, Jack strode beside me willingly as we crossed the Great Hall. He looked puzzled when we passed the queen's office and started up the stairs to the north wing.

"Where are we going?"

"To where Her Grace now spends every waking hour not required for business."

In the King's Tower, where her husband lay willing himself to die.

Chapter 27

SOMETIMES, IT SEEMED HE WAS AWAKE, BUT THEN THE world would twist and tell him he was dreaming. He heard voices, snatches of conversation that might have been real but didn't matter.

He preferred the other times, the dark times when he disappeared into the silence. Each fall into the void made him hope it would be the last—that the task he had set himself was finally done. Each time he was disappointed when the dreams/memories came.

In one, he lived again the sweat and blood-gunpowder reek of battle. In *another* he lay on stony ground, warmth pulsing liquid pain from his left thigh. Then would come a face, grim and scarred, deep bronze skin and startling silver eyes. Hands touching, moving. A voice chanting that set him away from the bleeding body so he could watch as the ball was cut from his flesh, the muscle and skin stitched together. Another chant to yank him unwilling back.

Between those were the ones he hated—Bart's face, and Danella's, lined with fear and worry. He wanted to tell them this was best, but he would have had to move further from the cradling dark to do it and he wouldn't.

And the ones of her.

Those, in particular, were the dreams (moments?) he wanted to keep away from. Her voice calling his name, speaking of love. Her fingers gliding over his skin or cooling it with scented water. Dreams—yes, they had to be dreams.

Time was meaningless. He neither knew nor cared how long it had been since the bullet slammed into flesh, shattered bone, tore vessels that pumped his life out by the heartbeat. Except that it had been too long.

Then she came. Not the voice or the hands but her, into his dreams. They were in the dim-lit hall of Raven's Cry, she in her wide-winged chair swathed in shimmering silk, he in its mate wearing his chain mail. He was angry. She had no right to be there.

"Again you invade my dreams," he growled.

"I'm not in your dream, Christopher. You're in mine."

"But—no, that's impossible. I'm not—"

"One needn't be Moldori to travel the maze of the Dream World. It's a skill almost anyone can acquire with a bit of practice, if they like. The Moldori have just learned to use it."

"Why would I want to?"

She sighed and flipped up her veil so their eyes truly met for the first time.

"I suspect you've come to say goodbye."

Chris barely heard what she said, so engrossed was he in studying her face. There were no deformities. He had abandoned that specious rumor long ago. Yet she was not the exotic beauty of his own dream, either.

Her hair was mouse-brown, an unremarkable compromise between the golden shades of House Rediman and the glossy blue-black of Moldor. Her eyes, though large and almond-shaped with a slight, intriguing tilt, were mud-colored. She took after Edrick with her strong square chin and proud straight nose. Those features that had been handsome on her father, however, were too bold for a woman. The Ugly Princess was not, in fact, ugly, but she was undeniably plain.

Belatedly, Chris's mind registered what she had said, and for some reason he was annoyed she knew his dark desire. He chose to hide his resentment under cover of feigned ignorance.

"What?"

"You are dying, my lord Earl Marshall, as you well know. The physicians and the healers and the Moldori shaman who are treating you all agree there is no reason for it. Never in the history of medicine have they all agreed on a diagnosis, so I must accept that they're correct."

He let his anger curdle into the bitterness it was rooted in.

"Well, why not? There are other men who can run your army, and I doubt anyone will be resorting to single combat as a means of diplomacy anytime soon. And the one thing I should have done, protect you, I failed at. Dagger Jack is right—I'm an anachronism, a leftover with no real purpose."

"You are also my husband."

"There are other men who can do that, too. Hell, Jack's blood is as royal as mine. Or, better yet, find some prince with an army big enough to make Decir think twice."

"There are no princes with armies as well-trained as ours, nor as loyal to their commander. It is you they fight for, Christopher, not me. And Jack is my brother."

This time his confusion wasn't feigned. "What?"

"Ten years ago, Marvin Overlack convinced my father that it was dangerous to have more than one potential contender for the thrown, no matter which side of the blanket he or she was born on. They murdered all my father's illegitimate children save one. That one was supposedly the orphaned grandson of the Count of Montrivert. So, they concocted an accusation of treason and had the young man and his aged grandfather arrested and condemned. The rest, I believe, you know."

He got up and paced the open area in front of the gently burning hearth, although even such slight activity made sweat stream down his face and soak his dress uniform. *When did I change?*

He remembered now overhearing Settleson remind Overlack of this very thing, and as he called an image of Jack Tarragent to mind he saw the resemblance.

However, that seemed only to make his decision that much more valid. He wasn't capable of the kind of intricate, twisted machinations that obviously governed the way politics progressed. He'd really known it all along, but he had accepted his father's assurance it would come to him in time.

"In any case, it wouldn't matter if there were a hundred princes with armies of millions clamoring for my hand. I decided many years ago, after listening to my mother tell the story of her marriage to my father, that I would never marry solely for political reasons. I have always intended to marry for love, and I love you."

"Wh-what?"

"Do you usually stammer so, dear heart, or only when you're ill and dreaming?" A smile that transformed her face erased any sting from the gently ironic question. "I said I love you. I think I've loved you from the moment you sat outside my gates, cold and soaking wet and cursing my poor Troll guards who feared you had come to kill me.

"At least, I think that must have been the beginning, because I can't remember a time when I didn't love you. I don't expect you to love me as well—"

"Not love you!" The resigned sadness in her velvet voice pierced his chest more painfully than the bullet had his leg. He all but ran to drop to his knees beside her, taking her hands and pressing his lips to the backs, the palms. "My God, I love you so much I ache with it. You're my first thought in the morning and my last at night and just the sound of your voice is more to me than life and honor."

She leaned forward to rest her cheek on his hair, and the scents of lavender and roses enveloped him.

"Yet you're leaving me, of your own will," she murmured.

His rational mind told him to get up, to force himself out of this dream-place and into the safety of the eternal darkness. Instead, he buried his face in her lap.

"I can't be just an appendage, Jahmelle, the queen's husband, the begetter of the royal family."

"Why not?"

"Because...Because..." Then her husky teasing tone sank in and did what it always did—sent warm currents to intimate parts of his anatomy. Even here, in this world outside reality, he felt the pulse and the ache and had to fight the urge to draw her down onto the thick carpet and strip away all the silk that lay between them.

"Christopher."

Her voice made his name music, but he couldn't face her.

"Christopher, does this have anything to do with the end of the tradition of the Royal Champion?"

Damn! Did she have to be quite so good at understanding what was going through his mind? Or was it something to do with Dream Dancing? Was this what they did, meet a man in his dreams and learn his innermost secrets?

"Even if there is no longer a Royal Champion, have you forgotten there is a duty to the crown and your country you've not yet attended to?"

He sat up, wracking his brain trying to recall what he might have left undone. Nothing came immediately to mind. He had taken great pains to ensure his life was in order before he rode off to try and end it. What had he missed?

"If I understand correctly," Jahmelle went on, her face grown hard and her eyes flashing, "the demons and their worshipers you saw so long ago still inhabit Abernal."

"I've no reason to think otherwise. I never found that priest."

Her eyes were locked with his now, and he could feel her outrage.

"Is it not the place of the Crown to eradicate this horror, my lord Earl Marshall?"

Like a flawed blade, Chris's despair shattered as he understood where she was going. For twenty years the search for the demons had been his private war, but for the last five his duties as Royal Champion, the necessity of his dancing attendance on Edrick, had kept him too busy to engage in it. Only, as he had long since realized and she had just noted, Abernal no longer needed a Royal Champion.

223

"Yes, Your Grace," he agreed, his voice harsh with tears of joy and gratitude that stung his eyes.

"And, as I cannot see to this myself, is it not your place as Earl Marshall of the realm to do so in my stead?"

"Oh, yes, Your Grace. By your leave, I will begin at once."

Jahmelle smiled, and again he was astonished at how it lit her face and gave her a beauty deeper than the shape of a nose or the curve of a chin. Her eyes twinkled with mischief and something deeper that made his thighs tingle.

"I believe we can wait until after we have completed our marriage duties," she said, and trailed the tips of her fingers ever so lightly across his bottom lip.

The lightning that shot down his spine was still charging his groin when he woke to find her lying beside him, her arm across his waist and her veils tumbling like air across his chest.

His recovery, once he set his mind to it, was rapid. Three weeks after he awoke from his months-long death-sleep all the wedding guests had been reassembled in the Great Hall. This time he had thoughts only for the woman beside him, whose hand he refused to relinquish even long enough to allow her to eat. The hunger they shared had nothing to do with food, and their appetites were whetted by their having mutually decided to wait until this night for their consummation.

The feasting and celebrating were at full bore when Jahmelle rose, bidding her guests continue their revels. Chris waited the required hour, shifting constantly to ease the pressure and enduring the wiseass grin on Bart's face. Finally, he slipped away and all but ran to the King's Tower where tradition said even a reigning queen must await her consort.

She sat before the cold hearth in the darkened bedchamber, her shrouding veils making her ghostly in the light of a single candle that was the only source of illumination. Tradition said she should have been in his bed, naked and waiting. He understood that with her it could not be. He had seen her in her dream, but that was not the same as seeing her here, touching her.

The bed curtains were drawn, and he knew from experience that inside it was dark as a cave. There was a lamp, set in a niche in the thick headboard so the bed's occupant might read on a cold winter's night without having to suffer the drafts. He suspected that lamp was unlit.

She stood as he softly closed and locked the door, pouring a glass of wine and bringing it to him.

"Thank you, my lady."

"I think, under the circumstances, that you might call me by my given name," she teased, walking back to stand by the window that overlooked the formal gardens. The drapes were pushed back to allow the warm summer night breeze to enter through the open casement, and her veil stirred as if alive under its touch. He followed and set his glass down on a tea table as he passed. He put his hands on her shoulders.

"Of course, Jahmelle," he complied, letting the syllables flow over his tongue like warm honey.

"You needn't stay," she blurted, trying to keep her voice calm. But he heard the quiver in it. What he didn't understand was the reason for her words. How could she not know it was taking all his restraint not to reach for the laces that bound her bodice and...

"It is the dearest wish of my heart to stay, Jahmelle," he said, putting into his voice all that his heart felt.

She sighed and caressed his cheek. "Yet how long will you love me once you've seen?"

"I've seen you already, remember?"

"You have seen a dream image," she corrected him. "Do you remember about dream images?"

It took a moment, but he did remember. When she had come to his dream to tell him where she was being kept prisoner, she explained that the Jahmelle he saw was one he had created, the image of her he wanted to see. What she was warning him of was that the face he had seen in the more recent dream was also an image, that the reality was quite different.

He could give in to her fear—and he had no delusions it was anything else—blow out the candle, let her slip into the lightless cavern of the bed and keep her secret. Only, if he did that would she ever truly believe he loved her?

Before she realized his intent, he grasped the hem of her veil and tossed it over her head, using just enough force that the gold circlet holding it in place came off with it.

"No!" she cried and covered her face with her hands as she turned her back to him.

"Look at me, Jahmelle," he demanded in his gentlest tone. "I love you, and I want to see you."

Her shoulders fell and her hands followed; and she turned slowly back to face him. Her face told in every stiff line how much of her will and courage it took for her to do it, and she winced when he drew in his breath at the sight.

It was the same face he had seen in her dream, and yet it was not. Her eyes, though perhaps a shade too full of intelligence for some men, were not muddy brown but an incredible shade of chestnut shot with flecks of green and gold. Her hair was the rich color of strong coffee and when he slowly pulled the confining pins from it fell in soft waves to her waist. Those features that in her dream image had been too strong, too masculine were, in truth, much softer, more feminine—her father's strong bones mitigated by the graceful ones of her mother's people.

What would it be like, he wondered as he began tracing the lines of those bones with his fingertips, to be sent away from your own kind and raised knowing you were spoken of far and wide as the Ugly Princess? That you were called "monster" and said to be a madwoman? What if your only companions were creatures who, though loving and kind, had no criterion for telling you if you were plain or beautiful? Could reassurances, even from a mother, be enough to dispel the thought there might be some truth to those tales?

She was trembling as he ran his thumb over the fullness of her lower lip and into her mouth, but it wasn't fear of rejection that made her shiver. Already he could see a telltale flush blooming on her cheeks, could scent her musk under the drift of roses and lavender. She took a deep breath and it, too, trembled.

He slid his hand to the nape of her neck and drew her to him, brushing his mouth over hers until she opened for his kiss. Hours, days—an eternity passed before he let her go and took one step back. Her bodice was unlaced, his hand already familiar with the curve of her breast. She swayed a little, her eyes glazed with the same potent need that boiled in his blood.

"You are beautiful, my love," he told her. "Never doubt that. You need not hide behind veils ever again."

"Ah, but then I would lack all mystery," she said, undoing the last fastenings of her gown and letting it fall with a soft sigh to the floor. She wore nothing underneath. "There are some advantages to being an ugly princess who must spare those who look upon her the sight of her ugliness."

She stepped nearer and unbuttoned his tunic, sliding it off his shoulders to join her dress. He clenched his fists as she ran her fingertips over his back, his chest, down his belly to the fastening of his trousers and swiftly set him free.

"Fine," he gasped as her hands moved again, "but I don't... want to ever...hear you refer to yourself...that way again." He picked her up and carried her to the bed, tossing her onto the satin sheets and noting peripherally that the lamp had been lit.

"Orders to your queen, my lord Earl Marshall?" she murmured as he stretched out next to her and began a comprehensive exploration.

"Orders from your husband, madam." He shifted over, moved within, watched her face as she responded, tormented both of them in his determination not to surrender until he had no choice.

"Yes, my lord," she said as she made one decisive move that put an end to his erotic teasing. "Oh...yes!"

END

ABOUT THE AUTHOR

ELIZABETH K. BURTON, formerly of Pennsylvania, now happily transplanted in Austin, Texas, decided to do freelance book editing while she finally launched her writing career. Little did she know she would end up on the other side of the "transom" as a publisher. Author of several published short stories, including a 1999 Writers of the Future finalist, four published novels and three novellas, Liz is currently following Dagger Jack Tarragent on a new adventure, a fate she wouldn't wish on anyone she likes.

ABOUT THE ARTIST

TAMIAN WOOD, winner of the 17th Annual Florida Print Awards, Best of Category, is currently based out of sunny South Florida. Using art, photography, typography and digital collage techniques, she creates book covers that appeal to the eye and the mind, to entice the book browser to become a book reader. She holds degrees in computer science and graphic design, and is a proud member of Phi Theta Kappa National Honour Society.

View the broad range of her design experience on her website at www.tamianwood.com.

www.ingramcontent.com/pod-product-compliance
Lightning Source LLC
Chambersburg PA
CBHW020834260626
47169CB00003B/977